THE DEPUTY SHERIFF

BAR 20

BOOKS BY
CLARENCE E. MULFORD

THE ORPHAN
BAR 20
BAR 20 DAYS
THE MAN FROM BAR 20
TEX
BRING ME HIS EARS
JOHNNY NELSON
THE BAR 20 THREE
THE COMING OF CASSIDY— AND THE OTHERS
HOPALONG CASSIDY
BUCK PETERS, RANCHMAN
BLACK BUTTES
RUSTLERS' VALLEY
HOPALONG CASSIDY RETURNS
COTTONWOOD GULCH

HOPALONG CASSIDY'S PROTÉGÉ
THE BAR 20 RIDES AGAIN
CORSON OF THE J.C
MESQUITE JENKINS
ME AN' SHORTY

The
DEPUTY SHERIFF

By CLARENCE E. MULFORD

AEONIAN PRESS, INC.
LEYDEN, MASS.

THE DEPUTY SHERIFF

CHAPTER I

CACTUS COUNTY, in its area, was almost as large as some of the smaller Eastern states; but in its population it was almost negligible. Its territory was spotted with grazing areas, mostly poor, some good, and a few very excellent. These largely were separated by desert stretches. Cities, it had none; small towns, a few; but mainly its habitations were single ranches, miles apart. At one time prospectors had scratched it rather thoroughly and found it wanting in the precious metals. Agriculture was practically unknown, and the chief business, of a productive nature, was ranching.

It was organized in a governmental and political sense. Its county seat was so far from the outlying territory, and the methods of transportation so primitive, that so far as the greater part of the county was concerned the county seat might as well have not existed.

In the Cactus Springs and Willow Springs sections, situated in the northern and western part of the county, the home of the sheriff was located, and he had hoped to spend most of his time there instead of in the office provided for him in the county seat. The present incumbent was Robert Corson, owner of the JC ranch, and he had hoped to make the town of Willow Springs his headquarters, following the precedent set by the former sheriff, who had stubbornly refused to leave for any length of time the village of Cactus Springs, where he had his home. Pressure, steadily growing, and the courts being in session, had made Corson waver in this determination and finally forced him to make his preparations to leave the ranch and take up his domicile at the seat of government.

He would leave behind him competent deputies and competent cattlemen to look after the ranch, and in all cases they were the same persons. Nueces, of the horse face, was boss of both. The ranch was safe under the direction of such a foreman and such an outfit; and the local peace was no more in jeopardy. These assistants, both on the ranch and as deputies, were Nueces and Shorty, and certain gentlemen of the saddle known as Burns and Bludsoe. All of these men knew the difference between the muzzle and handles of a six-shooter. As survivals of the fittest, they all had survived several fits, fits of intensity and duration, thrown by sundry other gentlemen of barely lesser caliber. Against all the signs and portents to the contrary notwithstanding, they all firmly believed that they would die in bed, at a ripe old age, with their boots removed before the end.

This was not just sheer egotism. The country more or less immediately surrounding and adjacent to the two little towns above named was now enjoying an unbroken reign of peace. Spasms had occurred, been promptly and properly diagnosed, and heroically cured.

Grass and weeds were beginning to grow on the last little rounded oblongs of earth which marked the final resting place of the foolhardily turbulent. The stage-coach came and went with monotonous regularity; store-keepers loafed in their front doors, ready to gossip with the first loafer who joined them. The click of pool balls and an occasional burst of laughter marked the Cheyenne, where tense atmospheres had been known to be its true index in days gone past. Willow Springs lived calmly in the sun, and one mark of its placidity and love of peace was its growing toleration for Cactus Springs and the inhabitants thereof. Citizens of the two towns did not embrace when they met, but they were prone to swap the makings and to talk pleasantly together.

Corson's time of departure drew near. He was miles to the south of his own range, riding homeward after attending to a relatively unimportant official duty, and thinking of the temporary separation from his old friends and his old stamping ground. His face wore a slight frown, for his thoughts did not please him. Turning a dense thicket of brush he drew rein sharply, his free hand instinctively dropping, under the stimulus of surprise, to the walnut handles of his gun.

"Do not e-shoot," said a pleasant musical voice, laughter rippling in the words.

The sheriff's frown disappeared and a quizzical grin took its place as the officer looked at the mounted Mexican.

"Señor Chavez," he said. "I am glad to see you,

unofficially. But officially I must ask you if yore presence in this county is for pleasure or business."

"Eet ees har-rdly a pleasure, Señor Sheriff; although eet ees not a business. I hav' been seeing my fr-riends; an' I was tol' that you would r-ride home thees way. I am her-re to tell you I am glad you ar-re the sheriff; an' sorry that you mus' go away. To say adios ees not a pleasure. No?"

"No," sighed Corson. "How are things with you?"

"Ver' good. I am not disturb'. You look well. How ar-re my ver' good fr-riends Señor Nueces and Shor-rty?"

"First rate. Señor, I am going down in another part of th' county to stay too dam' long to suit me. Is yore promise still good?"

"Eet ees. I tol' you, by messenger, that so long as you ar-re the sheriff I would not do business een thees county. That ees steel so, but, Señor Corson, ther-re ar-re others who do business een thees county, an' eet ees easy to say, 'El Toro deed thees. El Toro deed that.' Eet ees of that I weesh to e-spik, but I cannot do thees weethout—weethout, ah, thees damn' English! You know w'at I mean?"

"You mean, perhaps, that you can't tell me without telling me things that are not yore secrets?"

"*Si! Si!* I would like to e-spik, but I cannot e-spik; except thees: El Toro weel not come eento thees county, een any part of eet, while Señor Chavez may come and go as he please. Een other wor-rds, I weel not e-steal cattle in Cactus County while you are the sheriff. That ees the wor-rd of one gentleman to another. Her-re ees my hand on eet."

Corson, smiling a true smile, reached out and shook the lean, brown hand, finding nothing humorous in the other's claim to be a gentleman. Human nature is a strange thing: here was a cattle thief, a bandit, whose given word was as sacred as any vow ever made; here was a man whose measure of desperation, courage, and cruelty had never been plumbed, who was, on the other hand, kindly, friendly, loyal, and truthful. Between these two, this guardian of law and order, this sworn peace officer, and the other, a bandit and cattle thief, there was an understanding as firm as it was trusting; and each knew that the other, within his own code of honor, would render the assistance that one good friend gives to another. And each knew, too, one other thing: let duty order, let the promise be broken, and the war between them would be bitter past words.

"Eet may be that you weel be looking for me weeth papers of ar-rest, sworn to by liars, Señor Corson. Then what?"

"They will be for El Toro and not for Señor Chavez, and they will be good only in this county. I will have to search for you, in that case, and will have to try to arrest you. If I find you, an' take your prisoner, you will have to stand yore trial. That means that almost any jury will find you guilty of any crime on the calendar that you may be charged with. They will find you guilty automatically, evidence or no evidence. You know that."

"*Si.* You e-spik the tr-ruth. Eef eet be that ther-re ees mooch e-stealing een the south and east, you weel do well to look near Porter. Money loves money, Señor. Look near Porter. Shall we say adios?"

"Adios, Señor," replied the sheriff, holding out his hand again.

They shook, smiled, and the bandit pulled back his horse in a courteous gesture for his companion to ride on.

El Toro sat quietly in his saddle and watched the departing horseman until that official was out of sight. Then he raised two fingers to his lips and blew a shrill blast.

Over a rise two hundred yards away, from where they had been idly killing time on the other side, three men appeared and rode toward their chief, stopping when close to him.

"Rodriguez," said the bandit in Spanish, "we have business across the boundary, and no *business* of any kind in this county. We shall not miss it, for there is small profit in such long journeys while there is so much waiting for us nearer home. Pass the word on to our friends, and meet me in San Ignacio a week from to-day. For gringos to steal from gringos, it is not our affair; but when they steal from El Toro, or blame their own thefts on me, then that is different. I have put a bug in the ear, and done a friend a good turn. Take your companions with you, and guard well your fat carcass. Adios."

He wheeled and rode southward toward the international line on his way to a self-imposed exile from a territory in which he had but small interest. He had told the truth, warned a friend, and spiked an enemy gun. The day had not been wasted.

CHAPTER II

NUECES, his glittering badge of office exposed for all the world to see and to admire, dismounted before the open door of the Cheyenne and strolled in to the bar.

Steve, functioning behind the so-called mahogany, smiled as a matter of habit, and slid out the bottle preferred by his friend and customer, grunting something which passed as a word of welcome.

Nueces grunted something in reply, caught the spinning glass with one hand and reached for the bottle with the other.

"Mail in yet?" asked Steve, returning to his everlasting and unconscious mopping of a dry counter.

"No," grunted the puncher, and threw back his head. He sighed, drew a sleeve across his lips, and leaned lazily against the bar, one high heel caught on the foot rail.

The big clock ticked without competition in sound, unless it were that made by a score of flies buzzing on the specked and dusty windows.

Steve placed the rag on the backbar with one hand and then absent-mindedly picked it up with the other and went on with his mopping. After a moment or two he looked intently at the cloth, seemed to be surprised, and hurled it into the bin under the counter.

"Bob like th' county seat any better, last you heard?"
he asked.

"No," grunted the deputy. "He says it's all war-
rants, executions, sales, levies, papers an' politics. Th'
politics is th' worst. He says he never will get broke
to a cane-seated saddle that sets on a hinge and has
four tricky little wheels under it. Steve, I dunno but
what we made a mistake, puttin' Bob into a fool job
like that. He's a range-bred critter."

"What you mean?" asked Steve with only polite
interest. "We never knowed it was goin' to be a job
like that, did we?"

"No, we didn't——"

Sounds from the street made both men look curiously toward the door. A shadow darkened it momentarily and announced the arrival of Shorty. The newcomer walked straight to the bar, took the bottle from
Nueces' elbow, and pointed to the row of glasses on
the backbar.

"On me," he said, grinning.

"What you doin' in town?" demanded his friend
Nueces, frowning severely. "Don't you know that you
oughta stay on th' ranch when I ain't there?"

"Huh! Then I never would get off it, day or night,"
retorted Shorty.

"That so?" snapped his boss indignantly.

"You know it is. Here's how!"

"How, Shorty," said Steve, touching the glass to
his lips.

"Mail in yet?" asked the newcomer, glancing from one to the other.

"Reckon that's it now," said Steve, holding up a finger for silence.

From a distance came the low sounds of creaking leather, squealing brakes, the jingle of chain, and the stamping of the restless hoofs of a six-horse team.

"On me," said Nueces, shoving the bottle to his ranch mate and motioning for Steve to take it next.

Three sighs of contentment and satisfaction marked a rite performed, and then the tall foreman of the JC ranch, scraping his change into an enormous hand, pushed from the bar and started toward the door, his short friend close to his heels.

"S'long, Steve," he said.

"S'long, Steve," echoed Shorty.

"S'long, boys," grunted Steve, and mechanically picked up the cloth and fell to mopping off the bar.

"You know dam' well you should 'a' stayed on th' ranch," came Nueces' voice in a growl.

Steve chuckled at Shorty's reply and at the wrangling which grew softer and soon died out. He again looked down at the cloth in his hand, and this time hurled it to the floor.

The mail was in, and the crowd in the post office grew as it was being sorted. It was not long before Nueces had the mail for the ranch, among which was a letter from his boss. Standing in the doorway, a bar to incomers and outgoers, he tore an end off the envelope and began laboriously to read. A head popped up under his arm, for Shorty shrewdly guessed where the letter had been mailed. Neuces squeezed. Shorty, with his head in chancery, retaliated by a quick hip thrust and a heave of his squat but powerful body. Neuces left the floor and found it again instantly with his back. He looked up and grinned.

"Serves him right!" snorted an indignant citizen who had tried in vain to get through the door.

Nueces' reproachful gaze settled on this blustering person, and his face wrinkled.

"Tweet! Tweet!" he said, and then his long arm shot out, gripped Shorty's left leg, and heaved mightily.

Shorty apologized to the indignant citizen as they collided and rolled down the two steps before the door. Picking himself up, he surged back into the building, and was held at bay by a huge hand on his collar, his reach too short to bother the holder, who now complacently read the letter while his short friend raved.

"He's lonesome, Shorty," said the reader, releasing his grip.

"Hell!" growled Shorty, all his interest now on the news in the letter.

"He says for you to work a little harder, an' for me to see that you do it."

"Liar!" snorted Shorty, grinning.

"Says trouble's fixin' to bust loose down in th' southeast corner of th' county, but that he has already seen so many folks from down there that he is too well known in that section. Says that hobbles him." The reader paused to weigh and consider this statement.

"Well, keep a-readin'," prompted Shorty, interrupting his friend's thoughts.

"Says mebby I'll have to go down there in his place——"

"—*We*, you liar!" interrupted his companion.

"—*an'* fill up th' jails or graveyards. You will become boss of th' JC in that event, an' may God have pity on th' ranch."

"You know damn' well where *I'll* be, in *that* event," jeered Shorty. His face brightened. "Wouldn't that be luck, ham-head? Keep on a-readin'."

"There ain't no more to read, runt."

"You lemme see that letter!" retorted Shorty, his hand darting out and plucking part of the sheet from his friend's grip.

"There! You tore it!" reproached Nueces.

Shorty scrutinized both sides of the paper and returned it to his companion.

"Damn these three-mails-a-week towns! We won't hear nothin' more till day after to-morrow. Well, let's go down an' tell Steve th' news."

"Let's tell it to yore great-gran'father!" retorted Nueces. "An' you ain't goin' to see Steve a-tall. You've had enough likker now. *You* are goin' back to th' ranch, an' *work*. You hear that? WORK! Yo're goin' with me, an' yo're goin' now. Come on!"

"Trouble bustin' loose," muttered Shorty as he led the way to the tie-rail. He chuckled. "Say, Nueces, wouldn't that be slick, you an' me off hornin' plumb into somebody's private an' criminal business? Huh?"

"You ain't never happy till yo're stickin' that red nose of yourn into somebody else's affairs," retorted Nueces, swinging into the saddle.

"Red nose?" inquired Shorty, his accusing gaze fixed on the long nasal organ of his companion. "Huh! Long as it don't get purple *I'll* be satisfied!"

Two days later found the friends again awaiting the sorting of the mail, and the hoped-for letter did not arrive.

"Hey, Hank!" said Nueces, thrusting his face against the bars of the opened window. "Hank! You right shore there ain't no letter for us?"

"Didn't you find none?" asked Hank, peering into the box belonging to the ranch.

"No, I didn't."

"Then there ain't none," said Hank flatly.

"You shore it didn't get mixed up with somebody else's mail?" persisted the lanky puncher.

"Jest as shore as I am that yo're goin' to get mixed up with *this* male, if you get smart!"

"Let's get outa here, Nueces!" cried Shorty. "Our lives are plumb in danger!" He shoved his face against the bars, and put a thumb to his nose. "You mix up with Nueces all you wants, Hank, but you be damn' careful you never mix with me!"

"Hold fast, or I'll blow you away!" said the postmaster, grinning. "You fellers lookin' for some special letter?"

"Oh, nothin' particular," said Nueces, pushing back from the window. "We was just kinda hopin' it would come to-day."

"Then you stretch out yore hope two days longer," suggested Hank. "How's Bob makin' out, down to th' county seat?"

"Fine!" enthused Nueces. "He's buildin' a gallows for a hangin'."

"That so? Who for?" asked Hank with deep interest.

"Postmaster of Willer Springs!" said Shorty. "Come on, Nueces, we'll take th' news to Steve."

"We ain't got no news to take him!" retorted Nueces shortly.

"Then we'll go tell him so," said Shorty.

They did. Then they rode out to the ranch and killed another two-day interval, and then they were again in the post office, watching the mail as it was popped into this box and into that one. Shorty became inspired by an idea.

"Great gamblin' game," he said enthusiastically. "You take that half of th' boxes, an' I'll take this half. Bet you two bits that my section gets th' next piece of mail."

"Yo're——" Nueces chopped his words short as an envelope popped against the glass door of the JC box. Shorty beat him to it and they retired against the wall, triumphant and elated.

Shorty's slow spelling was not to be endured, especially as he spelled out loud for all and sundry to hear.

His companion snatched the letter, held it high above the short one's head, and quickly read it. He then leaned down and whispered into Shorty's receptive ear.

"It's come! I'm takin' Bob's place somewhere southeast of here! Let's get in th' saddle an' talk this over. Come on!"

CHAPTER III

PORTER was the largest town in the county, although it was not the county seat; but while it was not the county seat it was, nevertheless, the real seat of government, for it was the home of the leaders of the dominant political party. The political strings which reached out all over the county came to a common center here.

Nueces dismounted before the smaller of the two little hotels and obtained a room. He stabled his horse, an animal which did not bear a brand registered inside the county, and wandered along the main street. About mid-afternoon he saw Bob Corson on the other side of the thoroughfare, the sheriff's badge glittering in the sun. Corson was present in his official capacity of sheriff, and wanted everybody to know both him and his job. There was no badge in sight on Nueces' lanky person, and neither of the two recognized the other. One ambled north, and the other south—passing as strangers—but Nueces soon turned and crossed the street, walking along lazily, a few score paces behind his boss.

Corson entered the Cattlemen's Bar and went over to a table where three men were seated. They leaned back on their chairs and made him welcome. Talking idly, they called for and consumed a round of drinks, paying scant attention to the horse-faced puncher who ducked his head to clear the top of the door frame as he loafed into the room.

Nueces leaned against the bar and smiled down at the man behind it.

"Little rye likker," he said amiably.

"Well, Mr. Corson," said the patent leader of the three men at the table, "we're glad to meet the new sheriff and to see him in our town. Yore predecessor warn't worth much to us folks down here in this corner of th' county. He kinda let things slide 'round here, an' when you let things slide they generally don't get no better. We're right glad to meet you, an' talk things over. What you say we have a round or two more, an' then shift over to a place where th' chairs ain't so all-fired stiff an' hard?"

Corson nodded, knowing that it was not a question of chairs, but of listeners. He was present in his official capacity to be complaisant, not too smart, and to show a due regard for the machine which, unasked, had veered from opposition to his election and at the eleventh hour had put itself behind him to help him into his job. He knew that the shift had been made only when it was certain that the landslide in the upper and western parts of the county had made his election a certainty. He knew, too, that the machine preferred to ride with a winner, claiming his success as its effect, and claiming, as a corollary, those favors and consider-ations which machines expect from their favored can-

didates. He knew that the defeated candidate had been
the choice of these three gentlemen and what they represented; that one of the reasons why the ex-sheriff
had not been seen around Porter was because he had
been told to stay away. He knew, or strongly suspected,
that the continued presence of an honest and active
sheriff in this locality would be strongly resented, and
that such an officer could hope to accomplish little by
working in person: he would be out in the open and
his every move watched and outguessed.

In clearing out his desk in the sheriff's office when
he took charge of it he had come upon a little batch
of memoranda, not destroyed by his predecessor because that person had been arrested and jailed on the
day of the election and had not been able to take care
of the little slips of paper. These slips had contained
data which the maker had deemed vauable for his own
safety against certain contingencies: crooks fall out,
and have been known to turn against one another. The
ex-sheriff had bulwarked his safety by careful notes of
this thing and that thing; not enough to bridge in the
gaps and make a clear and connected story, but enough
to back up the telling of the whole story by one who
knew it, and to give the telling weight.

Corson had read these slips with deep interest, an
interest pointed and stimulated by El Toro's ambigu-
ous remarks made in that meeting south of the JC
range. He gathered what he could from them, determined the drift of the evil wind, and locked them in

the safe, the combination of which had forthwith been changed. Then he had written to his lanky deputy, met that person at dusk thirty miles from the county seat, and ridden slowly through the dark night, stirrup to stirrup with him, talking with fear of neither being overheard nor recognized. Just before dawn the two had separated, Corson to return to his office to pick up a few things before his immediate departure for the town of Porter; Nueces, to drift along by himself toward the same destination; Corson, to enter the town proclaiming his official position by every means within his power: vain, proud, conceited, welcoming attentions; Nueces, a drifting cowboy, careless, lazy, enjoying the spending of half a year's accumulated pay.

The four men at the table stood up, pushing back the chairs noisily, just as the lanky puncher, facing around, beamed upon the room and upon them, and offered treats for "the house."

The foremost of the four, frowning a little, was in no mood for the observing of the trivialities of this common custom; although not to do so might be to give offense.

"Excuse us, friend," he said, the frown melting away and a smile taking its place, a smile intended to be placating. "We've had more than we need already."

Nueces coldly looked the speaker over.

"An' I reckon that warn't much," he said. "They grow 'em tougher up my way." He turned his back and spoke to the bartender.

"No offense, friend," said the leader of the four, his smile set. "Next time we meet we'll drink you under th' table."

The lanky puncher turned, a grin slipping across his face.

"That's a bet, pardner; you are all hereby excused, temporary. My name is Simpkins, gents; an' I aim to make, a loud noise in this here town while my money lasts; an' it's due to last right well." He raised his re-filled glass. "Here's to our next meetin', an' that there's room for four under that there table."

The four men saluted him and moved on out of his sight.

"You shore aim high, stranger," said the bartender, grinning. "Them fellers was Ike Peavy, his brother Frank, Ad Hitchins, an' Sheriff Corson."

"All of which means nothin' to me," replied Simpkins (as we will know him from now on), "except th' sheriff. I allus like to get a good look at th' sheriff of any county I might be in. Useful information, sometimes."

"Yes; an' overlook th' real things," commented the bartender sententiously.

"An' that means?" asked Simpkins curiously.

"Yo're like a kid baby: can't take yore eyes off a bright an' shinin' star. Them three fellers with th' sheriff are th' men that run this county an' th' sheriff an' his whole office along with it."

"Hell," grunted the puncher, grinning wisely, "that ain't nothin' new. Not to me, anyhow."

"No, 'tain't; but it's shore somethin' worth knowing, just th' same," said the bartender.

"Mebby," grunted the puncher carelessly, "but there's somethin', right now, that's worth knowin' a blame sight more: where is there a genteel, refined game of draw poker, where a total stranger might be expected to have a Chinaman's chance?"

"Ad Hitchins' saloon," answered the man behind the bar, "at this time of day. In here, after supper. None of th' games, howsomever, amount to much until after dark, when th' boys get in." He slid the bar rag along the counter. "Th' big three hang out together, an' play a stiff game. If yo're lookin' for action, you can get it there. If yo're just lookin' for a sociable game, you can get it in here."

"Ad Hitchins?" muttered the lanky puncher, and then his face brightened. "Oh, yes: he's one of them fellers that just went out. Well, I'm issuin' forth to look over yore little town. If I like it I might buy it, an' if I buy it, an' like you, I might make you a present of it."

The bartender laughed.

"Well," he said, humoring the fancy, "if you make up yore mind to buy it, I just showed you who to pay yore money to."

"In which case I'll mebby not buy it; but win it. S'long."

"S'long, friend."

Simpkins wandered along the street, past the Porter Cattlemen's Bank, in whose directors' room his friend

Corson was acting important. The regular hang-out of the big three was Ad Hitchins's saloon, but on this occasion they thought it wise to impress the new peace officer. Simpkins kept on, and drifted in through the door of Ad Hitchins's Royal Palace Saloon and Gambling Hall. Here he loitered, becoming casually acquainted with the lone man on duty behind the bar and with the layout of the building. Suppertime found him somewhat maudlin, outwardly, and he weaved gently back to the hotel and was the third man through the door of the dining room.

Supper over, the lanky puncher sauntered out into the office, found a chair which seemed to have been made more to his own specifications than the others were, seated himself comfortably, crossed his ankles, and settled down into a quiet reverie, where he ran over in his mind the many things which Corson had told him on that ride through the night. Names, episodes, situations; the peculiar conditions of the cattle trade in this corner of the county; certain clues, the values of which were as yet unestablished; the temper of some of the men on the opposite side; the peculiarities of two of them, noted locally for their deftness with and love for firearms. So he sat while the big office clock ticked on and on; and finally, its loud, brassy bell breaking into his cogitations, he glanced up at it, yawned, arose, and walked carelessly out of the door, heading for Hitchins's Royal Palace Saloon, which shortly would come to life.

CHAPTER IV

THE Royal Palace was more ornate than the saloons with which Simpkins had been familiar. The barroom itself was not much different except in size, but when one passed through the wide double doors in its rear wall and stepped into the gambling end of the building, he left austere simplicity behind him and stepped into an atmosphere of embellishment which seems to be a tradition with gambling places.

There were no rugs in this gambling room, but the floor was of hard wood, well polished in an attempt to hide the countless scratches underneath. The walls, plastered and papered, were hung with draperies, and supported pictures of more than mediocre workmanship, and subjects of high art. The tables were of walnut, massive, with thick tops, and well rubbed with oil. The lighting was profuse, both hanging and wall lamps flooding the room with radiance.

Simpkins, having stopped at the bar for a moment, passed on into the gambling room and stopped again just inside the big doors. His surprise was fairly well concealed, and his slowly moving gaze went around the place in calm and nonchalant appraisal. When he had scrutinized the last picture his grin was frank and congratulatory; and he straightway looked the pictures all over again. Then the tapestries caught his attention and intrigued him: he wondered what was behind them, or rather who was behind them. To his suspicious nature they spoke of hidden watchers and of ambush. Only a fool would attempt a holdup in this room; and only a fool would reach for a gun against any friend of the house. One of the hangings moved gently, a little, rolling billow of movement, as if a slight current of air stirred behind it, the others hung quietly.

The moving tapestry was in the middle of the right-hand side wall if one were facing toward the double doors; it represented gleaners, standing in a field, with bowed heads and stooped shoulders, pausing momentarily in their labors. He had never heard of the Angelus, and did not know that he was looking at a reproduction of it. It was the only piece of decoration in the big room which did not reveal the charms of nudity, and was, therefore, believed less likely to attract or hold the attention of the class of men who gambled there. To a careless man this difference would have preached in vain; but to Simpkins it told a story. If the time should ever come when he felt obliged to start trouble in this room, his first movement would be to send a shot through the middle of the Angelus.

The hour was early, but already some of the tables were filled and the games were running. The roulette table was still uncovered, that game not being so popular as the others. A three-card monte layout, keno outfit, and a faro game called the first comers. Simpkins's gaze moved on. Three men sat idly at a large, round table, with two unbroken packs of cards lying before them. They talked lazily and enjoyed their cigars in a period of relaxation. They were the three men he had met and talked with earlier in the day, and they nodded to him.

Simpkins, returning the salutations, wandered over to the faro game and lost ten dollars in three minutes. He went on to the three-card spread and got five of them back again. Keno interested him for a little while, and then he moved back to the faro game and watched the run of the cards. He was intent on keeping cases in his own mind, and checking up with the case-keeper, and his absorption was profound. Tiring of this after a few deals, he turned and wandered back toward the double doors, but he paused as Hitchins leaned forward over the table and signaled with a crooked finger. Simpkins nodded gently and moved in that direction, stopping to lean lazily against a vacant chair.

"You don't seem to show much interest in th' set games," said the proprietor, smiling.

"Too much like buckin' a machine," admitted Simpkins, returning the smile. "Reckon they're all right, if a feller's only playin' for th' money; but me, I don't gamble just for money: I gamble as much for th' fun I get in playin' th' game. Faro-bank's all right; so is monte; but for me there ain't no game like th' good old-fashioned American game, without no fancy work or extras. Draw poker, with incidental jack-pots, is my first name. An' that ain't no joke, because my first

name is Drew, which somebody told me is kinda past
tense for Draw. If it comes to a choice, an' the corner
is tight, I allus prefer th' present to th' past. Which
is my declaration, flat an' frank." The smile on his
face robbed the words of all suspicion of being related
to a declaration of war.

The three men were chuckling, twinkles in their eyes.
They were looking upon a pilgrim from some distant
place, some far-off range, a pilgrim who had had his
eyeteeth cut, perhaps, on a regular bunk-house game;
a pilgrim who rather fancied himself, and who itched
to cavort, calf-like, on a strange range. Cavorting calves
in human form meant money in the bank, and, while
they were not in need, a bank account is always improved by growth, and it never attains its full stature.
There is always room for more.

On the other side of the table stood the cavorting
calf, frankly supported by the back of the chair. He,
strange to relate, was in no way concerned by the
yearning of bank accounts, not even his own. He was
not crazy. He could become as deeply interested in
the net earnings of Aces-Full, Preferred, as almost any
man who crowded the edge of a table; but that was
only when there was nothing of greater importance
to be considered. And he never let himself crowd the
edge of the table, unless it was with malice afore-
thought. Just now he yearned for poker, as he always
yearned for it; but upon this occasion there was more
than pleasure, or money gains, as a motive. It was
his fixed belief that a game of poker would tell an

intelligent and observing man more about the other
men in the game than any of the milder methods with
which he was familiar. Of course, there was no test
like the sudden and unexpected threat of deadly peril;
but a man could hardly go around pulling his gun on
strangers just to find out their reactions. Even in that
day and in that society it was not considered quite the
proper thing to do.

Ike Peavy, blowing through his cigar to straighten
the ash line, shifted his gaze from cross-eyed contempla-
tion of the cigar tip to the horse-like face almost ruining
its own smile.

"We kinda owe you an apology, Mr.—ah———"

"Simpkins: Drew Simpkins," prompted Nueces
kindly. "Sometimes said, Simpkins drew: which is fre-
quent fatal."

"Ah—*ha-ha*—yes," continued Mr. Peavy. "Yes;
yes—as I was saying—damn' if *that* wasn't good—as
I was sayin', we kinda feel that we owe you an apology,
Mr. Simpkins—Mr. *Drew* Simpkins—for not drinkin'
with you this afternoon. There wasn't nothin' personal
in it. We would like it if you would join us in a few
minutes in yore favorite game. Just now we are waitin'
for th' arrival of th' sheriff; an' when he comes th'
game will start."

"Five's a better game than four, Simpkins," said
Frank Peavy. "You better straddle that chair an' kinda
get yore breath."

Simpkins felt the Angelus moving gently behind his
back. It was purely imagination, but the effect was dis-

turbing. He eased himself to full self-support, let loose of the stalwart chair back, and grinned genially at the big three.

"Be shore glad to," he said, and one could see that he was pleased. He pushed up his hat and scratched gently under it with a long, skinny finger. "You boys got any objections if I kinda mooch around, lookin' closer at them pictures? I ain't never seen nothin' quite like 'em before."

"Go ahead; we'll call you when th' sheriff gets here," said Hitchins with a laugh. "They're well worth lookin' at."

Simpkins nodded gravely and sauntered away to make the circuit of the big room, the eyes of the three occasionally upon him. He did not pause before the Angelus, unknowingly following the precedent of many men before him; but he timed his arrival before it to coincide with that of another man who was hastening toward the faro game. They bumped gently, apologized automatically, and Simpkins maintained his disturbed balance by resting for an instant against the tapestry. As he moved on again he held the impressions of the brief contact. The wall behind the picture had creaked so softly that he barely had heard it. There was some kind of long, narrow projection on the wall, and it was not plaster. Could it be the molding framing a door? Better yet, could it be the molding framing a small window, a loophole? Either would do for a hypothesis, for in this case things unlike the same things were equal to each other. Door or window or loophole, it was all the same to a ready gun barrel behind the hanging. What of it? Many of the gambling places he had been in had had an armed man protecting the interests of the house; but they had been easy to discover; he did not like this hidden watcher. How could a hidden man see through the tapestry? Very small holes, perhaps, cunningly placed.

He moved over and watched the monte game, drifted on to the faro layout, and then again sauntered to the poker table, dropping into a chair on the other side of the table, where he could see the Angelus without craning his neck. He had taken a deal of trouble to change his seat, and now he relaxed gratefully, placid in the thought of a good deed well done.

Ad Hitchins stretched his legs and grinned across the table.

"Yo're a stranger in these parts, I take it?" he inquired, purely for the sake of making conversation. Some men dislike a continued silence.

"Yeah; I'm out to see th' world," drawled Simpkins, basking in the genial atmosphere. He showed signs of becoming confidential, the mark of the foolish and the unwary.

Frank Peavy chuckled.

"You've mebby got a lot to see," he said. "You have, if you see 'em all."

"Reckon so," replied Simpkins. "I aim to see much more of it very soon, though. I've been workin' right steady for a hull year an' didn't have no chance to spend my wages. I'm beginnin' now, an' I got a whole year for th' job. That oughta be time enough to see a lot."

Three minds worked automatically with the same thought: if this stranger could work for a year, and then live a year in comfortable and gambling idleness on his savings, he had not been a common cowpuncher working for common wages. Either that or he was a trusting fool with not many vices. If he had worked at an honest calling—oh, well: a night or two of hard luck at a gaming table might make a great difference in his cash reserve.

There was another mind thinking along the same lines. Simpkins knew what he was saying when he had said it. He fidgeted and looked a little anxiously through the doorway toward the bar, as if instinctively looking for a way out of his blunder. He believed that honesty was no asset in this company.

Ike Peavy put his own interpretations on the shifting look, and struck a little bell on a tabouret at his side; and a waiter left the bar and started toward them.

Simpkins grinned as his eyes took in this moving figure. He had turned like a flash when the bell sounded, closely scrutinized his companions through narrowed lids; and then, nodding, looked again toward the outer room. Now he chuckled.

"Mind readin'?" he inquired, motioning with a thumb toward the approaching waiter.

"Readin' yourn right then was easy," laughed Ike Peavy, and believed his own words. "I've spent half my life tryin' to read minds over th' tops of th' cards."

The stranger's reaction to the tinkle of the bell was now engaging his real interest: this fellow was suspicious, perhaps apprehensive, and despite his size and lazy mannerisms, was as quick as a bobcat.

"I've lost a couple of fortunes tryin' to read minds," admitted the other Peavy, his mien bespeaking sorrow.

"Yeah, you have," said the proprietor with heavy sarcasm; "but you've shore done picked up just one more than you've dropped, an' you got that one now." He beckoned to the waiter. "What'll you boys have?"

"Reckon this is on me," said Simpkins, reaching into a pocket.

"But I rang th' bell," objected Ike Peavy without much enthusiasm.

"An' I'm talkin' to th' waiter," said Hitchins.

"Well, let's match for it," suggested Simpkins, juggling a twenty-dollar gold piece in the palm of his huge hand. He thought he caught the gleam of the gold reflected on Ike Peavy's eyeballs.

"All right, then. Count me in," said Hitchins. "Odd man pays."

Simpkins did not change his expression as he swiftly thought that here was the old, odd-man game again making his acquaintance; but the stakes were too trifling, in view of what might possibly come out of this meeting. If there was to be any crookedness it would appear when the stakes were large: they would not cheat him for a round of drinks; in fact, to play it true to form, they should let him win.

Three pairs of hands reached out over the table top

toward its center, in each clasped pair a coin. Hitchins and Simpkins showed heads; Peavy, tails. Hitchins's chuckle was so full of real enjoyment that it told a little tale.

"Name it, friends," said the loser, and in a moment the waiter was on his way to the bar.

Simpkins reached idly for one of the decks of cards, found it sealed, and absent-mindedly toyed with it. Sealed decks meant nothing to a man of his experience: sealed decks can be as crooked as unsealed decks if the house is crooked and wants a plant.

"We only need one or two more for a whirl at th' great American," he suggested, his eyes lighting momentarily.

"Th' sheriff will be here in a couple of minutes," said one of the Peavys.

"An' th' house rules are?" asked Simpkins curiously.

Hitchins waved toward a framed card hanging on the wall near the big doors.

Simpkins regarded it gravely and slowly shook his head. He did not care to leave his chair, and if he gave the impression of not being able to read it would do him no harm.

"Can't read such fine print," he said, revealing a hint of embarrassment.

Hitchins looked closely at him for a moment and quickly explained the rules of play adopted by his establishment. The game was a regular Hoyle affair, all freak hands being ignored. Straights were legal hands and fell in their regular place.

Simpkins nodded and watched the waiter place the drinks on the table. His companions were talking carelessly of things known to themselves, occasionally including him in the conversation; and then Sheriff Corson entered the building and crossed the barroom toward them. He nodded smilingly as they looked up, and perfunctorily included Simpkins. One could see that he was a great man, and that he knew it.

"Sorry to have kept you waitin'," said the sheriff. "On my way here I met a couple of fellers that I've seen up in th' county seat. They want to be made deppeties, an' I had trouble breakin' away from 'em. Seems like a lot of folks want to deppeties."

"Who are they?" asked Ike Peavy curiously.

"Oh, a couple of fellers named Huston an' Brady."

"I know 'em," said Hitchins. "Right good men, too. We oughta have a couple more good deppeties down here. As a matter of fact we'd all take it right kind of you if you'd appoint them two boys."

Corson smiled and shrugged his shoulders.

"Anythin' you say, Hitchins; but I've already fixed it up with 'em. They're deppeties right now, an' when I get back I'll fix up their papers. I aim to stand in with th' reg'lar boys. I don't figger to buck th' organization. What is this game goin' to be?"

"Just a friendly fight," chuckled Frank Peavy. "Two bits an' a dollar. That agreeable to everybody?" he asked, looking from the sheriff to Simpkins.

Corson nodded and drew up a chair, while on Simpkins's horse-like face a placid and benign smile spread itself.

"That allus was my game," he admitted with a chuckle. "Stiff enough to make it interestin', an' still keep it in th' pleasure class; anythin' steeper is work, an' makes a man think too hard. It gives some value to a bluff, too." While he spoke he had broken the seal and tossed the cards in the center of the table. In a few minutes the game was on.

"Saw some nice HF critters trailin' out to-day," observed Ike Peavy, passing in turn and tossing his cards into the discard. "Fine, four-year-old steers. Their cattle shore run heavy."

"She's open," said his brother Frank, shoving out a white chip. He looked at Ike. "What you talkin' about? They got more different kinds of cattle than any ranch hereabouts."

"She's up another, just to make you feel at home," said Ad Hitchins, shoving two white chips into the pot. "Yeah, they shore have got all kinds; but, Frank, when they want to make up a uniform herd they shore can do it, providin' they're satisfied to make up a small one."

"I was raised on poker," said the sheriff rather importantly, sliding three chips from his stack, "so now *I'm* raisin' her. Three queens look awful good to me before th' draw."

"So do mine," chuckled Simpkins, seeing. "I only need two more queens to have a good hand." His laughter was low and contented.

"Reckon we're playin' with experts," said Hitchins, grinning. "That makes six queens already, an' Simpkins is hopin' to draw two more."

The game ran on.

The Royal Palace began to fill. The big front room was soon comfortably crowded and its noise steadily arose in volume. Men drifted in through the big double doors, most of them passing close to the poker table and pausing to exchange greetings with the three politicians. The casual interruptions constantly interrupted the game. The sheriff was flattered by these attentions and grew more important under them; the lanky stranger was affable, but he did not let his thoughts wander far from the cards. Apparently this was so, but in reality he paid close attention to the newcomers and quietly checked name after name from his mental list. He became acquainted with Brady and Houston, the new deputy sheriffs; he met certain others in whom he was professionally interested. He decided that poker was a great institution and found added zest in the game.

The big outer room was noisy, but the gambling hall was remarkably silent and decorous. The games were now running full blast, only the roulette table being poorly attended. Apparently it was there for advertising purposes more than for anything else. The faro bank and three-card monte layouts were crowded. Low, droning voices; the occasional click of chips; the sudden growl or pleased exclamation of loser or winner occasionally arose above the low hum of restrained voices.

The poker game ran on with its ups and downs, but was averaging remarkably close. There were big hands and runs of poor ones, but not a man in the game was a novice, and luck seemed to play no favorites through extended deals. When the play ended a little after midnight only the house was the real winner, and the difference between the heaviest loser and the biggest winner was not great.

Sheriff Corson lived up to his part, although he played a shrewd game—a game which awakened the silent admiration of the only professional present. As the minutes passed and as one introduction followed another he grew visibly more important, until the individual had become submerged by the dignity of his official position. The three politicians, having watched him closely without appearing to do so, now judged that he had been inflated enough by flattery and deference to play the part they had chosen for him.

Hitchins, the leader, stretched and then squared off to the table, looking from one to another.

"Well," he said, smiling, "instead of callin' th' game over, let's call this a recess, an' start a real game. It's still early, we've had a chance to study th' play an' get acquainted. What you say about raisin' th' limit, an' playin' a man's game?"

Corson looked a little doubtful. He glanced around the table at each face in turn, studying them briefly.

"Well," he said, and then hesitated. "I didn't bring much money with me, not knowing that anythin' like this was in the wind. Besides, things are a little tight with me, an' I didn't reckon I'd need much." He poorly concealed the struggle going on in his mind: the avid eagerness to win big money, and the contending fear of losing it. Judged by the standards of this house he was a weak member.

"Shucks!" laughed Ike Peavy genially. "Judgin' from th' brand of poker you been showin' us I don't reckon you'll need to hand out any real money, but if you do yore IOU'S are good enough for us."

Simpkins had taken no part in the conversation, but he had reached for and picked up a new deck, and was idly looking at the seal. His actions bespoke his agreement with the proposal for heavier stakes, and he was heartily in sympathy with the idea: never before had he played with money that was not his own, and to sit in a big game with the county treasury behind him and his expense account was very agreeable to him. He considered this game as a necessary introduction to the characters he was to watch and outguess, and in that light it became a necessary expense. He glanced idly at his companions, and when his eyes rested for a moment on Corson's face all his pleasant anticipations were blasted. Corson signaled for him to get out of the game.

Ad Hitchins looked at the lanky puncher, wondering just how to get rid of him without giving offense. Ad did not believe in arousing unnecessary enmity.

"We're goin' to play a mighty steep game, Simpkins," he said with a disarming smile. "I shore hope that you won't have to go back to work after it's over."

The two Peavys nodded and grinned. Ike chuckled reminiscently.

"I've seen five thousan' dollars change owners," he said, rubbing his hands.

"Many's th' time," endorsed his brother.

"That so? Well, you won't see no five thousan' of mine change no owners," replied Simpkins, grinning foolishly. "If you gents will excuse me, I'll go play penny ante with th' children."

"Well," replied Hitchins regretfully, "we shore don't want to drive you out, Simpkins. You play a right inter-estin' game, an' we'd like to keep it five handed."

"Man, you boys ain't drivin' me out!" assured Simpkins with much feeling. "I'm just pullin' my stake, vol-untary, an' wanderin' on. See you all ag'in, mebby, to-morrow night, an' take a hand with you in th' prac-tice game. Sorry to spoil this five-man combination, but—so long!"

"Well, suit yoreself. We'll be mighty glad to wrastle with you to-morrow night," replied Hitchins with a chuckle. He turned to the others. "I reckon we better move into my office. A big game allus draws a lot of onlookers, an' that interferes with th' play. What you say?"

Simpkins moved over to the faro table, where the two new deputies were guessing wrong. He watched the play, standing near Brady, and after a few minutes the player cursed his luck and glanced up at the on-looker.

"You just can't turn a run of bad luck," said Simpkins, sorrowfully shaking his head. "I've tried it, an' I know."

"Yo're right!" growled Brady, pushing back from the table. He pocketed his remaining chips and arose, looking inquiringly at his friends and fellow deputy. Huston nodded and left the game, joining them.

"Faro ain't got no respect for th' law," he said, grinning.

"Well, *I* have," said Simpkins, motioning toward the bar. "I'm goin' to buy th' law some drinks. What you say?"

Brady's hand brushed over his new badge of office, and his frown gave way. "I'd 'a' got this sooner if I'd 'a' knowed it was goin' to work like this. Yo're a stranger down here, ain't you, friend?"

"Yeah," answered Simpkins, "though I shore don't want to be."

"Reckon you don't have to be, then," said Huston, smiling. "Lookin' for work?"

"Hell, no! I just got through with a year of it!" protested Simpkins. "Don't you say 'work' to me!"

As they neared the big doors his companions glanced from the deserted poker table to a small door set in the farther wall.

"Big play goin' on in there, I reckon," said Brady knowingly.

"Too big for me, friend!" chuckled Simpkins. "I

rode her till they changed hosses, an' then I drifted. I got a year's pay on me, an' I shore aim to keep *some* of it. Well, what'll it be? Name yore pizen."

It was whisky, three rounds of it, and good whisky, judged by local standards, after which they wandered over to a vacant table, to talk idly and to get better acquainted. The two new deputies wore their badges of office in plain sight, and the moving crowd passed and repassed, exchanging banter with the two men. They seemed to be well known and to be well liked; but that meant nothing positive to their cheerful companion.

CHAPTER V

In the private room the four men had removed coats and vests upon entering and made themselves comfortable. Any game played in there was a purely personal affair and in no way was connected to the fortunes of the house. There was no kitty, and the chips, of special marking, had no redeemable value with the cashier outside. Poker was Hitchins's hobby as well as livelihood; but in this room it was his hobby only, and he played as a purely personal matter and not for the house.

The situation was somewhat delicate and quite difficult. The other sheriff had been a comparatively poor man, who would have found it next to impossible to redeem any sizable IOU's; but the present incumbent was a man of wealth, as wealth was measured in that part of the country. The other sheriff, once deep in debt, would have to remain there, and trust to the mercy of his creditors. This he had done, and he had found them lenient; indeed, he had found them so lenient that his IOU's had never been presented for redemption. This state of affairs had not been free from conditions, however, for he had to make certain promises and to live up to them to the strict letter.

He had agreed to remain away from that section of the country and to let it severely alone. He had made gestures, it is true, but they had amounted to nothing. The present sheriff, under the same conditions of loss, could write out his check, redeem his pledges, and be free from any obligation in connection with them.

Hitchins and his friends had discussed the situation from all angles, and finally decided upon an entirely different course of action. Had they dared, they would have openly and frankly bribed the new official and not have quibbled over a few thousand dollars more or less. They believed that he loved money; but they also believed that he was not to be bought. How, then, were they to obtain their ends and get him into a position where he would be obliged to take their orders?

As they sat around the table for a brief talk before beginning the game, Hitchins leaned back in his chair, reached behind him to a little paneled closet built in the wall, and brought out a box of chips and some new decks of cards. He tossed the cards in the center of the table and pushed the chip box toward Corson, finishing the movement with a salute.

"In this room the guest always takes th' bank," he said, smiling. "Seein' that you are th' only newcomer, that honor is yourn. There is no kitty. The house has nothing to do with this game, except that by tacit understandin' we have always followed house rules in th' matter of th' play. Now, sir: let us set th' values of th' chips. First, shall it be a limit game?" He was looking directly at Corson.

The sheriff wet his lips and glanced at the other players. He was torn between cupidity and fear.

"Why, what do you boys say about it?" he asked them, somewhat nervously.

"A limit game is safer, an' more sensible; but it cuts down th' power of th' bluff, an' to my way of thinkin' bluff is more than half of poker," said Ike Peavy. He smiled. "Not that I make any great practice of it."

"That's right," said his brother; "but, personally, I favor a limit. We can make th' limit high enough to make a good bluff stick." He looked at Hitchins. "What's th' idear of this game? Blood only, or blood an' pleasure? Why not play our reg'lar game? Don't seem fair to raise th' limit when a stranger sets in."

"Anythin' at all suits me," replied Hitchins. "What you say, Sheriff?"

"Well, what *is* th' reg'lar game?" asked Corson nervously.

"Five dollar ante an' a hundred-dollar limit. Th' whites are five; th' reds, twenty-five, th' blues, a hundred. We usually buy a thousan' dollars' worth of chips to start with."

"My Gawd!" exclaimed Corson, and thought a moment. "Why, I ain't got that much money with me," he objected. "I never expected to run up ag'in anythin' like this: but, if that's yore *reg'lar* game, I'd like to play it—if th' shock don't kill me!"

"Bein' banker, you don't have to have a cent to start with," explained Frank Peavy, grinning. He was finding a great deal of enjoyment in the situation. "You

only need money if you lose. That's why we make th'
newcomer th' banker. You only have to pay for th'
chips you have to redeem. If you have more'n yore
share of 'em, you don't need a two-bit piece. Ain't
nothin' much simpler than that, is there?"

"It shore is right simple; but suppose," said Corson
argumentatively, "that th' banker lost more than he
could pay? You boys are takin' a chance, with a rule
like that."

"There's no chance to it, a-tall," replied Hitchins,
chuckling softly. "We never invite a man to play in
here who can't make good his losses; either that, or
he don't take th' bank. So far's yo're concerned, there's
th' bank, without no strings to it whatever." His tone
and gesture were very flattering.

"All right, then," replied the sheriff, and fell to
counting out the chips. Three check books came out
and Hitchins took pen and paper from the little cabinet
in the wall. In a few moments the banker had passed
over chips for the checks, took a thousand dollars'
worth of the counters for himself, and placed the box
and the checks on the floor beside his chair—and the
game was on.

For a young man Corson had played a great deal of
poker, and he had played against all kinds of players,
good, bad, indifferent, and crooked. An intuitive value
of cards had been groomed and made proficient by
hours of playing; but, knowing this, he was hardly
prepared for the success which perched upon his hands.
He won and he lost, but after the first few rounds his

losses were light and his winnings large. He found
that Ike Peavy, despite the closeness of his play out
in the public room, had now a most unwarranted affec-
tion for two pairs; that Frank Peavy liked to gamble
with straights, either inside or outside; and that
Hitchins, a professional gambler who made an excellent
living at his trade, never seemed to vary his play.
Hitchins had a trick unforgivable in a gambler: when he
held a really dangerous hand, he had the habit of sitting up very straight and pressing against the edge of
the table.

At the end of the first hour Ike Peavy, frankly sore
and disgruntled, parted with his last chip, swore that
he would play no more, and found solace in the whisky
bottle. Being reasoned with against breaking up the
game, he grudgingly consented to buy more chips and
took another stack. Frank Peavy, also, was playing
his second stack, while Hitchins was down to his last
hundred dollars.

As it happened, the last deal was three handed. Ike
Peavy, his second thousand still intact, threw down
his hand and refused to play. Hitchins opened with
a white chip, and Frank Peavy saw it and raised. Corson saw, and raised in turn, and the raise was met.
Hitchins's last chip was in the pot when the cards were
dealt for the draw. Hitchins passed, Peavy bet the
limit, and Corson saw. Hitchins, swearing under his
breath, threw his hand into the discard and announced
that he was through for the night. Ike Peavy growled
an affirmative, his gaze fixed steadily on the proprie-

tor's face. On the showdown Frank Peavy won and raked in the chips.

"No more of this to-night," growled Ike. "I never saw th' cards run like they did since we closed that door. No matter what I held, it was a losin' hand. Let's stop th' damn game, an' talk. I've had enough."

"I'm agreein'," said Hitchins with a sigh of relief. "I couldn't seem to get started, an' everythin' I done was wrong."

Corson nodded, and watched Frank Peavy counting his chips, and silently counted with him.

"Nine hundred an' forty dollars," said Frank, sliding the small stacks across the table. "Here," he said, digging into a pocket. "Here's three double eagles; pass me back one of my checks."

Corson nodded and obeyed. He redeemed Ike Peavy's untouched second pile, and then, folding the other checks and placing them in a pocket, looked around curiously. Secretly he was very much puzzled and somewhat perturbed.

"I've played a lot of poker," he admitted slowly, "but I never sat in a game that ran quite like this one did." He glanced at the decks of cards on a chair and shook his head. "We've played two hours, an' used six new decks of cards. Nothin' seemed to change th' run of th' luck. I feel like apologizin'. Well," he said, laughing uncomfortably, "any time you believe you can get it back, yo're shore welcome to try for it. I just can't understand it, nohow."

"We know we're welcome to try for it," said Hitch-

ins calmly. "Well, Sheriff, how do you like yore job
of bein' law boss of th' county?"

The conversation ran along lines apart from poker,
and the Peavy brothers slowly regained their good natures, severely strained by their losses; and yet, Corson
found something unconvincing about their attitude;
in fact, there was something unconvincing about the
whole affair. The Peavy brothers even became genial
under the mellowing effects of good whisky, good cigars,
and pleasant company. Somehow they seemed over-
genial, as behove winners instead of heavy losers, and
Corson was tempted to recatalogue them. And so time
passed with discussions of politics, poker, and almost
everything else, except the local cattle business.

Out in the other part of the building Simpkins and
his two new friends still talked much and drank little
at their table. They were thus engaged when the game
in the inner room broke up, and after. Simpkins was
recounting a humorous experience of his own when
a tall, rangy puncher hastened into the barroom from
the street, caught sight of them, and made straight for
them, his peremptory gesture signaling George Brady.

"Hey, George! George!" he called. "Come here!"
and he stopped in his tracks for the other to come to
him.

Brady arose, grunted something to his companions
in the way of apology, and joined the speaker. After
a few moments of low-voiced and excited conversation
the two separated, the puncher to hurry out again, and

Brady to return to his companions, his expression not a pleasant one.

"Damn that greaser!" he muttered as he reached the table, and then, noticing the look of curiosity on the face of his new friend, he explained shortly: "It's El Toro ag'in. Damn that Mex cattle thief! He's just run off fifty head of IP cattle. Reckon we'll have to say good-bye to you, Simpkins, for a while. We got plenty of work to do."

"Hell," said Simpkins with restrained zest. "Swear me in, why don't you? I'm lonesome, an' kinda itchin' for a little excitement." He grinned expansively. "I was a deppety, once, myself. They fired me, though; fired me hard."

"Fired you?" asked Huston politely as he pushed back his chair.

"Yeah. They said I got careless when I found out that a friend of mine was in th' gang we was after. Anyhow, they blamed me for lettin' 'em git clean away. Hell, it wasn't *my* fault."

The two deputies exchanged smiles and shook their heads.

"We can't swear nobody in," replied Brady, who as yet was unfamiliar with the extent of his powers. "We ain't got time to wait for th' sheriff to do it." He snapped his fingers impatiently. "My Gawd! I near forgot that Ike Peavy an' his brother are both here. I got to see 'em, pronto. Wait a minute, Jim," he flung over his shoulder to his brother officer.

They watched him reach the door of the private

room, knock upon it, listen, and enter. They got a glimpse of a smoke-filled room, of a bright green table devoid of chips and cards, and of four men with their coats and vests off. Ike Peavy was on his feet, leaning against the table, his frayed cigar clamped between set teeth as he listened to what Brady had to say to him. They saw the standee turn to the sheriff and smash his hand down upon the table until the glasses jumped.

Corson protested and stood erect. Then he reached for his coat and vest, grabbed his hat, and strode toward the door, his companions duplicating his movements. The five men crossed the big gambling room, the cynosure of all eyes, and hastened toward the front door. Hitchins looked at a group of three men and shouted an order about getting horses, and the sheriff's mount as well, and the three men departed at top speed. As they neared the cashier's desk Hitchins checked his companion and said something about having to wait for the horses, and he took the official's arm and drew him aside. He might as well make use of the wait by getting cash for the checks.

The sheriff nodded and stepped to the desk, took out some slips of paper, endorsed them, pushed them across the counter and took bills in their place. He was not thinking of the checks or the cash, but automatically following his companion's suggestion while his mind was engaged with the news that had just come in. In a moment he and Hitchins swung from the desk, joined the impatient little group, and hurried out of the door and into the street.

Simpkins tagged along and joined the group outside the building, not being noticed in the general excitement. It was not long before they were mounted and riding out of town under the brilliant light of a glorious full moon in a cloudless sky. Conversation was general and no one appeared to realize that a stranger was with them until Hitchins, looking around for no particular reason, let his gaze rest upon the stranger.

"What th' hell are *you* doin' here?" he demanded with pugnacious curiosity.

"Just ridin' along," answered Simpkins, grinning with good nature. "I tried to get George to swear me in, back in th' saloon, but he said as how he couldn't do it. You reckon th' sheriff will?" His face was placid, but revealed a trace of eagerness. "I'm fair honin' for some excitement. You'll reckon he'll swear me in?"

"Swear you in?" asked Hitchins, his voice rising in anger. "Why, you —— —— fool! Who th' hell told you to horn in on this?"

"No need to get mad," reproved Simpkins. "You might need a good man before you get back; an' I'm shore rated as a good one. An extra gun might come in handy."

"Well, seein' as he's heard everythin' that anybody had to say," cut in Ike Peavy, "I reckon we better keep him with us. You never can tell about strangers, an' *he* stays with us!" His eyes glinted ominously. "Brady, since he's such a damn' good friend of yourn, you keep him with you every minute! You savvy? Keep yore eye on him every minute!"

"Great —— ——! He ain't no friend of mine!" retorted Brady angrily. "I never saw th' damn fool before
to-night!"

"He follered *you,* an' that makes him yore dog!"
snapped Hitchins. "Yo're responsible for him!"

Sheriff Corson dropped back among the wranglers.

"Why fight about it?" he asked with pardonable curiosity. "Seems to me that another man might prove to
be a good thing. Here, Simpkins: I'll swear you in as
a temporary special deputy. Hold up yore hand." He
rattled off a jumbled oath; Simpkins nodded and then
grunted affirmation. "All right, Simpkins, Brady's yore
boss," he said sternly. "You do what he says, an' stay
close to him."

The general wrangling slowly died out as the horses
pounded over the trail. The leader suddenly swung
from the main road and followed a fainter path which
left it at an angle. This led them to a group of ranch
buildings, where half a dozen men rode forward to
meet them.

"Hands off that gun!" snapped Brady to his "dog."
"Them's friends!"

Simpkins nodded and released the walnut, sighing
with relief.

Ike Peavy was now in the lead and he drew rein as
he met the foremost of the outfit.

"What you boys doin' here on th' ranch, with fifty
head run off?" he demanded angrily.

"We just got back, boss," answered the foreman of
the IP. "Lost th' trail in th' hills. Got to wait for day-

light. Them greasers are headin' for th' border, damn em!"

"Yes, an' they'll cross it before we can catch 'em!" snapped the owner of the IP. "Where'd they strike us this time?"

"Over in th' big arroyo," answered the foreman. "Dan was ridin' acrost it on his way home from town, an' he saw th' whole thing. Six greasers, they was; an' that feller Rodriguez was th' boss. They caught sight of Dan, drove him into th' bush, crippled his hoss, an' then rustled th' bunch they had rounded up."

"An' where's Dan?" demanded Peavy ominously.

"Here, Ike," called a voice, and its owner pushed up from the rear of the group.

"Couldn't you hold off a handful of greasers on yore own ground?" asked Peavy.

"It was six-shooter ag'in rifles, boss; an' they got my cayuse in th' first couple of minutes. He jumped an' pitched so damn' much that I couldn't hit a butte from th' saddle; an' I dassn't dismount or I'd be left afoot to fight a bunch of horsemen."

"How do you know that Rodriguez was there?" asked Frank Peavy, taking part in the conversation for the first time.

"Heard 'em call his name an' git cussed four ways from th' Jack for doin' it. Oh, it was El Toro's gang, all right. You'll never get 'em now. It's just another bunch they got away with."

"—— ——!" swore the ranch owner. "There's a man with three thousan' dollars on his head, *dead* or alive, an' there ain't a damn man in this whole country that's got guts enough to go out after it an' make a try for it!"

" 'Cept me," said a humorous voice. Simpkins's grin was hidden in the moon-cast shadow of his huge hat. "If there's anythin' I like, it's three thousan' dollars, an' a *dead* prisoner. You don't have to watch 'em when they're dead. Now that I'm a deppety, when this job is done I'm goin' to cost somebody three thousan' dollars, an' then play poker in that little room of th' Royal Palace. Man, I'm shore glad I come along!"

"Big wind to-night!" sneered somebody, and the crowd laughed. "Though there ain't no dust risin', at that."

"Th' big wind will raise th' dust, a puff of dust right off th' front of yore vest, you mealy coyote!" retorted Simpkins. "You make yore play! I may be Brady's dog, but I ain't yourn, —— —— you!"

"Here! Here!" snapped Corson. "Quit that! If there's any fightin' to be done, you save it up an' do it ag'in th' greasers!" He turned to Ike Peavy. "We might as well light off, eat a snack, an' wait for daylight; it'll be on us in a shake."

CHAPTER VI

When the sun pushed up over the low hills the posse was already on its way. The scene of the gathering of the cattle for the flight was first visited, and the self-important sheriff dismounted and spent half an hour moving on foot over the ground. Not a man present except the new special deputy had any knowledge of the expertness of the young official in this reading of sign, and would have been very much surprised and more than a little worried had they known it, and the sheriff gave no indication of the fullness of his art, but rather otherwise; he verified the tale of the IP puncher to that person's ironic satisfaction. The sheriff then asked a few more questions, went over some of the ground for the second time, and swung back into his saddle, his eyes for a moment engaging those of Simpkins. It appeared that he did not regard Simpkins very highly, for he regarded him with a frown; but Simpkins knew how to read that frown, knew what caused it, and he immediately discarded the sheriff's findings. The posse moved on again.

Following the trail ever southwesterly, they came at last to the international line and paused near one of its markers. The prints went on into Mexico, shrinking to nothing in the distance.

"There's no way to stop 'em now," muttered the sheriff. "They come an' go as they please, an' when they get south of this line they're safe." He turned to Ike Peavy. "What's this El Toro look like?"

Peavy's eyes glinted and an unpleasant expression came to his face.

"I reckoned you knowed what he looks like," he said slowly. "Wasn't there a lot of talk about you an' him bein' friends?"

"Mebby there was," retorted Corson shortly. His face grew hard. "*I* know what he looks like; but I want to find out if anybody down here knows."

The air was filled with words, and El Toro was described impartially, according to the guessing ability of the various speakers; but it was not upon El Toro that this structure had been so laboriously built. Rodriguez was the keystone, and there was no doubt but that he was well known, by sight, at least. And if Rodriguez could be connected with this raid, then it followed automatically that El Toro was responsible for it, since Rodriguez was his *segundo*.

"As for me bein' friends with El Toro," pursued Corson coldly, "you can believe that if you want. Th' man did me a favor an' I returned it. I canceled it, an' th' next hand is a new play. If you think that El Toro is behind these raids that you've been complainin' about, an' want me to stop 'em, you have only to say so. I'll come down here, an' stay here, with my own outfit an' men I know, an' stop th' rustlin' if it takes all my term of office. If you want this rustlin' stopped, I'll do it, no matter *who* is behind it."

Ike Peavy smiled evilly. "I'll see that bluff, an' I'll raise you th' limit!" He turned to the rest of the group. "You boys ride on back, ahead of us, except Frank an' Hitchins. Wait here, Sheriff: we'll hold a pow-wow."

The rest of the posse whirled and went back along its own trail, one member of it especially keyed up for action if the need should arise. When well out of earshot the IP owner turned slowly and looked the sheriff in the eye.

"I saw yore bet an' raised, Corson," he said abruptly. "Yo're too good a poker player to bluff ag'in strength. I got th' best hand, an' you know it. Th' only play you can make is to throw 'em into th' discard. It's freeze-out—an' yo're out, cold."

"I never was much of a hand at figgerin' puzzles," replied the peace officer; "but I'm figgerin' you for a busted straight, an', whatever th' limit is, I'm boostin' her ag'in. Now I ain't waitin' to be asked: I'm comin' down here with my own men an' clean this range to th' grass roots. That sound good to you?"

"Yo're leavin' this part of th' county th' first thing in th' mornin', an' yo're *not* comin' back," said Frank Peavy, his face set and cold. "We're goin' to holler for help, but yo're goin' to be stone deaf. Yo're stayin' up where you belong: an' that is in yore own end of th' county. That sound good to you?"

"I don't know what th' hell yo're talkin' about, an' I doubt if you do, either," retorted the sheriff, seeming to have trouble to hold back his anger. "It don't make sense, nohow. If you've got anythin' under yore hat beside hair, talk plain."

"You don't have to know any more than you do right now, an' that ain't anythin'," said Ad Hitchins, grinning. "You can make any excuse that sounds good to you, but yo're not goin' to pay any attention to any calls for help that come from down here. *We*'re aimin' to handle El Toro ourselves, an' in our *own* way, an' we don't want to be bothered by no damn' sheriff's office. You leave town to-morrow, an' you leave in a huff. You can even call us a lot of names; but you *go* away, an' you *stay* away. That sound good to you?"

"I'll go when I please, an' I'll come back when I please!" retorted Corson, his official dignity again in evidence. "*I'm* th' sheriff of this county, an' I run my office to suit myself!"

"You'll do as yo're told!" snapped Ike Peavy. "You will, or you'll lose yore job, an' go behind th' bars. That won't be no new experience for you, neither!"

"What do you mean?" asked Corson, his eyes narrowed and the pallor showing through his tan. "Spit it out, an' spit fast!"

"All right," drawled Ike Peavy, his voice silky. "We've got three one-thousan'-dollar checks with yore name in endorsement on th' back; an' we deny that you ever won 'em at poker, or at any other game. We gave 'em to you in that little private room, with th' door closed, an' they wasn't no presents, by a damn' sight. Our story is that you've been bribed, Sheriff: an' you took th' checks an' you cashed 'em as quick as you could. We'll swear to that, an' we're three to yore one. You'll stay away from this section, an' you'll do as yo're told!"

The sheriff sat slumped in his saddle, simulating the surprise of a lifetime; and he really was surprised, at that. No one spoke, but let the situation sink in, and let him search frantically for a way out. He never thought faster in his life. He stared into their grinning faces, his own gradually becoming the picture of defeat. The cockiness went out of him; the dignity departed and his official pomposity collapsed like a top balloon. He sighed, groped for the reins, kneed his horse, and without a word swung into the trail of the others. His three companions, smiling exultantly, bunched up closely and followed him at a distance.

"Ad, you old coyote," said Frank Peavy in open and joyous admiration, "you shore got a head on you. She slid like she was greased!"

"Well," said Hitchins, chuckling in rare good humor, "we couldn't bribe a man as rich as him; but, by G—d, there is allus a way if you'll take th' trouble to look for it! We figgered him, an' we figgered right; that's all."

"Everythin's all right for a year," said Ike Peavy reflectively. "It looks like we've got to reëlect him, time after time. There ain't no use throwin' away a good tool, after you've got it sharp an' ready to work."

"No, there ain't," said Hitchins quickly; "an' if we pound him too hard we'll turn th' county ag'in him, an' nothin' on earth will reëlect him. We dassn't call on him

for help very much, or very loud. We'll grumble a little
an' let it get forgotten. Anyhow, we can allus be too
proud to ask for help in our own troubles. I near choked
when I saw him cash them checks. Gawd, what a fool
he is!"

"Let's push on an' give him some company," suggested Frank Peavy, taking the lead.

"Sheriff," said Hitchins as they rejoined the dejected
official, "we don't want you foolin' around town here
for just one reason: we don't want no arrests. When
that greaser thief, or any of his gang, get caught, we
aim to hang him, forthwith an' pronto. Down here
there ain't no sympathy for expensive trials that run
up taxes, an' we ain't got no use a-tall for technical law-
yers. We live here, an' we aim to run this part of th'
country in our own way. Frankly, we all prefer lynchin'
an' we aim to put th' fear of God into rustlers, an' not
feed 'em at th' county's expense. We ain't intendin' to
be hobbled by no sheriff's office, an' we don't give a
damn for no court. You just stay away from down here,
mind yore own business, an' nobody will ever hear about
them checks. Yo're mighty sore now, but you won't be
after you get used to th' idear. Why, hell! Look at th'
trouble we're savin' you!"

Corson turned an angry face to the three.

"Don't you coyotes reckon that I'm worryin' none
about what goes on down here," he rejoined. "I don't
give a damn if yo're robbed of yore last peso! I don't
give a damn if you lose every head you've got! Th' only
thing I'm thinkin' about is them checks. If I reckoned

you had 'em with you, I'd take 'em from you so damn' quick you wouldn't know what happened!"

"You mean that you'd try it," sneered Frank Peavy, stung a little out of his cold and calculating balance. His hand had dropped to the butt of his gun as he spoke.

The reply was a blur. They found themselves looking into two dull steel tubes, and the hooked thumbs fascinated them.

"Mebby I better go through you after all!" snapped the sheriff. "You might have 'em on you!"

"You know better than that," said Hitchins, somewhat changing his opinion of the peace officer. "We turned right away from that counter an' left 'em with th' cashier." He smiled a little. "Anythin' happens to us, an' they'll speak for themselves, an' for more than bribery. Right now there's a signed an' sworn statement pinned to 'em, an' it'll hang you."

Slowly, reluctantly, the sheriff let his guns fall and shoved them back into their holsters, nodding understandingly.

"You win!" he admitted, and then he laughed, sneeringly, bitterly. "It serves me right for mixin' in with a lot of dirty politicians."

"You can call us worse than that if it'll make you feel any better," said Hitchins, pushing on.

Back in town again, Corson left his companions without a word and went to the hotel. Once up in his room he shed his depression with his coat and fought with himself to keep his laughter silent. After he was able to give sensible attention to what he did, he took the poker winnings from his pocket, made a compact roll of the bills, and wrapped them in a handkerchief. They would go into his office safe in that condition, and with them would go a written memorandum.

Midnight came and passed, and then Corson's door slowly opened and the sheriff moved softly across the hall in his stockinged feet, pushed open a door on the other side, and gently closed it behind him.

Simpkins was about to light a cigarette, but feared the flare of the match. He turned his head quickly and watched the door. It was slowly opening, and he grinned a welcome, although the darkness hid it. An hour later, alone again, Simpkins waited a few minutes to be certain that the sheriff had regained his own room, and then slid out of his clothes to enjoy a sleep which would be deep and untroubled.

CHAPTER VII

CORSON entered the dining room for his breakfast, glanced around, saw Simpkins eating heartily at a table near the front window, and chose a table at the other end of the room. It was at the close of the breakfast hour and the two men had the room to themselves. Simpkins looked up, grunted a welcome, and went back whole-heartedly to his gustatory labors. The sheriff nodded to him perfunctorily, gave his order, and when he was served ate silently and in preoccupation. He did not seem to be in very good spirits.

Simpkins finished, pushed back, and arose. He took several toothpicks, pushed them down into a vest pocket against a future need, and moved toward the door. About to pass near the sheriff's table he paused, considered for a moment, and then sauntered toward the peace officer.

"Mornin', Sheriff," he said, giving the impression that he realized that he was addressing royalty.

"Mornin'," grunted Corson without any encouragement.

"Want to ask you somethin'," said Simpkins a little nervously.

"All right: ask it," growled the peace officer, idly

watching the proprietor, who had just entered the room and was unnecessarily fussing with the appointments of a near-by table.

"It's true that there's a reward for that El Toro hombre?"

"It's true; there is."

"An' it's—it's three thousan' dollars?" continued Simpkins hopefully.

"It is," grunted the sheriff.

"Dead or alive?" persisted Simpkins, still more hopefully.

"Yes."

"Make any difference where he's got?"

"What you mean?" demanded the sheriff with a frown.

"I mean, do I have to catch him inside th' county?"

"There's nothin' said about that."

"Would it be better to?"

"Reckon so."

"Well," said the lanky puncher with a grin, "I could allus drag him across th' line."

"Reckon you'd have to, anyhow. They'd shore want to see him before they paid out any reward on him."

"That's so, too. You goin' after him, yoreself?" asked Simpkins with ill-concealed anxiety.

"No!" answered the sheriff, fairly snapping the word.

Simpkins's sigh of relief was audible, and brought a smile to the proprietor's face. The latter found this conversation of more than passing interest, and he believed that the interest would be shared by Ad Hitchins and his friends. He must tell them about it as soon as he could.

"Reckon I will, then," said the puncher, his enfolding grin threatening his ears. "There ain't no use of bein' a special deppety sheriff for nothin'."

"You ain't a special deppety anythin'!" retorted the sheriff. "You was appointed temporary, for that one job. Th' job's ended; an' so is yore appointment."

Simpkins hitched up one of his belts in indecision, was about to ask for reappointment, and then, realizing that the sheriff's humor was not propitious, asked a question instead.

"Then I ain't no officer, a-tall?"

"No. Adios," grunted the sheriff, and then, feeling sorry for the lanky fool in front of him, gave a warning. "I said Adios: I said that because I reckon yo're fool enough to go after El Toro. If you *do* go after him, it shore will be *adios* for you."

"Meanin'?"

"You'll know what I mean after you find him, *if* you ever do."

"Oh," muttered the puncher, scratching his head. His eyes grew hard. "Reckon mebby I will. Well, so-long, Sheriff."

"So-long," grunted the peace officer, feeling of his coffee cup to see how much it had cooled.

The proprietor watched the lanky puncher amble out of the room and then went over to the sheriff's table.

"That coffee cold?" he asked. "Lemme get you a fresh cup."

"It's just right. Don't like it so damn' hot," replied the sheriff with unjustified irritation.

"Stayin' with us very long?"

"Not five minutes longer'n I have to!" snapped the peace officer.

The proprietor managed to restrain his smile, nodded understandingly, and turned away. He had reached his desk and was idly tidying it when the sheriff entered the office and approached him, hand in pocket.

"What's my bill?" he demanded, and paid it in gold coins when he had been told.

Ten minutes later Corson stepped out of the back door and headed for the stables, and five minutes after that he rode past the side of the hotel, turned into the main street, and soon thereafter was to be seen no more. An hour from town, a cautiously following rider stopped, turned, and rode back to Porter, going directly to the Royal Palace Saloon to make his report; and up on the second floor of the hotel a window shade fluttered gently as Simpkins turned away from it.

Hitchins listened to the report in silence, pulled up his belt, looked at the few early bar-flies loafing near the front window, and motioned to the man behind the bar.

"Set out th' drinks on th' house," he ordered, and wheeled to go to his private office.

Up at the hotel the proprietor fussed around his desk, waiting for the lanky puncher to come downstairs and go out, and impatient to make his report to the gambling-house proprietor. His eyes strayed to the ceiling, and his ears were alertly tuned for the creaking of the stairs.

Up above, Simpkins saw that the loops of his gun belts were filled, wiped and oiled his guns, jammed them into their worn sheaths, wiped the grin off his face, and went awkwardly down the protesting stairs. He nodded to the proprietor, passed out of the back door, and strode to the stables. In a few moments he rode off, under the watchful eyes of the hotel-keeper, stopped at the general store, made a few judicious purchases in the food line, put them in his blanket roll, and headed south out of town. Coincident with his disappearance was the hurried exit of the hotel-keeper, who turned his steps up the street in the direction of the Royal Palace Saloon.

Simpkins held to his course, although he drew steadily away from his real objective, which lay more to the west. Mile after mile was put behind him, and at last he reached a monument at the side of the road. Beyond it lay Mexico. He crossed the boundary and pushed on for several miles, until he had topped and ridden down the far side of a low range of hills which extended east and west. Following along the ridge and hidden by it from the view of anyone who might be riding to the north of the boundary, he at last came to the continuation of the trail which he and the rest of the posse had followed the day before.

To follow that trail to its end, if it had been made

by El Toro's band, would have been a dangerous pro-
ceeding for any man living in the lower part of the
country; but it was not dangerous to Simpkins. He
was known and liked by the bandit, and also, in his
own mind, it had not been made by any of that worthy's
riders.

He rolled a cigarette, lit it, and pushed on, following the prints of the hoofs. After a few miles the trail
turned, ran westward for two or three miles farther,
and then swung to the north, following a dried water-
course, which had been gouged deeply in the friable
earth by the rains of countless numbers of years. He
knew these infrequent rains in the Southwest, so few
and far between, and so furious when they did come
that they poured sheets of water down the slopes,
filled the arroyos with seething floods, to carry all before them, and quickly to disappear.

The trail led upward over a gentle slope, left the
arroyo, and disintegrated into its several individual
prints, which wandered off in all directions and became
the ordinary tracks of range cattle casually grazing.
Here the drive had ended, back on the range whence
it had started.

Simpkins grunted with satisfaction, and a grim smile
slipped over his homely face. The raid had been faked.
There was reason why no empty cartridge shells, no
telltale grouping of horse tracks showing an offensive
in one direction, had been found where the posse had
searched. He cast around, picked up the tracks of the
horses, and followed the shoe prints, riding slowly and

thoughtfully. It was mid-afternoon when he cautiously
rode up a rise and stopped where he could barely see
over its crest. Far in the distance lay the ranch houses
of the IP; but the horse tracks did not go that way:
they led straight for Porter, and did not make the
mistake of connecting the outfit of the IP with the raid
on the ranch.

Simpkins grunted again, turned his mount, and rode
down the slope; and not much later he was riding, roundabout, for the town, his mind busy with one of the puzzles he loved so well. He had learned a fact, which
could be coupled with other facts; but while they were
of absorbing interest in themselves, they did not tell
him the answer to the questions he was asking himself:
answers that could be proved in a court of law. Had he
ridden around the country, asking for information, he
doubtless would have learned the answers more quickly,
and at the same time exposed his hand and, perhaps,
rendered it valueless. He had his own answers, but
so far they were only personal opinions, and no matter
how true they might be they needed verification and
proof before they would be true to others.

Reaching Porter he put up his horse and wandered
idly down to the Royal Palace Saloon. Coming in from
the dazzling sunlight, he required a moment to adjust
his vision to the softer light of the big room, and the
group which sat around one of the tables in the rear
slowly took on definite facial details. Ad Hitchins was
gazing at him with studied directness, as were the

other two, who the puncher saw were the Peavy brothers.

Simpkins moved over to the table and dropped into a chair, raising his hand to the bartender.

"What'll you all have?" he asked carelessly, while the functionary behind the counter paused for further instructions.

"Nothin'," said Hitchins shortly and gruffly.

"Nothin'," echoed the other two in one voice.

Simpkins looked his surprise, lowered his hand, and shook his head at the bartender, who thereupon resumed the polishing of glassware.

"You said somethin' about seein' th' world," said Hitchins slowly and meaningly.

"Yeah," replied Simpkins with a foolish grin.

"Then you better move along an' do it," said the gambler coldly.

"Huh?" asked Simpkins, his face blank. He seemed to doubt his ears.

"You'd better move along an' do it," said Ike Peavy, parrot-like, while his brother nodded unequivocal endorsement.

"Oh, there's lots of time for that," said Simpkins, the grin returning. He stretched out his long legs and relaxed in the chair, settling himself comfortably.

"You want to copper that idear," said Ike Peavy. His voice was hard, his gaze level and unfriendly. "Boot Hill, out back, is chock full of fellers that stuck their noses into other folks' private business."

"What do you mean?" asked Simpkins, hoping for specific reasons. He was pleased with himself. If he could definitely connect their animosity against himself with his morning's activities, it would go far to verify some of his suspicions.

As if they read his mind their animosity faded, or, rather, it took on the aspect of anxious friendliness. Hitchins's pitying smile turned mournful.

"Simpkins," he said, shaking his head sorrowfully, "you ain't got a chance. Th' minute you begin takin' too much interest in El Toro, some greaser will rise up in a patch of sage an' drill you as calmly as he'd kill a fly. Either that, or you'll step around th' corner of a buildin', or through a door, an' slide up on th' blade of a knife. You better pull yore stakes while you can. I'm tellin' you yo're foolin' with a dangerous business. Now, then, we'll have that drink on you, feelin' that we've done earned it."

"Gosh! After that talk about th' knife, I need one, too," replied Simpkins, the look of alarm slowly fading. "That El Toro must kinda run this country."

"He does; but if th' sheriff was worth a damn he wouldn't," growled Frank Peavy. "He comes down here, looks around, an' goes home ag'in. Make mine rye."

One round called for another, and the four men sat and smoked and talked, taking things easy. Simpkins seemed to be of two minds, and he grew restless as time passed. He continually brought the conversation back to El Toro and to that person's activities, a subject which appeared to be wearying to his three companions, but they humored him, as they might humor a child.

"Look here! You want to put that greaser out of yore mind," said Hitchins somewhat unpleasantly; "or somebody'll blow it out."

"Shucks!" exclaimed Simpkins a little boastfully. "That's been tried more'n once, an' I'm still alive. Let me tell you that three thousan' dollars is three thousan' dollars. Hell! That's all I was able to save outa a whole year's work." He caught himself and looked a little vexed at his slip. No cowpuncher, working honestly at his trade, could earn, let alone save, that sum in a year.

Ike Peavy's quick glance at his friends apprised them that they were not oblivious to the slip of the tongue. There was only one way that a man could work with cattle and earn, and save, that much money. Even as foreman of a good ranch, as wages went in those days, Simpkins could hardly receive more than one hundred and twenty-five dollars a month; yet he had saved three thousand dollars. Ike Peavy was wondering whether he should press the subject, when Hitchins took the lead away from him.

"That's all right, but th' money won't do you much good if we have to cover you up in Boot Hill," said the gambler. "You've done so much talkin' about gettin' that bandit that if I was you I'd shore pull stakes an' ride on to see th' world." He smiled grimly. "An' you don't want to start with Mexico."

CHAPTER VIII

AFTER his talk with the three politicians Simpkins determined to spend most of his time in the saddle, and in consequence he rode forth from the hotel the following morning, bound for almost anywhere, since one direction seemed to be as good as another. He wanted to locate the small ranchers, talk with them, get acquainted generally and learn the more important details of the country. Coincidental with his departure from the hotel, a Mexican from another part of the county was riding into town from the southwest, a lean, brown youth with snapping black eyes and teeth that gleamed like a rift of snow on a tree-clad mountain slope.

They met before the vacant lot which stood between the general store and the last saloon on the trail, and Simpkins received a slight shock. It was one of El Toro's most trusted couriers, by name Felipe. To be seen and recognized in Porter was to be revealed in all the perfidy of an officer of the law, even though it was in the days when officers of the law were not perfidious. Unpleasant premonitions filled the puncher's soul. His scowl was automatic, reflexive; and then it faded, for the Mexican answered the frown with a smile, and the white teeth seemed to heliograph.

Simpkins caught the friendly momentum of the in-

stant and seized it by pressing a finger to his lips; and
then he was past and riding on, a clear after-image on
his retina revealing the almost imperceptible nod of
assent which was the answer to his plea.

"Felipe," he muttered, and then mauled the matter
thoroughly in his mind, flopping it from one side to
the other, and even peering under it. Felipe might be
expected, from his scanty accumulation of years, to be
filled with the surging irresponsibility of youth, to be
careless in his talk; but Felipe had been well trained, and
the few times in which he had thrown himself against
the point-studded training collar had taught him much.
Now he did his master's bidding with a singleness of
purpose which awoke admiration in those who knew
him well. This thought emerged from the mental wel-
ter in Simpkins's mind, and the puncher found the day
rarely beautiful.

A hoof-marked path turned aside from the main
trail, and the rider swung into it, to follow wherever
it led. It was a lazy path, for it climbed no slopes that
it could go around; but, like human destiny, it had both
a purpose and an end. For a while it seemed to be interminable, ever leading southeastwardly; and then its
end came into sight.

An adobe house, pink as a tooth powder, stood
against the base of a small hill and emphasized the
patch of greenery which evidently marked the location
of the spring. To the right of it stood a corral, a crazy
thing of shreds and patches, apparently held together
by the cohesion of the ether; but rawhide strings, cut

by a thrifty soul, do not show up well against a background of the same general color, and that corral would have stood up against an amazing amount of punishment.

A red-haired man, down on hands and knees, was searching the earth like a hound, quartering and re-quartering, circling and re-circling. He was preoccupied to the exclusion of all else, and advertised it so patently that the horsemen, obeying a sudden whim, rode up to him and then gently maneuvered the horse until its belly was over the rancher's back. Then Simpkins shouted in an exceedingly loud voice.

Jim Pettingill arose hastily, found that he was no Sampson, and jumped aside from under the horse like a jackrabbit leaving hair in a coyote's teeth. He had thought, panicky, that it was an avalanche; but now he was reassured, and his mental connection between past and present, suddenly appearing, took on a tint of anger.

"What th' hell you doin'?" he asked his guest.

"How'd you get under my hoss?" demanded Simpkins with strong suspicion. It was always best to put them on the defensive right at the start, and let them wriggle, like a worm on a hook.

"——— ———!" said the ranchman emphatically, admitting to himself that he was much befuddled.

"I must 'a' been asleep in th' saddle," explained Simpkins, and then hurriedly checked himself. That sounded like he was breaking ground: all right, breaking ground was good tactics if one stepped in again, swiftly and unexpectedly. He stepped in. "An' so must *you!*" he accused.

"Must me what?" asked the rancher, and then his red face grew redder. The fool words did not sound like he had thought they would.

" 'Must me what!' " jeered Simpkins. "I said you must 'a' been asleep, not musty what!"

The rancher grinned. He had been lonely, at times, out here away from everything; but the presence of another damn' fool cheered him.

"I was huntin'," he explained, the grin growing.

"Flaggin' antelope?" inquired Simpkins with grave simplicity.

"Flaggin' hell!" retorted the rancher with spirit.

"Good for you! I never knowed it could be done."

"There's a hell of a lot you don't know," retorted the ranchman. "Fact of th' matter is, I lost my collar button," he explained.

"Collar button?" asked Simpkins with justified curiosity, as he looked at a shirt whose neck band must have been used for a bandage, or some other necessary purpose. It was not there.

"Yeah, a collar button," said Redhead in grave explanation.

"Oh, a collar button?"

"Yeah."

"Where'd you have it last?" asked Simpkins, again eyeing the collarless shirt.

"In th' house, in a tobacco sack on th' shelf."

"Which shelf?"

"Th' shelf over th' winder."

"Then what you lookin' out here for?" asked the horseman, yearning for knowledge.

"Told you I was tryin' to find it!"

"Thought you was tryin' to plant it, from yo're actions. Anybody been here but you?"

"No."

"An' you didn't take it off th' shelf over th' winder?" persisted the horseman.

"No!"

"Then how th' hell could it get out here?"

"I don't know; but anythin' a-tall can happen in this damn' country!"

"That's the first thing you've said that's had any sense to it," said Simpkins brightly. "An' lemme tell you somethin' else, Red: yo're th' only man in this whole county that owns a collar button, an' I don't blame you for wantin' to hang onto it. But, after all, what good is it?"

"It's a keepsake," explained Red.

"Well, it ain't lost; it's somewhere in th' county. I'm thirsty."

"Bottle or spring?" asked the rancher.

"You got a lot of hard, common sense under that red hair, an' I feel like I'm goin' to cotton to you, though Gawd only knows why. I vote for th' bottle."

"Well, you want me to bring it out to you?" asked Pettingill with a trace of belligerency.

"No, sir; you might drop it!"

In a few moments, through the influence of a common multiple, they were on the way toward friendship, and they talked of this and that and whatever. Simpkins's garrulous ramblings eventually reached a point, which they so often did.

"What makes you think anythin' can happen in this damn' country?" he asked, a trace of reproach in his voice.

"I think what I know!" replied Pettingill.

"But do you know what you think?"

"Gimme that bottle! You had more'n was good for you when you first got here; though how in hell you got that hoss over me I don't know."

"You got a bad habit of jumpin' to conclusions. Are you shore that you know what you think is right?"

"My Gawd!" said the ranchman. "Friend, first thing you know you'll be pickin' snakes outa yore—outa yore —outa yore coffee!"

"I used to believe that, too," replied Simpkins, re-membering an almost forgotten supersition of his boy-hood. "Only it wasn't coffee: it was water. I used to put hairs, horse hairs, into bottles of water an' hang 'em in th' sun, so they'd turn into snakes. Th' hired man on my daddy's farm was a great snake raiser, only he never raised none. He taught me that trick. Now-adays I just look into th' coffee, if th' cook don't happen to be bald-headed; an' bald-headed cooks are scarce."

"You must 'a' been livin' off by yorseself, like me, only yo're a damn' sight worse than I am," said the host. "Man, don't you know there's only one liquid that makes snakes?"

"Snakin' you back to th' present, what makes you reckon that anythin' can happen in this country?" persisted Simpkins, following the true scent.

"Greasers," explained Pettingill.

"Greasers?"

"Yeah, *greasers!*" He spat the word out almost like an epithet, and his face revealed his hatred for it and what it stood for.

"Try to be more siplicit," said Simpkins gently.

"Huh? Siplicit?"

"Meanin' simple an' kinda detailed," explained Simpkins. "I make 'em up when I need 'em."

"Uh-huh. Would you mind throwin' standard hitches for me?"

"Gawd, but you do scatter!" reproved Simpkins. "Well, back you come once more: you remember th' question?"

"Simple, but kinda detailed?"

"Man, you ain't no fool, after all!" enthused Simpkins.

"Ain't I?" mused Pettingill. "If you hadn't rambled up I'd be on my way right now, headin' back to a country where they leave th' post holes when they steal th' posts. All I had left was that collar button, an' I was aimin' to pack it out before they got that, too; but I reckon it's too late. I cached th' whisky outside, or that would be gone, too."

"Looks like you an' me oughta have a talk," suggested Simpkins. "How come yo're all set to get outa th' country, an' what else have you lost beside that damn' collar button?"

"Every head of cattle I owned, an' four hosses," replied the rancher. "I come down into this place with four thousan' dollars an' some odd dimes. Bought yearlin' heifers, mostly, an' branded 'em JP. Lived on nothin', an' worked hard. Come th' third year an' I had a nice little herd. Sold a few head to keep goin'. Didn't even play poker with th' boys, though I knowed quite some good fellers. Poker bein' my main hobby, that shore was real self-denial. I got th' four thousan', in th' first place, in a poker game. Borrowed a hundred for a grub stake, prospectin'; learned there wasn't no gold where I aimed to go, an' fell by th' wayside. Played poker thirty hours straight, kept a-liftin' th' limit, split with th' man that staked me, an' then come down here. Now I got near what I started with, minus th' four thousan' an' a hoss. That means a few odd dimes. When I leave I'll have to walk, because I can't buy a hoss, an' hoss-stealin' ain't healthy."

Simpkins nodded and kept quiet. He was all ears.

"This is rough country: hilly, with arroyos an' draws. More cattle around than can be seen from one spot. Nobody bothered me, an' I didn't have no call to get suspicious. Sometimes it seemed that a lot of head were missin'; but, as I just said, th' cattle can get out of a man's sight right handy, an' stay out of it. Still, they did seem kinda thin an' scattered, an' I took to ridin' around, lookin' for 'em. Last spring I dug down into my pocket an' hired a round-up crew. When th' bad news busted I knowed that I'd lost half my cattle. I did quite some hard ridin' then; an' then damn' if my hosses wasn't stole. I walked to town to get a couple more, an' when I got back I found this shack had been cleaned right down to th' ground: they didn't even leave me a skillet! Next mornin' I rode out to look around, an' there wasn't no cattle left. I follered th' trail across th' line, an' had my hoss shot out from under me. It took me all that day an' most of th' night to get home ag'in, an' then I found that my other hoss was missin'. Now even my lucky collar button's gone, an' I should be gone, instead of sittin' here talkin' to another damn' fool."

"Greasers, huh?" muttered Simpkins, rubbing the stubble on his chin.

"Yes, greasers, damn 'em! An' damn that fat-head of a sheriff! An' me votin' for him, like a fool, just because I reckoned it would be a good joke to elect a man that was settin' in jail. He oughta go back in ag'in! I figgered he couldn't be worse than th' other feller, but there ain't no choice."

"Figger yo're kinda sore," commented Simpkins, not without cause.

"Sore? I'm so sore I'd like to kill half a dozen of them damn' thieves! I'd like to stay here an' go on the warpath. Losin' that collar button puts a blazer on me, an' now I'm gettin' out while I got boots to walk in."

"You've had lots to say about that collar button," replied Simpkins. "You talk like it's big medicine."

"It *is* big medicine! I found that button under my chair when I sat down to that big poker game. I picked it up, an' just for fun put it on top of my first pile of chips. Man, you should 'a' seen that stack grow! Then I started a new stack, with th' button on top of it, an' it growed right up even with th' other. Stack after stack, till th' house had to come over an' buy 'em back, so they'd have some to sell to customers. Over eight thousan' dollars in thirty hours! If I had that button I'd go to town, borrow a stake, an' drop in at a place I know about. I'd own th' town at th' end of a week, an' never have to work no more."

"I'll tell you how you can make a stake," said Simpkins. "I'm after that three-thousan'-dollar reward that's on El Toro. I can't be ridin' over th' country, an' in town listenin' to th' gossip: not at th' same time. I'll stake you to a pile of chips, a room an' table board. If you lose, all right: you won't owe me nothin', an' you won't be no worse off. If you win, you stay in town an' make a livin' playin' poker. Any gossip that you hear about fellers bein' missin', cattle bein' lost, or anythin' else that you figger is interestin', you save it up an' tell me. What you say?"

"I'd be a sucker not to take you up; an' it strikes me that yo're a sucker to make such a play. Of course, if I win, I'll split even with you; but I shore won't win without that collar button."

"Is that so?" inquired Simpkins with heavy sarcasm. "You had that damn' button right along, here in th' house, an' you lost all yore cattle an' hosses. I figger you got rid of it just in time. What kinda button was it, anyhow?"

"Gold, with a diamond chip set into it."

"Sorta pretty little knick-knack, huh?"

"Shore was."

"You mean shore is," corrected Simpkins. "Such a pretty little knick-knack that most fellers wouldn't throw it away, huh?"

"Yes."

"I tell you that yo're better off without th' damn' thing. Its luck went sour, an' th' feller that stole it ain't got no damn' idear what's fixin' to light onto him. You cheer up, Red; an' you get th' feel of this."

Simpkins dug down into a pocket and drew out a fat roll of bills. He started to peel the layers, stopped and looked intently at the money, and shook his head.

"Bills are numbered. They *can* be traced. I'm so damn' suspicious that I'm afraid to go to sleep, almost. Reckon hard money is more in our line, because we ain't supposed to be thick enough to be stakin' each other. Here," he said, shoving the roll into one pocket while he dug into another with his left hand. "Here, Red: here's th' stuff that talks in all languages, an' right out loud. It'll be a relief to get th' weight off'n me." He was digging into other pockets and bringing to light more coins, and he stacked them in front of him and pushed them over toward his companion.

"You must be an awful successful train robber," said Pettingill. He lifted the glittering coins two at a time and restacked them. "Thirty-two, I make 'em." He eyed them thoughtfully. "Don't seem right to take advantage of a child like you. Three hundred an' twenty dollars for nothin'. I'm glad you dropped in, even if you did try to tromple me to death."

"Not for nothin'," reproved Simpkins. "For yo're say-so. Mebby I'm a child, but I shore outgrowed th' notion of makin' a god outa a collar button. Besides, I allus did have a likin' for gray-blue eyes an' red hair."

Pettingill chuckled as he pulled the coins toward him. There was warmth in his smile, friendship in his eyes, and a glow in his heart.

"I allus believed that a hoss was a noble animal," he mused whimsically, the smile growing as he looked squarely and frankly at the homely face in front of him. "And if you don't look like a hoss, then I'm a liar, an' I've got medals for tellin' th' truth. Shake, Stranger!"

"Simpkins was my father's name," said the visitor, crossing his fingers.

Pettingill glanced from the telltale motion, his expression saying that he absolutely ignored it.

"You must 'a' inherited yore father's trustin' disposition," he said, laughing gently as their hands met and closed across the home-made table in a man's grip.

"Yeah; he sold patent medicine from a wagon!" chuckled Simpkins.

"Then you shore oughta know somethin' about medicine: I'll take yore say-so on th' collar button; if you say it's bad luck, then *I* say so. I aim to keep my eyes on poker hands, an' my ears open promiscuous."

"I thought you had more sense than you showed," replied Simpkins, grinning. "I not only know about medicine, but I make it; an' them I make it for, take it—even if I have to shoot it into 'em. You bein' so talkative to-day, suppose you tell me all you know about this blame' country: th' little ranchers, the mejium ranchers, an' th' big ranchers. Tell me about their brands an' their drives. Tell me them things, 'specially, that you reckon they wouldn't want you to tell. For instance, what scandal do you know about th' IP? Is it growin' awful fast? Is it makin' lots of money? Who put Ad Hitchins in th' driver's seat in this country? Who greases his axles, an' who hands up th' reins to him? Spit on yore hands, an' get goin'—we got all day, so you won't have to leave very much out."

The shadows crawled up from the west, shortened, stood still, and moved eastward. The low hum of voices rose and fell. An almost domesticated lizard moved across the roof of the hut in short, swift dashes, but mostly it froze and seemed to listen. On the top of a distant hill a coyote slid into sight, its delicate nostrils turned toward the house; and in a moment it disappeared like a ghost. Boxes scraped on the clay floor as the two men who used them for seats pushed them back and stood up.

"Then you've flat made up yore mind to give up this shack?" asked Simpkins, leading the way toward the door.

"Pronto, an' permanent, without no strings of any kind or nature whatsoever a-tall."

"Then I reckon I'll unroll my blankets an' take possession," said Simpkins. "I ain't got no collar button
to lose. Hotel life is confinin', an' there ain't many
places hereabouts where there's a spring like that one.
It's a reg'lar gushin' fountain; an' if th' soil is th' right
kind there would be a right smart crick headin' down
th' watershed."

"Yes, th' spring's a big one; biggest I know of for
miles around," replied Pettingill. He raised his arm
and pointed. "Th' crick is fair-sized, for a ways. That
scabby salt marsh is where she sinks. 'Bout a mile, I
reckon."

"You got a head, but you only use it to hang a hat
on," said Simpkins. His gaze drifted from the distant
sink and ran along the verdant ribbon which marked
the course of the stream, and stopped at the spring.
The little brook ran strong for more than three quar-
ters of the distance, which bespoke an earth not nearly
so porous as it might well be. By building a low dirt
dam half a mile below the spring a man might be able
to have a permanent pond for the drinking of many
cattle. He had seen such ponds, where, after a few
inches of water had collected, cattle had been driven in
and around and around, puddling and packing the bottom until it was tight and firm. Water is the keystone
of a range, and a necessity along a drive trail. He who
controls the water controls the rest.

"Red, I like this here location," said the lanky
puncher; "but I don't like it so much that I want it if
you do. When you get ready to move to pastures new,

suppose you sell me th' place? An' if you change yore mind, an' get on yore feet financial, an' figger to buy you some more cattle, an' make a lot of money raisin' 'em, then you let me know; but, in between times, I'd like to win this ranch at poker, with th' gang lookin' on. You bein' busted, an' me a stranger, you could easy claim th' place is worth more than it really is, an' fool me into puttin' up real money for it. I don't want to win it permanent, but just temporary."

"I don't know what yo're talkin' about, an' mebby you don't," said Pettingill, smiling. "Get yore breath an' tell me some more."

"Well, Red, there's a thought buzzin' 'round under my hat," went on the visitor; "an, anyhow, we don't want th' title to that spring to get outside th' fambly. So, if I come a-pesterin' around you when yo're playin' poker, an' make sarcastic remarks about you, they don't mean nothin' a-tall, except that I want to get into a wrangle with you an' win all yore money. If you'll just remember that I'm talkin' to th' gang an' not to you, an' that I don't mean a word of it, then we'll pertend otherwise an' let nature take her course. I want to win this here ranch. Th' reason I want to win it is because I reckon somebody wants it awful bad. They want it so bad, an' dassn't come out an' show it, that they're wastin' time stealin' yore cattle, an' yore cookin' outfit, an' even that damn' collar button; an' all th' time there's so much bigger game to be won with th' same effort an' risk. In th' first place this water is right valuable for grazin' stock; but I've a most unexcusable idear that it's worth even more in another way. After I look over th' lay of th' land hereabouts, I'll know more about that. Just now I want a place to drop my saddle an' unroll my blankets, outa th' sleet an' th' snow."

"Sleet an' snow!" exclaimed Pettingill, breaking the seemingly endless monologue. "That's somethin' they ain't seen down here for th' last three hundred an' fifty years to my own personal knowledge."

"An' I thought you was a young feller," reproved Simpkins. "Well, then, outa th' rain."

"Ha-ha-ha!" boomed Pettingill. "That's near as bad. It's two hundred an' eight years, come next Sunday, since we had any rain."

"Damn' if you ain't a wet blanket!" retorted Simpkins. "Then outa th' wind! I'm goin' to have a reason to stay here, lemme tell you! See if you can put th' brakes onto that!"

"No, by Gawd, I can't. You win!"

"Well," said the cheerful puncher, "you hoof it for th' dens of th' devil an' th' sinks of iniquity, an' get you some action in a poker game. Me, I'll just move in, an' around, an' about, an' likewise roundabout. But you tell me this: In all yore wanderin's, lookin' for yore stolen cattle, have you ever seen what you thought was a cattle trail anywhere near here? A kinda set cattle trail, like it was used kinda reg'lar?"

"Shore. She runs up from north of th' Rio Grande country, through Frijoles arroyo, cuts acrost th' corner of th' CD ranch, an' peters out ten, twenty miles above.

Howsomever, it ain't been used for years; not in my time, anyway."

"Any water on it?"

"That's why she ain't bein' used. There ain't none north of th' Grande, except a little puddle on th' CD."

"Very well, Mr. Pettingill. I've enjoyed yore visit an' am glad you called; but if you'll get th' hell outa here, an' go back to town, I'll unload my can of tomaters an' settle down. You don't know me an' I don't know you, an' if anybody sees me here I'm just a-squattin', findin' it deserted like. So-long, an' good luck."

CHAPTER IX

LEAVING Pettingill to ride shanks' mare to town, Simpkins carried his blankets into the shack, placed his
scanty provisions on the shelf near the sheet-iron stove,
which no one had stolen as yet, rustled in some twigs
and branches of scrubby brush, and determined to collect some of last year's chips for a steadier and more
reliable fire. Then he mounted and moved up over the
hill, riding hither and yon as his fancy dictated, content
to learn the lay of the country immediately surrounding the house. He returned well before dark, cooked
a meager supper, and after he had cleaned up the culinary mess went outside to the box which served as
wash bench and sat down upon it with his back against
the wall.

It was rather too early to expect visitors, but he did
not lose sight of the possibility. The spring was a large
one, larger than any he ever had seen, and the volume
of water it discharged was considerable. It was also
cold and sweet, and had no taste of copper or iron or
gypsum or anything else which might be expected in
that part of the country. Pettingill had told him that
it flowed steadily all the year round, and to him this
suggested that its source lay deep and did not depend
upon local surface seepage.

The drive trail mentioned by Pettingill came in for its share of thought, and he determined to examine it; not that he expected to find much, but more for the purpose of cataloguing it. He would also take a look at the CD ranch and, perhaps, have a talk with its owner, Charles Dailey. So he sat and thought and smoked as the heat of the day turned to a distinct chill, which at last drove him indoors, to roll up in his blankets and go to sleep. Plainsman that he was, he could awaken at the least unusual sound, or at any hour set by himself. Dawn found him awake. Nothing had occurred to disturb him.

The chill was swiftly disappearing under the level rays of the sun when he rode forth, headed for the south-bound cattle trail and the Dailey ranch. In due time he came to the trail and found nothing to show that it had ever been used to any great extent, and nothing to indicate that it had been used recently. It bespoke abandonment, although this was not positive: he knew what wind-drifted sand could do to trails.

Dailey's adobe ranch building appeared as he topped a rise. It was squat and ugly, crowded against a fenced-in spring, which barely gained upon absorption and evaporation, and provided hardly more water than was needed for culinary operations. Simpkins knew that such a spring was likely to become impregnated with whatever foreign matter it might contain, since it tended to be left in the spring by evaporation instead of being swept out of it and kept from accumulating. A man could, however, keep it fairly sweet by bailing it from time to time. From the looks of it, Dailey, himself, might be greatly interested in Pettingill's sweet, generous, and unfailing water supply.

Dailey appeared in the door, rubbing sleepy eyes. At first glance he struck Simpkins as being what was commonly known in the Old South as a "poor white." Out in this country he was hardly more than a shiftless squatter, with neither ambition nor energy. Simpkins wondered what a man like Dailey would do with the big spring, even if he had the ambition to make a play for it.

"Mornin'," said the rider, pulling up.

"Mornin'," grunted Dailey, feeling for his plug tobacco. He brushed off the lint and sand, worried off a piece with poor teeth, and turned it in his mouth as he put the plug away.

"Greasers bother you any?" asked Simpkins abruptly.

"Nope."

"Have they ever bothered you any?"

"Nope."

"Have you lost any cattle?"

"Nope."

"Where's this old cattle trail lead to?"

"Mexico."

"Used much nowadays?"

"Nope."

"Why not?"

"Dunno."

"Ain't it a dry trail?"

"Yep."

"What's th' longest drive between water?"

"Dunno."

"You ever use it?"

"Nope."

"You own cattle, don't you?"

"Yep."

"Who do you sell cattle to?"

"Who're you?" asked Dailey.

"Name's Simpkins. I'm after El Toro."

"Hump!" grunted Dailey, his eyes glowing ominously, his scowl dark and frank. "You a law coyote?"
he demanded.

"Nope."

"Ain't no damn' deppety of one kind or 'nother?"

"Nope," lied Simpkins easily.

"Then you aimin' to jine up with that damn' thief?"

"Nope."

"Then what th' hell you want with him?"

"Dunno," answered Simpkins in further mimicry,
and then he laughed. "Why, I want him because he's
worth three thousan' dollars to somebody. I need
that money."

"Reckon you'll earn it, Stranger," growled Dailey,
stepping back, a hand going out for the edge of the
door. "Yo're name's Simpkins, accordin' to you: it
oughta be Simpleton." The speaker took another step
backward and closed the door in his caller's face, and
the interview seemed to be terminated.

Simpkins eased the big hat up on one side of his head and gently scratched under it. His face puckered and then a grin enveloped it. Judging from Dailey's limited knowledge, the ranchman was right. Simpkins pressed his knees against the sides of his horse and rode on again, following the old cattle track southward. He had intended to ask the rancher more about the trail, but whatever opportunity there had been for this had passed. So he rode on, looking at the occasional CD cattle that came into sight, and in his mind he imposed the Peavys' IP on Dailey's CD, and found that the two brands would not blend. At any rate, neither of these two ranches stole from the other, if they trusted to re-branding to cover it.

Mile followed mile until the forenoon was about halved, and then he found that the trail bore off sharply in an eastward direction instead of going on to strike the river. He pulled up, asking himself questions. At the angle in which the river and trail now ran they would not meet for more than threescore miles. It was a dry trail, according to Pettingill, and here stretched away an unnecessary sixty miles of it in addition to what he had covered. Why was the river shunned? Why should any trail boss endure so long a dry drive, when it could be shortened, so far as water was concerned, by at least two thirds of the distance? It was not reasonable, and yet, there it was. Down where the trail left the river it could continue along the north bank of the stream until it reached a point south of him, and then turn and head north. It seemed inexplicably crazy; but he knew that trail bosses are not crazy, except perhaps one or two of them who had fired him off the payroll in the days of his youth.

The way to get answers to questions is to go after them. Simpkins left the old track and headed south on a straight line for the river, observing and cogitating. He would ride up a little slope, top a rise, and go down the other side; up another little slope, top another rise, and down again. The country grew more sandy, and as rise succeeded rise the windrows of sand became more prominent. Then the sand grew less and he was riding over a soil different from any he had crossed that day. Ordinarily he would not have noticed this, for the difference was sensed rather than seen; but now he was suspiciously alert. Trail bosses love water like a sot loves liquor—for their cattle, of course—and yet they had forsworn the river. A higher ridge lay ahead of him, a thrusting kind of ridge, more like an old broken-down rock wall. Detritus made his horse pick its steps and angle up the steep slope. When he reached the top he drew rein and stared, his attitude of mind proclaiming that there was no such animal. It could not be, yet there it was.

He faced a botanical freak, a nightmare of fact, a thing so unexpected and beyond his experience that for an instant he groped mentally. He was looking down upon a low, flat country, extending for miles; and he was looking down upon literally miles and miles of dense-growing loco weed. It dominated every other growth and the sight struck him almost like a blow. He had seen loco weed, and plenty of it; but never in his wildest dream, sober or otherwise, had he ever envisioned a sight like this. The trail bosses of many years, choosing this trail only in the spring because of better chances for water, instead of being crazy, had wanted to keep their cattle from becoming so. Here was a bar to bovine progress as unbreakable as steel chains. This section of the country was automatically and definitely removed from any further search of his. He let his breath loose in a gusty sigh, wheeled abruptly, and rode back the way he had come, taking with him a feeling of revulsion. He would stop again at the CD and have another try at its owner.

When he reached the CD ranch house Dailey was bracing a corner post of the corral, and the ranchman looked up as his ears apprised him that he had company. For a moment his stolid gaze rested on the horseman's face, and then the rancher squinted up at the sun, and seemed to be cogitating. Then he turned his back on the caller and calmly went about fixing the post.

Simpkins smiled, threw a leg over the pommel, and prepared to stay awhile. He rolled a cigarette, lit it with a flourish, and then took the deep interest of the idle onlooker where physical work is being done.

Dailey tried the post, stepped back to look it over from all angles, and then slowly turned to face his visitor.

"You here yet?" he asked.

"Yeah."

"What you want?"

"Water."

"Huh! That all?" the speaker's expressionless eyes were fixed squarely on the horseman's face in a gaze direct and hostile.

"Reckon so. Why?"

"Dunno. Water's up to th' house."

Simpkins let his host take the lead and slowly followed him, his leg still over the pommel. At the door he slid from the saddle, stood erect to stretch his body, and then took the dipper of poor water from the ranchman's hand. Emptying the container, he made a wry face and returned the dipper.

"Alkali," he grunted. "I ain't had a good drink of water since I come down to this part of th' country. Reckon there ain't much of it drunk down here," he added, grinning.

"Well, it's good to them that likes it," growled Dailey, stating an undoubted fact. "Git used to it in time. Foller th' trail?"

"Till it turned east," answered Simpkins. "Kinda wondered why it didn't keep right on an' strike for th' river. Pushed on south to find out."

"Larn why?"

"Yeah. I never saw a sight like that before."

"Pizen for cattle," offered Dailey.

"So I've heard," replied Simpkins, holding back the sarcasm and trying to speak simply.

"Find th' Bull?"

"Huh?"

"Find El Toro?"

Simpkins chuckled. "Not yet. Ain't really started out to get him yet. Kinda gettin' myself located, like."

"You'll get located, all right," grimly replied the rancher. "Well, seein' you ain't got nothin' to do right now, you might kinda ride along and let me git to work."

Simpkins threw back his head and laughed, stepped to his horse, mounted, and wheeled.

"Obliged for th' drink. I'll buy you one of a different kind when I see you in town. So-long."

"S'-long," replied Dailey, and entered the house.

Simpkins wondered if he had time to visit one of the other ranches which Pettingill had mentioned, decided that he was working too hard, and pushed on in the direction of his new home. He had covered half of the distance when he remembered Dailey's squint at the sun, and for the next few minutes he gave this subject his close attention.

Dailey, he decided, was timing him. The reason for that was—what? The most logical answer was that the rancher was interested in knowing about how far the puncher had ridden. And if that were so, then why? A man is naturally interested in anything which might affect himself, but twitching noses and itching ears were plentiful enough, and Dailey did not appear to come under the latter classification. Anything he showed interest in could properly be suspected to affect himself. Then, if he was interested in anything which that trail might reveal—Simpkins snapped his fingers at the thought, and put it aside for a moment—he might be inquisitive enough in the appearance of an inquisitive stranger to follow discreetly and see where he went.

"Ain't I th' damnedest fool?" asked Simpkins of himself. "Allus suspectin' folks: well, I might as well settle it right now."

He pushed on, studying the trail ahead, and when he saw a place that looked to be good for his purpose he turned aside from the trail, rode around the end of a ridge, and back along the other side. After a quarter of a mile of this retrograde progress he swung back toward the trail and waited in a little draw, shielded by the vegetation along its rim.

Ten minutes later a horseman rounded a turn in the trail and rode alertly forward. Simpkins chuckled and let the other ride past; and then, gaining the trail, pushed ahead rapidly, keenly watching the other for the first sign of discovery; and when it came he took the play away from Dailey by hailing cheerily and spurring on. The rancher's slow turning was quickened, and he looked behind him to see the stranger's grinning face.

"This is kinda lucky," said Simpkins. "If you'd told me you was goin' to town I'd 'a' waited for you an' had company all th' way. I saw somethin' back there off th' trail that looked funny, but when I got over to it I found it was only a shadow."

"Didn't aim to go to town," growled Dailey, "till I looked into my coffee tin. A feller's allus gittin' out of somethin'," he complained.

Simpkins thought that they both were getting out of something, or trying to, but he kept his thoughts to himself. He nodded.

"Yeah; an' it seems like th' farther a feller lives from town, th' more often he does get out of things. How long you been ranchin' down here?"

"Four, five years," growled Dailey, faced with a journey to town that he did not want to make.

"Doin' good?" asked Simpkins, wishing that he was going to Pettingill's little shack instead of the hotel.

"Just about fillin' my mouth. If I was younger I'd pull out. It ain't no place for a poor man, with only a few head."

"Then El Toro ain't bothered you?"

"No; why should he pester with a feller like me?" asked the ranchman pessimistically. "What do my few head amount to with him?" He glanced out of the corner of his eye at his companion before he continued. "Anyhow, I reckon that loco crop down yonder would stop him."

"Yeah; reckon it would," grunted Simpkins, the picture returning to his mind.

And so they chatted, but as warily as two fencers feeling each other out, and drew steadily nearer to town to the satisfaction of neither.

CHAPTER X

SIMPKINS and Dailey jogged into town, the latter a little in advance, Simpkins having let him take the lead. The ranchman headed straight for the hotel and drew rein outside of it, waiting for his companion to leave him. After a few minutes the rancher looked around in irritation, frowning at the patient puncher.

"Well?" he asked, somewhat sharply.

"Well," echoed Simpkins simply.

"This here's yore boardin' place, ain't it?"

"Reckon so," answered Simpkins, smiling. "I'm aimin' to buy you that drink, but I don't hanker for th' likker that's sold in here. Also want to play a little poker with some of th' boys. Go ahead."

"Get good likker an' plenty of poker at th' Royal Palace," growled the ranchman, and pushed on again.

"Too high-toned," objected Simpkins, who wanted to learn more about the hang-outs in the town, and wanted to learn them under the guidance of his companion. He would not be so much a stranger in a certain element if Dailey introduced him. First impressions are important.

Dailey grunted something and continued, and soon turned down a side street. He stopped before a false-fronted dive and tied his horse to the rail, his actions duplicated by his companion. Simpkins was second through the door, but once through it he stepped toward the smelly bar with the directness and celerity of a magnetized needle toward its pole.

"Ha!" he sighed, beaming satisfaction. "What'll you have, friend?"

"Same old thing," growled the ranchman, nodding to the bartender.

"I'm stringin' along with him," said Simpkins in answer to the barman's unasked question. He looked about him and nodded. "This is th' kinda place that suits me," he affirmed contentedly. " 'Tain't all dingle-dangled with fancy fixin's. A feller ain't afraid to spit on th' floor once in a while." He pushed the bottle on to his companion and then filled his own glass in turn. "Well, here's how!"

"How," grunted Dailey, and tossed the raw liquor off at a single gulp. "Fill 'em ag'in," he said, licking his lips to get the last drop.

Simpkins obeyed and now turned to face down the bar and toward the deep rear room, where smoke hung in clean-cut clouds above the tables, to break up and eddy with every movement of the habitués.

Somewhere a snicker sounded, followed by low laughter, and his eyes searched for and found the table, where four men had temporarily ceased their card game to watch him. Under his level stare they sobered and after a moment's hesitation returned to their game. They had no hostility for him, but only derision; the

horse-faced fool thought he could earn the reward on
El Toro. But there was something deeper than that,
and he sensed it without being able to name it.

Dailey had taken advantage of his companion's
momentary occupation and had left him to walk down
the long room and join the four scoffers, an action which
plainly said that he was tired of Simpkins's company.
They made room for the ranchman, and the low laughter arose again as the newcomer talked confidentially.
He bought some chips from the winner and fitted easily
into the game.

Simpkins pushed away from the bar and wandered
into the big back room, looking curiously about him.
He saw Pettingill glance up curiously and back to his
cards. This table was full, but the one next to it was
not in use, and Simpkins choose it, dropped into a chair,
and idly picked up a deck of cards lying near him.
He watched the game next to him with disinterested
curiosity and smiled occasionally when some particu-
larly big hand or big play came along. After a while
he became accepted as a friendly-disposed stranger, and
from time to time a player would look at him and grin.
The inevitable happened: one of the players went broke
and could no longer continue; and as this person arose
to leave the table, one of his companions looked invitingly at the stranger and nodded inquiringly toward
the vacant chair.

Simpkins drew in his long legs, changed chairs, and
slid down into his new seat. He found a place for his
feet and knees, and relaxed.

"Ten cents—an' a half dollar?" he inquired, more for formal confirmation than for anything else.

"Yeah; ten—an' a half," replied the dealer, whose stack of chips indicated that the speaker was a favorite son of the god of chance.

Simpkins dug down into a pocket, drew out a roll of bills, stripped one off and tossed it to the man holding the deck.

"As many as you can spare," he said.

"Not me!" exclaimed the fortunate one in threatened panic. "It's bad luck to sell before th' game's over!"

Pettingill grunted and moved a hand toward his pile of counters. He counted out ten dollars' worth, pushed them over to the newcomer, slid a ten-dollar gold piece after them, and pocketed the bill.

"Bad luck!" he scoffed, gently reproving the dealer for holding to unfounded superstitions. He himself did not expect anything but hard luck, now that he had lost his lucky collar button; but to pretend to find hard luck in the innocent selling of chips—bah! It was all nonsense. He dismissed superstition from his mind and began to wonder if this was the time to lose his ranch to his new friend, and he decided that he might as well do it now as later. His opulence was not guessed at by his companions, for he had taken the precaution to change most of the gold pieces into paper money, and this was tucked away safely. No one, knowing his circumstances, expected him to have more than a few dollars, and they might even wonder where he got those. If he should lose a little more money than he had shown—being careful, however, to lose it to Simpkins—no one would suspect him to be playing a part.

Simpkins smiled at him as he stacked the chips.

"Much obliged. Reckon I'll have to treat you gentle, so you won't blame me for buyin' 'em from you, an' bustin' yore luck."

Pettingill studied the horse face for a moment, and the semblance of a grin appeared on his own.

"You spit on yore hands, cowboy; an' ride yore damnedest: I don't want no favors in this game, an' I'll show you that I don't."

"An' I'm tellin' you now, feller," said the dealer, sliding the cards deftly from the pack, "that if yore ante ain't in there before I get through, it'll cost you double. Them's th' rules of this here table."

Simpkins threw in a chip with a gesture of fright, and laughed low in contentment. He was in the game he loved, and loved for its own sake, aside from the angles of winnings or losses.

The afternoon passed and the lamps were lighted, no man thinking of his empty stomach. Deal followed deal, and as the hours passed the identities of the players changed. Two men had been forced to leave the table, sullen and disgruntled; but their places had been taken and the game went on. The honors seemed to be divided between Pettingill and Simpkins, and the former, elated by his run of luck and discounting the loss of his collar button, knew that the time had not

come for him to lose his ranch. He couldn't lose it,
the way the cards were running. Then came the inevitable period when the game eased up, when the hands
ran small, and when relaxation aided loss of interest.
Somebody discovered, all at once, that he was hungry
—ravenously hungry, and he put his hand over the discard as the next man to deal lazily reached for them.

"I'm hungry," he said, looking around. "Anybody
else feel like eatin'?"

Affirmation came like a chorus, and the players, leaning back in their chairs, grinned at each other.

"Then we'll eat an' play afterward; we'll feel more
like playin', then." The speaker raised his voice and
looked toward the bar. "Hey, John! Send out for five
suppers, an' do it pronto, will you? We're goin' to
have a party, an' we're goin' to have it here."

They pocketed their chips and talked, the conversation dwelling on the game and its high lights.

"My Gawd!" said one of them, turning to Pettingill.
"You must 'a' won a hell of a lot."

"Not as much as you reckon, mebby," replied Pettingill, whose stack was but little larger than it was
when he had started. He had sold chips many times
and pocketed the money, and he felt that anything
like an accurate check on his winnings was impossible.
Then, too, the players had shifted, and his biggest
winnings had been in the earlier part of the play. But
unless he lost steadily and heavily during the rest of
the night, which he devoutly hoped that he would not
do, he could not hope to make anyone believe that

he was so reduced financially as to be forced to put up his ranch. That would have to be done in some other way.

"Is that so?" sarcastically asked the first speaker.

"Yes. I ain't won near as much as you fellers reckon," persisted the ex-rancher. "I've won more hands than any of you; but them that I lost were tail-twisters! My Gawd! Don't you remember that ace-full that I lost to Simpkins' two pairs of five spots? You don't have to believe me, but that one play damn' near put me in th' poorhouse."

"Shore; I know th' poorhouse you mean; it's got marble walls, an' rich carpets, an' pictures, an' colored winder-glass, an' fountains in th' garden; an' th' moon comes up an' roosts on th' southeast tower every night! Hell, yes! I'll buy yore winnin's right now for two hundred dollars, cash. Come on, dig 'em up an' lemme gamble!"

Pettingill abandoned his pretense, since he could do nothing else.

"Well, ain't I got a right to press my luck?" he demanded seriously. "Look here, Blascomb, have I had anythin' but hard luck since I come down into this damn' country? Ain't I lost every cow-critter an' hoss that I ever owned? Ain't I been drove outa business an' forced to quit?"

"Forced to quit?" asked Blascomb curiously; but it was no surprise to him. "What you mean?"

"I mean that I quit th' ranch this afternoon, an' am now figgerin' on makin' a better an' a damn' sight

easier livin' playin' poker with children like you. You
can tell th' town that Mr. Pettingill, Esquire, is now a
gambler—an' long may he wave!"

A ripple of interest ran through the big room, although in most cases it was more or less masked; but
the room hushed, hungry for more information.

"An' a right smart good livin', too, judgin' by th'
way you've been bulldoggin' us to-day," said one of
his companions, as an excuse for an ironical smile which
he could not hold back.

"So th' JP has Just Petered?" chuckled another.
"What you take for it, Jim?"

"Oh, couple thousan'," answered Pettingill, keeping his face straight.

Laughter, high and explosive, burst out and filled
the room.

"How many head you got?" asked Simpkins in sudden, purposeful interest. He pushed up against the edge
of the table.

"Not none," admitted the owner of the Just Petered.

"Hump!" said Simpkins. "You own th' land?" he
persisted.

"Hundred sixty acres, an' use as much as I want."

"Bought it for four bits an acre?" asked some inquisitive soul.

"Just grazin' land?" asked Simpkins.

"An' a spring," said Pettingill, giving his whole
attention to this hungry sucker.

"Give you a dollar an acre, an' another hundred

sixty for th' water rights, sight unseen, if you got some kind of a house on th' land," offered Simpkins.

"There's a 'dobe shack on it," replied Pettingill. "It's worth more'n three-twenty, Simpkins."

"I'll pay you three-twenty cash," suggested Simpkins, "or put up five hundred ag'in it, an' throw three cold poker hands. Th' best two out of three takes th' whole thing."

"Yo're lucky to-day, Jim; take him up!" cried a voice in the rear of the room.

"Don't you do it, Pettingill! I can get you more'n that for it!" shouted another, pitched high in excitement. Its owner got up, paused for a moment as he reached the table, repeated his words, and then fairly ran from the building.

Pettingill looked worried, and knew that he would have to move rapidly if he passed the ranch to Simpkins without arousing suspicion. When Ad Hitchins's right-hand man hastened on a matter like this one, it was to take the news to his boss; and his boss would outbid any would-be purchaser of the JP.

Pettingill picked up a deck of cards, cut high to Simpkins's low, took his five cards, held them tightly against his chest where no one but himself could see them. He worked the pips into sight and looked across at his adversary.

"Play 'em cold, or draw to 'em?" he asked.

Simpkins sensed the need for haste.

"Suit yoreself," he answered.

"Cold, then. What you got?"

"Pair of fives," answered Simpkins, exposing the hand.

"Damn it!" growled Pettingill, and shoved his hand into the deck. "That's one for you."

The second hand was dealt swiftly and as the deck struck the table Pettingill laughed. "Looks like one for me, Simpkins! Three treys—look at 'em!"

Simpkins looked sorrowfully at the hand, gathered it up with his own cards, and shuffled.

"Hoss an' hoss," he growled, and again the cards fell swiftly.

"Hell!" snorted Pettingill, frowning ferociously at three eights, a winning hand nine times out of ten in a two-handed game. "What you got *this* time?" he asked tensely, listening for footsteps.

"King high, an' not nothin' else worth mentionin'," answered Simpkins, tossing his hand face up on the table and sighing. He was reaching into his pocket to pay his losses when Pettingill, swearing savagely, jammed his cards into the pack and looked around.

"Hell of a note when a man can't beat a single king, with a ranch hangin' onto th' play!" he said. "My luck shore has turned! Oh, well." He twisted in his chair and looked at the bartender. "Hey, John! Bring us pen, ink, an' paper."

The ink was hardly dry before two events took place simultaneously. Two men from a near-by restaurant came in the rear door loaded down with dishes and food, while through the street door burst Ad Hitchins's right-hand man, one fist shoved deep into a pocket.

"All right, Pettingill!" he cried. "Auction off th' JP! I'll start th' biddin' with five hundred cash!"

"Five thousan'!" yelled a penniless bum from a corner.

"Six thousan'!" yelled a voice, bursting into laughter.

"Six thousan' an' two bits!"

"*An*' four bits!"

"Six thousan' *an*' one dol-l-a-r-s—in Confederate money!"

"Seventeen thousan' dollars an' *no* bits!"

"What th' hell's th' matter with you fellows?" yelled the right-hand man. "I'm makin' real bids, an' biddin' real money!"

"All right," drawled Simpkins, the bill of sale safely in a pocket. "Go over in a corner, an' bid to yoreself."

"Come over in *my* corner!" shouted the bum hopefully.

"What you mean?" demanded the right-hand man very unpleasantly as he glared at the lanky puncher.

"Th' Just Petered ain't for sale," answered the new owner.

"What th' hell *you* got to say about it, anyhow?" demanded the right-hand man ominously, so ominously that Simpkins pushed back in his chair.

"A hell of a lot," drawled the new owner, "seein' that I just won it."

"Yo're a liar!" shouted the right-hand man, his face working.

Simpkins's right shoulder humped and then fell back

again, and the right-hand man did a half flip from a right-hand punch which came up from the floor and stopped against the point of his jaw. Simpkins slowly stood up, his hands resting on his hips just above his belts.

"Anybody else objectin' to me ownin' th' JP?" he asked, smiling coldly at the crowd.

"No!" roared the bum; "but shore as hell somebody's goin' to object to you keepin' any cattle onto it! By Gawd, but that was a *punch!* I could hear her whistle, an' my hat near blew off my head. But ain't you forgettin' somethin'? Is this here transfer of th' JP goin' to be a dry one?"

Simpkins flashed a look at the bartender.

"Set 'em up for th' boys, John," he ordered. Humorous cheers, ripples of laughter, the rising and falling hum of conversation filled the room while the two men from the restaurant slid dishes on the poker table and chatted on terms of equality with the men they served. Someone helped the right-hand man to his feet, shook him, and doused him with whisky which would almost bring back the dead; and his exit was unnoticed in the general hilarity.

CHAPTER XI

THEIR supper over and the table cleared, the five men once more faced each other over the cards. The three losers were eager and tense. One of them, looking slowly around at his companions, and figuring in his mind like the gambler he was, proposed that the limit be raised. He felt that his luck must change: the pause for supper, he believed, had acted as a stop, and the game would start anew.

"Two bits an' a dollar?" asked his right-hand companion.

"Yeah. That suit all of you?" He smiled at the affirmations and picked up the deck.

The game got under way and an hour later one of the losers dropped out, his place being eagerly taken by an anxious onlooker. The cards began to run erratically and the play slowed. Simpkins, sensing a change in the run of luck, began to play tightly, staying on no pair under tens. This kept him out of the majority of the hands, and when he did stay he lost more than he won. He raised his entrance cards to queens, and still he lost, but not heavily. The handwriting was plain enough: he was in for one of those poker droughts, so often met with.

Pettingill still won, being in the saddle of a determined run of luck, where he could fill almost anything he tried for. He had long since lost all track of his winnings, but his pockets bulged with bills and gold. For him it was one of those occasions when two pairs before the draw was worth all the raising he could force, for on this day and night two pairs became full houses with remarkable ease. The filling of his four-card flushes was almost automatic, and he was shrewd enough to press his luck while it remained with him.

Time ran swiftly on and ten o'clock came and went. The chairs had long since grown hard and uncomfortable, and the players squirmed and shifted more and more. The heat and the foul air of the room, not to speak of the poor light, began to tell, and at last one of the players, the man who had proposed raising the limit, leaned back in his chair and looked with heavy eyes at his companions. He had recouped some of his losses.

"What you say we play one round of jack-pots, an' then quit?" he suggested.

"Lord, yes!" sighed Simpkins among the grunts of affirmation.

"Seein' that this is th' wind-up," continued the jack-pot proposer, "suppose we raise her ag'in?"

"Four bits, an'——" Simpkins's prodigious yawn cut his words; "five dollars," he finished, and quick nods endorsed it.

On the first pot Simpkins picked up two pairs: kings and treys. All evening he had failed to help two pairs, and he never had thought much of that combination. He opened for the limit and every player saw and raised. He looked at them comically.

"Lot of bloody-minded assassins," he accused. "I'll see you. I was goin' to play this hand pat, but I can't do that with you jail-birds. Hell! Gimme three, to a straight flush." Then and there he proved that he knew poker, for in the course of human events there are times when it is wise to throw away the smaller pair, if the larger have the dignity of queens, kings, or aces. His back was to the wall, and he felt that two pairs were not worth a lead two-bit piece.

He checked without looking at his cards, and with curious eyes and mild apprehension saw the rush of raises. Picking up the first card of the draw, he saw an eight-spot. Sighing, he placed it face down on the pair of kings.

"Just a minute," he said, seeing the raises. "Just a minute," he repeated, and apprehensively picked up the second card. It was a king. "Now I will go on from where I left off," he chuckled, and raised in turn.

He was the center of four studious and curious gazes. The next player decided, audibly, that Simpkins was a horse thief and trying to steal the pot. He saw and raised.

"You can't steal a pot like this, Uncle Tom," he remarked with a grin.

"Not Uncle Tom," corrected Simpkins. "Uncle Drew. Drew bein' my first name, an' I just did. Th' past tense is Draw—or is it th' present tense? Anyhow,

I just did, Simon Legree, I just did: an' you should 'a' seen what I got!"

"I think you got a cramp," said the next player. "She's up ag'in."

Pettingill closed his eyes in pain. It is most unpleasant to have unquestionably the best hand before the draw, to back it heavily, and then come to the realization that the draw had shifted values. He saw, not daring to drop out. That is the worst of a hand like that.

It went around to Simpkins without being further raised. He smiled pleasantly at his suspicious companions and picked up the third and last card of his draw. His face was as full of expression as is a jug of molasses.

"Drew is my first name, but I forgot to tell you fellers that my middle name is Jesse. I was born in Missouri, an' my old man thought a lot of Jesse James. Held his hoss one time an' got a dime for it. But I've reformed, temporary; I'm not goin' to steal this pot, after all; I'm goin' to win it. She's so tough now, that she might as well be tougher. I'm raisin' th' limit once more."

"What's five dollars to a man with a fortune?" muttered the next player. He picked up his chips and found they were a dollar short of the required amount. His pockets yielded nothing in the line of legal tender, and he turned to the man behind him. "Lend me eight bits, Frank, so I can put my brand on this maverick."

"Eight bits with that hand?" inquired Frank in

pugnacious disgust. "Here," he said, dropping a handful of bills on the table. "My Gawd, man! You allus want to kiss luck right on th' snoot! Play it! Raise him!"

"No, Frank; a good poker player will throw away a good hand if he reckons it ain't good enough. I can't do that because I ain't got th' nerve. I'm callin', Jesse James." He watched the others level up, and then his eyes turned to Simpkins. "What you got, Wild Bill?"

"I got th' hand that made Moses jump off th' Ark," said Simpkins, slowly placing his cards on the table. "One king, two kings; an eight of spades; three kings, four kings. Peter, Paul, Luke an'—Percival. Call him Percy, for short. Do I win th' silver-plated six-shooter?"

"Henry Plummer had nothin' on you," sighed the next player. "This here is one of them times when a jack-full is a tearful sight."

"Damn three aces!" swore the next man. "You just can't throw 'em away, an' when they ain't good they're pizen!"

Pettingill tossed his hand, face down, on the table. "It's th' first time in my life I ever threw away a straight flush; but bein' a heavy winner I was ashamed to play it." He grinned ruefully. "A pretty necklace of diamonds, only th' eight spot was a five."

The dealer threw his hand into the discard, rolled a cigarette, and waited. Simpkins cleaned the table, and they started the second round. Half an hour later the game was over, and Pettingill, after the lean and bitter years of his attempt at ranching, had won what to him seemed like a fortune. He did not know the figures, but his stuffed pockets were hint enough.

"They can steal my cows, an' my hosses," he said; "but by Gawd they can't steal my money! They'll pay it to me, too, for them cows an' hosses!"

"What you mean?" demanded a cold-eyed man, who had straddled a chair near by and watched the game. He sat on the chair as he might sit on a hobby horse, and his forearms were crossed on its back, his hands close to his open vest.

"Just that," answered Pettingill. "Th' Mexicans do steal cattle. Shore. But th' Mexicans that stole *my* cattle had plumb white skins an' talked English. I'm in town to take payment, an' I've got th' first installment!"

A hush settled upon the room, and while some of the stares were direct and challenging, others were shifting and uneasy. Simpkins listened with both his ears, his glance flicking here and there. Pettingill, he thought, was drunk: drunk with elation over his winnings, drunk with elation from having stepped from poverty to affluence.

"Meanin'?" persisted the cold-eyed man, his posture erect and alert. He was looking at the lucky winner with an appraising directness which to Simpkins was a warning.

It was Simpkins who answered him.

"Pettingill ain't got no gun," he drawled, his horse face unemotional, calm, sphinx-like. "I have. I'll do his talkin', or back up his words. He said white men stole his cattle, an' not Mexicans; an' he figgers he's come to th' right place to get his money for 'em. I figger that he's wrong; but he shore has a right to his own idears. It's yore say-so, now."

"He's loco!" growled the cold-eyed man, not relishing the interference. "He's lived by hisself so long out there he's loco as a desert rat of a prospector. That's all right; but he oughta have sense enough not to come into town, win our money, an' then accuse us of stealin' his cattle. Everybody knows that El Toro's back of all this rustlin' that's been goin' on."

"Mebby," replied Simpkins, exchanging stare for stare, and waiting for that delicate change in the eyes which announces a sudden deadly decision. "Mebby. I've heard talk here an' there about rustlin' goin' on; but from th' way it shapes up it don't amount to nothin'. A few head here, an' a few head there. Don't seem to be no worse than any place else in th' cow country; don't seem to have no head behind it. Wherever there are cows there are cow thieves. If El Toro is behind this rustlin', as I reckon mebby he is, then he's a tinhorn!"

"Is that so?" cried a man at another table, half arising in his excitement. "I've lost three hundred head in th' last two years! Ike Peavy's lost more than that! Hen Fowler lost over sixty head just two weeks ago to-night! Frank Fessenden lost a hundred head last month! Sixty head, or even a hundred head don't mean very much, mebby, to ranches like th' IP, but they wipe out little fellers like us. Ike Peavy told me that

th' only thing that's kept him goin' is his poker winnin's, over in that back room of th' Royal Palace.
It's got so I feel like shootin' greasers on sight!"

"That's right, Bolton," cried another small rancher.
"It's been goin' on for th' last three, four years. They
ain't wiped us plumb out, because that'd make us quit,
like Pettingill, here; they leave enough to make us keep
on strugglin'. Hell, it's like we was workin' for them,
without pay or keep."

"Is that so?" shouted Pettingill, standing up. "They
wiped *me* out, didn't they? Took every last head, an'
even raided my shack an' cleaned it of pots, pans, an'
beddin'!"

Bolton shook his head in sympathy, but stubbornly
maintained his attitude.

"I don't know why they did that," he said. "Mebby
you didn't grow cows fast enough for 'em, an' they
got tired of havin' you around. But over our way,
they play a different game. An' they're goin' to play
a still different one, too: we're bandin' together an'
watchin' that northwest trail. There'll be some empty
saddles th' next time they try it!" He had spoken in
heat, carelessly, blunderingly, and low growls apprised
him of it. He shook his head again and sighed. "Oh,
well; what of it? They would 'a' found it out th' next
time they called. If they're scared off, then so much
th' better. Mebbe they'll give our part of th' county a
rest. Gawd knows it's time we had one."

Fessenden and Fowler moved to his side and expostulated in low voices. They were joined by the cold-eyed man, who abandoned his chair for another next to the complaining ranchers. When the crowd began to drift toward the bar, and then on toward the door, its units to drift home to their beds, the four men were still talking and arguing. Simpkins and Pettingill, remaining at the card table, talked idly and watched them carelessly.

"Who is th' gent that tried to call yore talk?" asked the tall puncher in a low voice.

"They call him Paso Tom," murmured Pettingill. "He rides for Peavy, but hangs out in th' Royal Palace about half his time. Has some kinda drag with his boss, I reckon. Bad hombre, takin' him all around." He shook his head slowly.

"He shore is listenin' hard, right now," commented Simpkins. A quizzical grin slipped across his face. "I'm kinda disappointed, Red. They ain't nobody tried to buy my new ranch from me yet. I've owned it four, five hours, an' not a buyer has showed up. Oh, well; I allus was kinda impatient." He chuckled. "I know where I can get a right good price for it, if I hold out."

Pettingill laughed suddenly, loudly, and grinned when the startled gazes of the four conferees rested on him. He was about to laughingly tell them the joke, when Simpkins's bony knee drove against him.

"Did you ever see such a run of luck?" he boasted, and thereby covered himself very neatly.

The cold-eyed man slowly arose, rested a reassuring hand on Bolton's shoulder, and wandered over to the

grinning, happy pair at the big table. He drew back
a chair, dropped into it, and smiled.

"You shore did have a run of luck, Jim," he said.
"I reckon it was due you, too. You been playin' in
blame' hard luck in th' cattle business, out on that ranch
of yourn. But you made a mistake about th' ranch:
you could 'a' sold it for good money, instead of losin'
it th' way you did."

Pettingill sneered.

"That so?" he demanded. "Then why didn't somebody make me an offer?"

Simpkins chuckled.

"They wasn't ready, mebby, Red. You see, if you
got to th' point where you'd made up yore mind to
throw it up an' pull stakes outa th' country, you'd not
expect to get much for it. You'd have to take th' best
price that was offered, an' that wouldn't be much,
I reckon. That's an old game. That's a game that's
played everywhere, an' some folks call it business."

Paso Tom nodded his unhesitating endorsement.

"Shore; it *is* business, ain't it?" He looked at Pettingill. "If you hadn't been so all-fired set, you could
'a' sold it to Big Jake to-night for what it was worth."

"Or mebby more," murmured Simpkins, smiling in-
nocently.

"That's right!" exclaimed Paso Tom quickly.
"Mebby more!"

Pettingill patted his pockets and laughed exultantly.

"I don't care nothin' a-tall about th' JP," he said.
"I reckon I was damn' lucky gettin' rid of it, seein'

how much money I can earn in town. One shore thing: I didn't have no luck while I owned it. Now, if I only could get hold of that——"

Again Simpkins's sharp knee drove against him and effectively stopped the audible wish for the recovery of the collar button.

"—damn' El Toro," went on Pettingill without a break, "I'd be all square."

"An' you'd be drivin' across my lines," reproved Simpkins. "I'm aimin' to get El Toro, an' I don't want no competition; an' I don't reckon I'll have much. You stick to poker, Red."

Paso Tom laughed gustily at the thought of any one man getting the notorious Mexican bandit; of one man going up against an organization of such size, power, and perfection.

"Well," he said, lazily arising, "let's stretch our laigs. Let's git outa this place an' go over to th' Royal. That monte layout is a-callin' to me. What you say?"

The Royal Palace, a little noisy in the outer room, was quieter and more decorous in the gaming hall. The faro layout and monte spreads were doing business. The big, round table in the center of the room was not in use, but Ad Hitchins sat at it, smoking a cigar, while he idly watched the play along the side walls. He looked up as the footfalls passed through the big, wide doorway. He saw three men: Paso Tom, and two men with money. The first of these was Pettingill, the fool who had jumped the wrong way and made more trouble than he had any idea of; the second was

the lanky, horse-faced stranger, who thought El Toro
was a babe in swaddling clouts. He was also a pestif-
erous nuisance and would bear a little watching.

Hitchins smiled and spread his hands invitingly. The
three men stopped at the table and moved apart. Paso
Tom started for the chair at Hitchins's right, but
found six feet six of cowpuncher in his way. He hesitated and took the next seat. Pettingill dropped into
the first chair he came to. He could see the faro bank
and monte players; but his new friend faced the Angelus, and his right leg was off the side of his chair,
its knee nearly on the floor. Simpkins removed his hat
and placed it on the floor beside him, and as his hand
came up again it shook the holster in passing.

"Pretty picture," he commented, glancing carelessly
at the tapestry. "Real calm-like, an' peaceful."

"Yeah," grunted Hitchins, holding back an ironical
smile.

Simpkins's innocent gaze passed on and rested on
the gamblers.

"Like flies around molasses," he chuckled. "What's
th' faro limit?"

"It's just a small game," answered Hitchins, "unless somebody wants it raised. We do that every once
in a while for Ike Peavy. He likes a heavy game. He
won eight thousan' dollars over there one night. It
came in right handy, too, I reckon. Ike was pretty hard
hit by th' rustlin'. He's talkin' about tryin' it another
whirl, but I dunno when."

"This man is a fool," thought Simpkins, an idea

exploding in his mind. Only a fool or a crook volunteers information, and if the information is important and pat, then he is more likely to be a crook. So he corrected himself: Hitchins was not a fool—he had no reason to suspect that he was talking to a man who loved puzzles, and so far had solved every one he had tackled. It would be most interesting and enlightening if he could learn in advance the date of Ike Peavy's next big winning in the Royal Palace. Aloud he said: "Takes guts to play a big game like that. I'd be near scared to death."

Hitchins raised his eyebrows.

"That so?" he asked. "I heard you was playin' a pretty big game to-night."

"I'm surprised *you* would reckon it was big," replied Simpkins, tense with expectancy. Hitchins was working around to mention the transfer of the JP. This would mean nothing in itself, for men had come and gone while the game had been on, and some of them must have dropped into the Royal Palace and gossiped. Almost everybody in town by this time knew of the new ownership of the ranch. It would be quite natural for Hitchins to mention it; seeing that he was in the company of both the old and new owners, it would be unnatural not to mention it.

"I made a clean-up," boasted Pettingill. "Man, but I did! I'm blame' near qualified to set in a game in that little room yonder. Yes, sir; I'm shore heeled for gamblin'!" He opened his coat in an attempt to counter-

balance the heat of the room; and Paso Tom caught
sight of a bit of sweat-stained leather slanting down
toward the left side; and the discoverer of the shoulder holster flashed a quick glance at Simpkins, who,
earlier in the evening, had told him that Pettingill had
no gun. However, that might just have been a guess.

Hitchins was smiling at the ex-rancher.

"Good for you, Jim," he said, referring to Petting-
gill's winnings. "You keep buildin' 'em up; an' when
you get 'em piled right high we'll make a try for 'em
in that little room." He turned to Simpkins, his smile
growing.

"Well, you get El Toro yet?" he asked banteringly.

"No," drawled Simpkins. "I don't seem to be able
to get a start, though I ain't tried real hard. He scat-
ters so," he complained. "He's all over th' country, I
reckon, pickin' up a few head here an' there. If he'd
keep to one section I'd salt him down so hard he
wouldn't spoil in hell." He frowned and then chuckled.
"But I'm gettin' a line on his drive trail. I'm goin' to
put in some time around Fowler's an' Bolton's an'
Fessenden's, over west."

Hitchins kept his face straight and looked the puncher
squarely in the eye.

"I get news, sometimes," he offered. "First time I
get a hint I'll pass it on to you." Despite himself his
eyes hardened, and he turned to glance at the faro bank.

Paso Tom had been fidgeting and now he broke into
the talk.

"Pettingill lost his ranch to-night," he said abruptly.

Hitchins's eyes left the faro bank, passed quickly over the monte spreads, and rested in gentle surprise on the ex-ranchman's face.

"You did?" he asked. "How's that?"

"Yeah, I did," answered Pettingill with a laugh. "Th' damn thing wasn't worth more than a couple hundred dollars. I bet it ag'in five hundred cash, an' lost. An' I'm right well satisfied."

"We'll be sorry to lose you, Jim," said Hitchins.

"Hell! You ain't goin' to lose me. I'll be stayin' around town, makin' easy money. I'm a gambler now, Ad!" He laughed with delight and aimed a thumb across the table. "There's th' sucker, over there. Simpkins owns a ranch without a cow critter or a hoss! All he's got is a brand, with no place to put it on!"

"That so?" inquired Hitchins in mild surprise, looking at the new owner of the JP. "You aimin' to settle here permanent?"

"Workin' out a new idear," replied Simpkins, scratching his head. "If it goes, all right; if it don't, all right. It's never been tried, out here; but I understand there's money in it, back East."

Three very curious faces were turned to his own, and it was a treat to read them.

"Goin' to have that spring assayed," he explained. "If it turns out good, blamed if I don't bottle th' water an' ship it East. If it's th' right kind of water there's big money in it."

Three roars of laughter burst out simultaneously,

three faces were convulsed. Hitchins was the first to recover himself. Still red from his laughter, he turned in his chair and looked at the fool beside him.

"Not figgerin' th' long wagon haul to th' railroad, th' first thing you want to do is to get th' freight rates on carload lots of that damn' water between here an' New York an' Boston!" Again his face suffused and his laughter filled the room, to the detriment of the faro and monte games.

Simpkins was somewhat stunned, and then began to view his new idea from the bias of freight rates over a twenty-five-hundred-mile haul. One could see the brilliant idea slowly die. He shook his head gently and reprovingly.

"An' I never thought about th' damn' freight a-tall!" he growled. "Reckon a cow-puncher oughta stick to punchin'. Well, I can do that, all right. I've got th' ranch, an' now all I need is a cow!" He joined in the laughter at his own expense and called out to the bartenders. He was a sport: if the joke was on him, and he most certainly believed that it was, then he would buy the drinks. In his mind was a central thought, about which other thoughts were milling: Ad Hitchins had no previous knowledge of the transfer of the JP; he had to be told by one of the principals, and was surprised by the news; and this in spite of the fact that the whole town knew about it by now. And yet Ad was smart enough and keen enough to think of the long haul and the freight rates like a flash. There are peculiar rifts in the human understanding, queer kinks, and

almost unbelievable streaks of dumbness. Hitchins, he
believed, had made a mistake by concealing the fact
that he had heard all about the transfer. Now Simpkins
sat back, waiting for the play, whose prologue had
been involved and laborious. He believed that the curtain was about to rise.

"You got capital enough to start a ranch on a big
enough scale to keep you in bacon an' beans from th'
beginnin', without havin' to sell off cattle you oughta
keep?" asked Hitchins.

"Reckon mebby I could hire out," explained Simpkins.

"There's more men than jobs," countered the gambler and business man.

"Well, I wasn't hardly serious, at that," said Simpkins. "You see, I got th' blame' thing on my hands.
What else can I do with it?"

"Do with it?" retorted Hitchins. "Sell it an' let
somebody else do th' bulldoggin'. I don't 'specially hanker for it, but I'll give you a fair price for it an' hold
onto it till values go up. You don't want to forget that
this is th' West, an' values out here are bound to rise.
It may take time, but that's nothin' to me. I can afford
to wait. Anyhow, what's a few hundred dollars?"

"Not very much," agreed Simpkins. "Not enough
to be interestin', let alone talk about. I met a queer
cuss to-day," he said, changing the subject abruptly.
"Feller named Dailey. Owns th' CD, on that old dry
drive. I was askin' him about that trail, but he only
knows one word: that was 'Nope.'"

Hitchins was studying the speaker and there were little glints of hostility in his eyes.

"Dailey *is* a queer cuss," he affirmed. "Don't see how he makes a livin' out there. Pettingill failed, an' he'll fail, an' so will you. How come yo're interested in that eastern section when El Toro does his raidin' over west?"

"Ain't that th' best reason I could have? I told you when I first came that I was seein' th' country," answered Simpkins blandly. "I reckoned I'd start in right at home. Now that I own a ranch somewhere in that section, I'm glad I looked it over. I'll be damn' careful never to drive cattle over that trail, or let 'em wander south toward th' river."

"You better sell out," said Hitchins. "That country ain't any good a-tall. No water, plumb poor grazin', an' too much loco. I'll give you five hundred for th' JP."

"Never owned a ranch before," growled Simpkins, who knew that he did not own one then if he played square with Pettingill. "But Red's had so much to say about that spring that I ain't figgerin' on sellin'. If I needed money I'd keep th' ranch an' lease th' water rights. I understand it's a right good spring. Throw a ridge of dirt across th' crick, Pettingill says, an' a feller could make a real fine reservoir." He was describing a picture that had been in Hitchins's mind for weeks, and was there now, detailed and vivid.

Hitchins flushed at this blundering mind reading, and anger stirred him. This damned blunderer was as bad as Pettingill. Since he could not be led, then perhaps he could be driven. The gambler's jaw set and he stiffened with sudden purpose.

"You'll never build that dam, an' you'll never raise cattle on that ranch," he said flatly. "Pettingill can tell you all about th' latter; an' if Pettingill had built a dam it would 'a' been blowed up. I know th' drift of things down in this part of th' county: El Toro seems hell-bent to discourage ranchin' over there. Don't ask me why, because I can't tell you; I'm only mentionin' facts."

"Then Dailey must be a friend of his," observed Simpkins, letting the bomb fall casually.

"Dailey!" snorted Hitchins, his face pale. Little streaks of color thrust across it and then it suddenly flamed. "Dailey! To hell with Dailey! He's got a few scrub cows, th' poorest of th' poor longhorn run. Bought trail-weary, footsore cattle an' th' calves that were dropped on th' bed grounds. Paid a dollar or two a head for th' grown animals an' mebby two bits for th' calves. He's got a couple of scrub bulls that we've tried to buy, so we could shoot 'em an' not risk th' quality of our cattle. Dailey! By Gawd!"

"Well, if Dailey can stick it out, then I can, some day," growled Simpkins. "Besides, if that trail ever comes to life ag'in, an' they head over my way, I can sell 'em water at a cent a head."

"You won't last ten minutes after El Toro makes up his mind that he wants that—that he wants you out of th' way!" retorted Hitchins, his anger grow-

ing. He was accustomed to having things go the way
he pointed.

"I'm glad to hear that," replied Simpkins, his memory treasuring that slip, that hesitation: he thought
he knew the word that Hitchins had choked back. "If
he comes after me, then I won't have to go after him.
A man's allus better off, fightin' on his own ground.
Why, Hitchins, I wouldn't sell that ranch, *now,* for a
cold thousan' in cash!"

"You'll sell it to-night for five hundred; to-morrow,
for four hundred; day after to-morrow, for three hundred," countered Hitchins, holding himself in as best
he could. "She drops a hundred a day, till it hits zero.
After that you'll be glad to *give it away!*" His eyes
blazed.

"You actin' for yoreself, or El Toro?" asked Simpkins coldly, his gaze resting idly on the Angelus.

"What th' hell you mean?" cried Hitchins, partly
rising.

"Why, you say El Toro won't let me use th' ranch,"
answered Simpkins. "Then *you* try to buy it off me.
If he won't let me use it, then he won't let you. Hell!
You've got me all tangled up! I don't savvy you a-tall."

"I told you I wanted th' ranch to hold for risin'
values!" snapped Hitchins. "But if I was fool enough
to put good cattle on a range like that, I've got men
enough an' friends enough, an' money enough, to protect it. You ain't. That's a mighty big difference, an'
you'll mebby find it out."

"Yeah, reckon it is," admitted Simpkins, convinced

of the truth at last. "One man would be kinda pressed, I reckon. Well," he sighed, slowly and sorrowfully shaking his head, "then I won't do no ranchin'. I'll have to hold it for higher prices. Much obliged for th' idear."

"Five hundred to-night," repeated Hitchins, his words clipped off; "four hundred to-morrow, an' a hundred a day less after that. You ain't got th' chance of a bat outa hell."

"But I don't want to sell out!" stubbornly persisted Simpkins. "I'll lease it, range rights an' water rights; but I want to keep on ownin' that ranch."

"Yes!" snarled Hitchins, his rage again climbing. "Yes! An' after you lease it, an' th' leasee builds a nice dam for you, then you'll refuse to renew, an' get a reservoir for nothin'!"

Simpkins almost held his breath, and was hoping that his companion would not realize what he had given away; and, in order to keep him from realizing it, the new JP owner changed the subject.

"You say El Toro's over west. What's his home range, his home town?" he asked.

"San Ignacio," answered Paso Tom, breaking his silence. "An' man, she's tough! She's hell with bells on."

"Good place to keep away from, I reckon," said Simpkins.

"Then you won't sell?" asked Hitchins smoothly. He had got hold of himself, realizing that he was

really concerning himself with another man's troubles.
He had only to raise his hand . . .

Simpkins shook his head emphatically.

"I've never owned a ranch before, an' I'm goin' to
hang on for a while. If I can't raise cows, then I can
shore raise hell as long as I last; but I ain't aimin' to do
either very soon. Looks like I kinda got to get that Mex
bandit on my own account as much as for th' reward.
Aw, th' hell with it! Let's talk about other things."

CHAPTER XII

AFTER the talk with Hitchins in the Royal Palace, Simpkins and Pettingill left the gambling hall and walked around to the latter's hotel, where they talked for a while and then parted. Simpkins got his horse and rode out of town instead of spending the night at the other hotel. He struck straight for his new ranch, so straight that he went cross-country instead of following the regular trail, which was easily accomplished in the moonlight. He had begun to grow wary.

Drawing rein on the side of the hill to the north of his adobe hut, he sat quietly in the saddle and studied the little depression before him. It was almost as light as day. The hut lay bathed in the moonlight, one side bright and the other black, the shadows like a puddle of ink. As yet he had made no overt act which reasonably connected him with serious interference with the plans of the men he was opposing; but he had made some large and wide gestures, and he had become the owner of the little ranch, and he had refused to sell it. The expressions on Hitchins's face were warnings enough for any man with sense.

He dismounted and swung down the side of the hill farthest from the hut, keeping its crest between him and the building. Reaching the bottom, he followed the

base of the hill around until he was in the rear of the
house, and then he began a cautious advance. The rear
wall of the building had no window, and for reasons
of his own that was a pleasant condition. To walk up
to a window or door might be foolish after his talk
with the proprietor of the Royal Palace.

His progress was slow and silent. Reaching the house
he slipped along to the corner of the dark end and
pushed his hat out past the wall. After a moment he
grinned foolishly, put it on the ground, and inched
along the end wall. At the second corner he stopped,
crouched, carefully lay down, and then, his face close
to the ground, he looked around the corner. There
were no tracks before the house that told him anything; but the ground was hard and was no telltale.
Nowhere had he seen any horse since leaving his own.
He lay still and hushed his breathing, listening intently.
Minutes passed and still he did not move; but he did
feel a growing sense of self-ridicule. This became
stronger, and he was about to call himself a fool, get
his hat and horse, and then go in and roll up in his
blankets, when a sound caught his attention.

He flattened again and listened with new interest.
Again the sound came to him, but it did not come from
the house. Somewhere a horse was moving, and he was
certain that his own mount was too well trained to move
against its inhibitions; it knew better than to move
against the rope, as represented by the bridle rein
dangling down before its eyes. Again he caught the
sound, and this time he located it; it came from the

direction of the trail, from the front. He chuckled and waited.

Time slid past. Then sounds of the moving horse caught his eye, and he focused on it. A man was slipping along the face of the northern hill, angling down toward the shack. Behind him was another, close to his heels. They reached the little corral and were lost to sight for a moment. Then they reappeared on hands and knees and crept toward the hut. Evidently Ad Hitchins did not believe in procrastination.

Simpkins was tempted to throw a bullet into the sand in front of them, and grinned as he pictured their actions under such a play; but he thought better of the impulse. That would be volunteering information, and that was against his rules, unless the volunteering had a solid reason behind it. He would let them come on, for it was possible that he might learn something worth while if he had the patience to wait. He was glad that he had chosen the shadowed end of the house for his own approach. As long as he lay prone and did not move, as long as he did not raise his head from the ground, and as long as they did not search around the house, he was safe from being discovered, and if he was seen he would have the advantage of surprise. His thoughts were interrupted by the nearness of the two men, who now were close to the house. They were so close that he recognized them: they were Big Jake and Paso Tom.

They came on slowly but steadily, guns in their hands, and they were as silent as ghosts. Simpkins complimented them, mentally, on their plainsmanship and waited. Then they were so close to the door that he lost sight of them, and the moment that happened they became really dangerous: it was problematical where he would next catch sight of them. Would they follow around the wall? If so, which way would they come? Would they stay together, or would they separate and go in opposite directions? He eased his guns out of their holsters, rolled over slowly and silently, and squirmed until he was in a position where both end corners of the building were in his range of vision. The seconds slipping past now began to drag a little.

"Hell," said a voice from inside the house, the growling voice of Big Jake. "We've lost a good night's sleep, an' had all our trouble for nuthin'. He stayed in town an' ain't took possession yet." A sigh, sounding suspiciously like one of regret, served for punctuation. "I was hopin' I wouldn't have to wait very long to pay him for that smash on th' jaw that he gave me. Oh, well, that'll come later. Now I can light up an' have a smoke."

"Like hell!" snapped his companion. "Don't you strike no match, an' don't you make no cigarette smoke around here for him to smell. No tellin' where that hombre is. You can wait for yore smoke, can't you?"

"I can, but I ain't aimin' to," retorted Big Jake. "Didn't I tell you that he's in town? Didn't we watch th' trail?" The stink of a sulphur match wafted through the door and drifted around to assail Simpkins's nostrils. Inside the house the squizzling and slowly lighting match for a brief moment cast its faint rays over the room.

"Whose blankets are them?" asked Peso Tom quickly, his hand dropping to his holster.

"Pettingill's, I reckon," answered the smoker, exhaling gustily.

"Would he leave 'em behind when he knowed he was quittin'?" demanded Paso Tom irritably.

"Did he know he was quittin' for shore, before he got into that poker game an' lost his ranch?" asked the smoker with a trace of contempt in his words. "Look here, this Simpkins coyote won this ranch _to-night_. He ain't left town. Therefore, them ain't his blankets. Don't you reckon he'd wait for daylight before he'd come out here to look over his new ranch? Wouldn't you?"

"Then we could 'a' waited, an' beat him out here in th' mornin'," growled Paso Tom. "Still, if we did that, he might 'a' got here before us. Seemed to me that you was awful anxious to come out here to-night."

"I was, then; but not because of Hitchins, or anybody else," replied Big Jake. "I had my own reasons for wantin' to be right here in this shack when he rode up to it; an' they was damn' good reasons."

"You reckon one of us oughta ride in an' watch that hotel?"

"What for?"

"Well, there's a drive goin' up to-night, ain't there? Somebody shore oughta keep him in sight, hadn't they, in case he got to smellin' around?"

"Huh! Yo're as bad as th' other old wimmen that's worryin' about him an' that drive!' retorted Big Jake contemptuously. "What does Simpkins know about any drive? He's just a damn' fool puncher feelin' his oats, an' I've got some oats, lead ones, that he's shore goin' to feel. Shucks, he's got a lot of wages in his pockets that I figger to spend for him, an' he's goin' to fool around, like any other puncher, till he goes broke. Then he figgers to drift on, lookin' for a job. Yeah, he will: if I don't end his wanderin's for him." A snort emphasized the words. "If he ain't stopped, he'll sell out to Ad, blow th' money, an' vamoose."

"Huh!" exclaimed Paso Tom thoughtfully. "Judgin' by th' job we got, I don't figger Ad's aimin' to buy this place. Reckon he figgers it's his, right now."

"He'll buy, if he has to, just to save a ruckus. He don't want to do anythin' that'll mebby turn too many eyes onto us. He'll buy if he gits th' chance, an' we're here to take possession in case he fails, an' also to make Simpkins see that there ain't a hell of a lot of value to th' place. When he finds he can't use it he'll sell out cheap an' move on. That's th' way Ad figgers. If I don't figger that way, that's my business."

"Dailey reckons he ain't no common puncher just lookin' around," suggested Paso Tom.

"Hell! Dailey's another jackass, like th' rest of 'em!"

"That's all right, but we've got to have this water, an' we got to have it soon. We've got to shift our drives, an' we got to keep strangers from pesterin' around in this part of th' county. Th' big brand won't be worth a damn as soon as somebody figgers it out. You know that as well as I do."

"Nobody's goin' to figger it out as long as El Toro gits th' blame for th' rustlin'. Somebody shore will rib up Simpkins to go after that greaser, an' then he won't never be seen ag'in; unless I beat th' greaser to it. Oh, hell, what's th' use of talkin'? We've beat him here an' we'll chase him off when he shows up—we will if I don't miss my shot!"

"Better not shoot him, Jake; pass th' word to some Mex an' let them do it," counseled Paso Tom thoughtfully. "That's one of them things that might turn too many eyes on us an' our game. Better not do it, Jake."

"You'd preach a different kind of sermon if he'd hit you on th' jaw, right in sight of all them fellers!"

"Mebby; but, Jake, he's got Dailey worried, an' Hitchins is beginnin' to fret. Why do you reckon he rode down that old trail like he did?"

"'Cause he was curious an' didn't have nothin' else to do."

"You reckon he's a law coyote?"

"Naw!" exploded Jake.

"Mebby he's a Cattlemen's Association man?"

"Naw. If he is, he won't live long down in this country. There ain't nobody down here that belongs to th' association. There ain't no use worryin' about him: it won't be long before some Mex leaves him layin' out in th' sage, if I don't git him first. Turn in. I'll take th' first trick."

"Hitchins was all riled up when he found out that

Pettingill lost this place to him," said Paso Tom; "but when he found out th' coyote had been ridin' down that old trail he shore was rileder."

"Turn in. I'll take th' first trick."

The rest of the conversation was idle, desultory, without pith or point, and it soon ceased as one of the guards rolled up in Simpkins's blankets and dropped off to sleep.

Simpkins was thinking hard and straight. He could creep along the front of the house and dispose of the two guards before they had any inkling of his purpose; of that he was confident. To do that would be to force the issue before he had filled his hand. It would put him squarely on the defensive after a declaration of war, expose his interest in local affairs, curtail his activities, and keep him desperately busy with nothing to gain. He had title to the property, and when the time came to take possession he would do so, forcing matters; but it appeared that the time had not yet come.

He inched backward, careful not to brush against the scrubby desert growths, and when he had turned around he started toward his horse, slowly, cautiously, intent on silence. Foot by foot, yard by yard, he put the house farther behind him, and at last crept over the crest of a little rise a hundred yards from the building. Here he went on at better speed, and it was not long thereafter that he arose to his feet and stepped out briskly. Reaching his horse, he led it down the slope of the hill and, mounting, circled to the south and struck west on a gamble.

There was a drive going on. Where, how, what, and why? Who were making it, and where were they going? What did Paso Tom mean when he spoke of the "big brand"? Why were they going to shift their drives? Was it because of what the rancher, Bolton, had said about him and his friends banding together to watch that other trail for rustlers? Was Bolton an honest rancher or was he playing a part? How, exactly, was Ad Hitchins mixed up in it? He found more questions without positive answers, and rode steadily ahead in the hope that he would find answers to some of them before another day had passed.

Dawn found him riding on, and when the sun rose a little later he was no better off than when he had started. He had found no drive or signs of a drive, and he circled wide as he headed back toward town. About an hour later he espied a ranch house and its outbuildings nestling in a small depression in the rolling hills. Riding up to the door, he was about to dismount when it was flung open suddenly, and he found himself looking into the sullen and suspicious face of Bolton. His reception reminded him of his call on Dailey: evidently householders down in that part of the county did not wait for callers to dismount and knock before opening doors to them.

While the two men exchanged looks, Simpkins tried to catalogue the rancher. It was more than possible Bolton had taken no part in the cattle stealing which had been going on in that section of the county; indeed, the man seemed to be a victim of it; but the lanky

puncher had found so many actors around the town
of Porter that he did not care to take anyone into his
confidence and risk the exposure of his hand. According to the conversations he had heard only a few hours
before, there had been a drive run off that night; and
the ranchman's appearance did not give the impression
that he had spent the night in sleep.

He looked sheepishly at the rancher and grinned
somewhat ruefully.

"You mind feedin' a weary pilgrim?" he asked hopefully.

"What you doin' 'way out here at this time o' day?"
countered Bolton, not without truculence. He stood
squarely in the doorway, blocking it. His arms, akimbo,
assured a quick draw.

"I've been castin' around, tryin' to blunder onto some
trail that will lead me to that Mex cattle thief an' three
thousan' dollars, U. S.," answered Simpkins, throwing
a leg over the pommel of the saddle. "I can't seem to
get a line on him, nohow. I've been hopin' to kinda
stumble onto him; but I reckon I've got to try somethin' different."

"Yo're either a damn fool or a knave!" retorted
the ranchman with engaging frankness. "I only wish
I knowed which! Well, you might as well light down.
I'll feed you, though I know I shouldn't."

"If I share yore salt with you, you won't have to
worry none about me, mister," replied Simpkins, sliding from the saddle.

"Mebby," grunted Bolton, stepping back into the room, and motioning for his caller to follow.

The visitor obeyed the ungracious invitation, stepped outside again to wash for breakfast, and then, reëntering, glanced about him curiously.

The building was a two-room adobe: kitchen and bedroom. It was neat, well kept, and sparsely furnished. The bed clothing in the bunk was made up, and without a wrinkle. If it had been used last night it had been made up without airing. Breakfast was not ready—in fact, the fire was just beginning to give results. If the bed had been slept in it would not have been made up until breakfast was well under way, or over with: at least, that was Simpkins's experience with bachelor housekeeping: a hungry man thinks first of his food, and the day is not squared off until after he has broken his fast. Bolton's eyes looked tired and heavy. Some men show the loss of a night's sleep more than others, and it was plain to be seen that Bolton was not in the habit of remaining up the clock around.

Simpkins wandered into the kitchen and sniffed eagerly at the bacon, which only now was beginning to sizzle purposefully. The water bucket was empty when he dipped into it for a drink, and without saying a word he picked it up and started through the door with it. The well lay to his left, between the house and the little corral, dug down through a slight rise in the ground so that the slope of the land around it would not let the corral drain into it. The water was cold and clear; but what took Simpkins's interest was the horse in the corral, not yet turned loose to graze. This would not be done until after the ranchman had used it to rustle in a fresh mount. The animal showed dried lather on its flanks and was tired and dejected. Appearances indicated that it had been ridden hard all night. Its brand was a BB, with the first letter turned around.

Reëntering the kitchen, Simpkins placed the bucket on its box and stood back, waiting. His host had the small table set with its rough utensils, and the bacon was ready, although not crisp and brown as the guest liked it. Bolton placed it on the table, opened the oven door, and took out a pan of corn bread. Here was a facer: how long did it take to cook corn bread after it was mixed and ready for baking? Simpkins did not know, but his suspicions were disturbing to his deductions.

"Draw up," growled the host, pouring the coffee. "That corn pone must be all dried to hell an' gone, but I warmed it up, anyhow."

Simpkins beamed as his suspicions died. Here was another fool who volunteered information: innocent, casual information, which often had the explosive properties of dynamite. The world was full of them, thought the puncher; but as a rule they make more trouble for others than they do for themselves. He was pleased by the thought that this was one occasion when the rule was reversed.

"It'll taste good to me, anyhow," he answered. "Corn pone is a treat I don't often get. Sugar?"

They ate on in silence, their minds as busy as their jaws. At the end of the meal Simpkins tossed his tobacco sack across the table and waited for his turn at it.

"I'm right tired an' sleepy," growled Bolton, believing that it might be better to give his own explanation to an obvious fact. "Just couldn't get to sleep, nohow, what with one thing an' another stirrin' in my mind. I never could stand a sleepless night."

"Makes a difference, I reckon, whether a feller's tryin' to sleep," replied the guest. "Layin' in bed an' tossin around must take more out of a feller than bein' up, doin' somethin'. I've been fussin' around all night like a fool." He also thought that he might as well explain an obvious fact. The earliness of his arrival at the ranch had established that as a fact in his host's mind, and he had practically admitted it before. He placed his elbows on the table and looked frankly across at his host.

"Wonder if you can tell me somethin' I want to know?" he asked. "I could ask in town, but I don't take much stock in some of them fellers. Yo're a rancher, an' I reckon you've been losin' cattle. Least of all you said so, last night in th' saloon."

"What is it you want to know?" asked Bolton suspiciously.

"I told you that just blunderin' around, hopin' to stumble over a trail to El Toro wasn't pannin' out like I wished, an' that I'd have to try somethin' else. Where's th' best place to go to find that greaser?"

Bolton looked at him apprisingly.

"San Ignacio," he said shortly.

"Tough town, ain't it?"

"All them border towns are tough, 'specially over th' line; an' they say San Ignacio is tougher than most. Chances are you won't come out alive. If they find out *why* yo're there, you'll die quick."

Simpkins leaned back, yawned, stretched, and managed to push his chair away from the table. When his outstretched hands fell one of them rested on the table, but the other hung down at his side, out of sight. Without letting his face or his eyes betray him, he was ready for anything, although he hoped that if he had to draw, it would be only to get the drop on his host and keep him from making a great mistake.

"Just what did you find out last night, ridin' around th' country?" he quietly asked.

Bolton's reaction to the question surprised the lanky puncher. The ranchman broke, much as an overstrained dam, and poured out a flood of bitter words which seemed to carry him along with it. They burst from the very heart and soul of the man; they painted the story of years of purposeful struggling, from the beginning up to the now; they told the tale of this man's ranching, and of trickery, theft, and even murder. They served as a safety valve to a man who for too long a time had carried too great a pressure, and they served as a measure of the man's desperation, for he unburdened his soul to a stranger, to the visitor who sat silently listening on the other side of the cheap table. Bolton ceased as abruptly as he had begun, and slumped back in his chair, weary, almost exhausted, and for the moment caring little what happened.

Simpkins knew that he had learned the truth, so far as Bolton was concerned. The true status of the ranchman was plain even to his suspicious mind. Bolton was not a thief, but was an honest rancher, striving to succeed in his business; instead of being a thief he was the victim of thieves.

"I didn't know just how to figger you," admitted the lanky puncher after a moment of silence. "All these fellers down here are strangers to me, an' most of 'em seem to be crooked. Everybody's yellin' El Toro, an' I know that he's a cattle thief. I started out to try to find th' greaser, an' I still hope to find him; but that will be a side line, kinda. At that time I didn't care much about th' way things were goin' down here: my interest was in th' reward. But now I own a ranch. I aim to have it used for what a ranch is for. As things go, cattle can't be kept on it; but I aim to have 'em kept on it. What's th' answer? Why, that I got to fix things so cattle can be kept on it. All right. Now, Bolton, you listen to me; an' you keep yore mouth shut, tight shut. If these sidewinders reckon they can drive me outa this country they're loco. They want that worthless ranch. Do you know why?"

Bolton was looking at his visitor in growing comprehension, at last overcoming the apathy induced by his own burst of rage and hopelessness. The first thing he sensed was sympathy and friendliness; then he began to get hold of the fact that here was more than sympathy:

this guest was not a passive sympathizer, but an active one. He was an outsider, a stranger, who was able to look at things through eyes not trained to see things in one way only; he was capable of judging men and events in a manner entirely free from bias, carefully prepared bias. The built-up stage play was not shaping his thoughts. Now he was not just a stranger, but a fellow rancher; and he looked most uncommonly able to take care of himself and of any trouble that chanced to break loose in his immediate vicinity. Let's see: he had asked a question. It was—oh, yes: Why did "they" want that worthless JP ranch?

The ranchman slowly shook his head.

"I dunno," he muttered.

"Well, I know; but I'm not tellin'," said the guest. "Not even tellin' you. Th' greasers may run off cattle: yes, a few head here an' there. El Toro ain't got nothin' to do with that. Not a thing. But th' cattle that a few scatterin' greasers are runnin' off don't amount to nothin'. Most generally th' brands tell a story, to a man that knows how to read it. Th' brands down here don't tell a damn' thing. Th' IP, Ike Peavy's ranch, could steal from th' JP, but they couldn't run th' brand over into their own. Th' JP could steal from th' IP, an' change th' brand; but th' JP ain't got a single head. You could steal from them both, an' alter both brands to yore own. I happen to know that yore herd is blame' near petered out. If you stole cattle, yore herd would grow instead of shrink. This feller Fessenden, with his FF, th' first letter turned around, he couldn't change

any of th' above-named brands into his own. Neither
th' IP or the JP could change his into theirs. You
could, but you ain't done so. Charley Dailey can't change
any of 'em into his; an' they can't change his into theirs.
You can make th' CD mark into yourn by doublin'
its size and addin' onto it from below. You ain't done
it. That leaves just one more: Henry Fowler an' his
HF mark. When he figgered out his brand he saved
hisself makin' a mark. You know what it is: an I an'
an F, with a H bar connectin' th' two. That makes it
HF ." The speaker's left index finger traced it quickly
on the table top. "Now th' only fellers that could steal
cattle an' change th' brands into their own are th' fellers that are losin' cattle instead of gainin' 'em."

Simpkins rolled another cigarette, lit it, and puffed
at it thoughtfully, giving his companion a chance to
speak, and gravely watching him. A smile twitched at
his homely horse face, and he continued.

"Well, Bolton, what does all this palaverin' mean to
you?" he finally asked.

The ranchman shook his head and remained silent.

Simpkins chuckled and let his right arm and hand
come up into sight and join their brother members on
the table top.

"It means just one thing," he said complacently.
"An' it means that I'm goin' to find out what an' where
that one thing is. If I do find it out, it'll mean that
you an' Fowler, an' Fessenden an' me will be able to
watch our herds grow by natural increase, steady an'
reg'lar; it will mean that we small fellers can sell a

few head of beef once in a while, to put flour in th' flour barrel an' beans in th' pot. It means that we'll grow, like we oughta."

Bolton nodded, a wistful smile breaking over his face: sell a few heads of beef once in a while without reducing his herd further toward the vanishing point!

"I allus was a feller for lookin' ahead," continued Simpkins, "but not far enough ahead to figger out where I want to be buried. My lookin' ahead is kinda fenced in, inside of th' game I happen to be sittin' in. Now, it may turn out from that kinda figgerin' that I don't want to live in town, or on th' JP. I can't say about that, yet. It may turn out that I'll need a job, for a couple of reasons. I want you to give me a job with you, punchin'; but I don't want it now. I'll want it when I ask for it, I'll want it right quick, an' I don't want no pay; though nobody but me an' you will know *that*. What you say?"

Bolton nodded, his mind full of questions, and his eyes asking them; but he was too big a man to force an ally's hand. He was pretty well convinced, by now, that a new factor had entered the county and the puzzle; and that this new factor, besides showing promise of being worth something, was also friendly to him. This satisfied him, so far as words were concerned.

"You got a job, when you come after it," he said slowly.

"Good! Now then: where did you an' yore friends hole up last night, when you was waitin' for a raid an' a drive?" asked Simpkins.

Bolton answered the question as well as he could, seeing that they had moved about considerably.

"Yeah. That was purty well north of here, wasn't it?" asked the puncher.

"Yes: north an' west. We been watchin' that part of th' country pretty hard th' last week or two. Before that we was keepin' an eye on th' south part, lookin' for drives toward th' line."

"Just ridin' around here an' there, huh?" asked Simpkins.

"Well, no. You see, there's a pass through that low mountain ridge, north of here a couple of dozen miles. Any herd would have to use it if they headed it up that way. There's a trail leadin' through it." He scratched his head. "It looks like it's bein' used considerable, but that might not mean anythin'; that trail is a reg'lar drive trail, with honest herds goin' up it."

"Uh-huh," grunted Simpkins. He stretched. "What you goin' to do to-day?"

"I was figgerin' on makin' up a lot of lost sleep."

"Me, too," grunted the puncher. "We'll close up th' house. Then you gimme a blanket an' I'll roll up on th' floor. I want to be fresh an' wide awake when I go off huntin' El Toro!" His laugh rang out and filled the little house.

Bolton grinned at him, not exactly knowing why; but he felt like grinning and he grinned. Then he, too, laughed; not such a hearty, booming laugh, but a laugh, just the same. It was an excellent index to the way he now felt.

CHAPTER XIII

SIMPKINS rode steadily along the drive trail which led into the pass mentioned by Bolton. His course was generally northward, bearing a little to the east; then the eastward trend became more noticeable, and when he came to the pass just a little after the noon hour his shadow was on his left hand. The pass was not much of an affair, just an easy slope to a crest and then down again; but on both sides the low mountains were rocky and covered with igneous stones of a nature harmful to hoofs.

He loped down the farther slope and saw that the trail held to its northeastward direction. In mid-afternoon he came to water, and he estimated that the dry interval behind him was close to twenty-five miles. This was a long, hard day's drive for cattle, but nothing to make a trail boss anxious, so long as this water could be depended upon. Fifteen miles would have been a comfortable drive, twenty a fair stretch. He rode his horse into the little stream and let it drink, and then went on again. Later in the day he was riding past scattered cattle, and went out of his way to read their brands, without learning anything of interest. At dusk he entered the little town of Bradley, found its poor hotel, and was soon walking about the streets.

He found what he wanted and entered. The saloon was the most pretentious in the town and was beginning to fill. A faro game was running in a corner, a pool table was the center of another small group, while a poker game or two completed the activities. He stopped at the bar for a moment and then drifted to an unoccupied chair and dropped gratefully on it, looking idly around the room.

Men came and went, and the crowd gradually grew until the big room was comfortably filled. Punchers, bull-whackers, gamblers, and a few indefinable types made up the complexion of the gathering. The bits of conversation he overheard were common to the cow country and aroused no particular interest in him. He arose and wandered over to the faro table, where he watched the play without interest. The pool game drew him and he dropped into a convenient chair, wishing that Shorty was on hand to show these cue-blacksmiths how the game really should be played. Shorty could make the beginning of a fortune in this town at his favorite game. The last man to shoot stepped back, chalked his cue, and glanced at the quiet stranger.

"How'd'y," he said casually.

"How'd'y," grunted Simpkins. "Didn't you see that two ball combination? Number three an' eleven?"

"Yeah, I did; but I was afraid of bustin' 'em up too much if I missed th' shot," answered the player.

Simpkins nodded and watched the game. When it was over the two losers dropped out, their places taken by two more of the waiting group. The man who had spoken to Simpkins racked his cue and took the chair next to the lanky stranger.

"Damn!" he grunted, but he was grinning. "Last pool game I'll be in for quite a while, to-night." What he intended to convey was that this night would be the last opportunity for him to play the game for some time to come.

"Yeah?" asked Simpkins politely.

"Yeah. Goin' up th' trail with th' second drive. It'll be like old days."

"Railroad?"

"No; range stockin'. We cross half a dozen railroads, I reckon; but none of 'em head up our way. I know that we cross two Union Pacifics, anyhow."

"Grinnell, an' Ogalalla?" asked Simpkins to keep the conversation going.

"Nope; not that far east. We miss th' head cf th' Republican entirely. Yo're thinkin' of th' Great Western Trail."

"Yeah, reckon so. You drivin' over Raton Pass?"

"I don't know. This end of th' drive is a new one to me. It's my first trip up th' trail from this part of th' country. I allus used to head up outa Texas, up Dodge way."

"Shucks," grunted Simpkins. "Be cheaper an' quicker to rail 'em through, wouldn't it?" he asked.

"No; not where we're goin'."

"All in one brand?"

"Yeah; eighteen hundred of 'em. Three an' four year olds."

"My Gawd!" said Simpkins reverently. "Eighteen hundred, all in one brand! I didn't know there was any ranch in this part of th' country big enough for that. That sounds like Texas."

"Well, there is, stranger. It's Bradley's old ranch, over east of town. Syndicate owns it now in th' old brand. This town's named for old man Bradley. Old cuss, he was. They sent him to Washington as th' territorial representative, an' he wore his cowhide boots all th' time he was there, an' damn' near caused a scandal with 'em."

Simpkins chuckled, picturing the type, which even now, he was sorry to admit, was growing scarce.

"My name's Watkins," Simpkins offered. "Have a drink?"

"Well, I don't want to lose my seat, or my turn at th' table."

Watkins put two fingers in his mouth and whistled a piercing blast. Among the frowning faces turned toward him was that of a bartender, who scowled, but obeyed the two high-held fingers. In a moment the drinks were at hand, coupled to a warning.

"This place ain't no damn' honkatonk, stranger," reproved the bartender, forgetting to make change. "Folks get throwed outa here sometimes."

"Hope this ain't one of 'em. My name's Watkins," said Simpkins, a foolish grin on his face. "Obliged for th' warnin'. Hey! Wait a minute! Suppose we split that four bits change, an' each take half of it?"

"All right," grudged the bartender, frowning. "But don't you whistle ag'in!"

"Not any more to-night," promised Watkins.

"Nor any other time!" snapped the bartender ominously.

"Th' next time I whistle," said Watkins, still grinning, "there'll be such a good reason for it that I won't get throwed out." He listened to the grunt of the departing barman and faced his companion. "My name's Watkins," he said for the third time, this time pointed.

"Mine's Egan. Dick Egan. Ol' White-eye is fixin' to ride you, Watkins," said the other, his gaze shifting to the bartender.

"He ain't got hands an' laigs enough to stick in th' saddle," replied Watkins good-naturedly.

"He's an ex-prizefighter from th' East," volunteered Egan.

"Well, there ain't nothin' *ex* about me," replied Watkins. "You fellers lookin' for a good hand to fill up some hole in yore drive crew?"

"No; we been turnin' 'em away," answered Egan regretfully. "Seems like 'most every puncher hereabouts has got th' itch to travel with pay. Here comes th' town marshal. Don't you whistle at *him!*"

Watkins looked at the incoming dignitary with no particular interest.

"Got a sheriff livin' here in town, too?" he asked. "Let's see: what's his name? Carter, or Carson, or Corson, or somethin' like that?"

"Naw! Corson's sheriff of th' county just west of

here," answered Egan, then and there having no doubts,
if he ever had known any, of his companion being a
stranger to this part of the country. "Hello, Bob," he
said to the man who had stopped beside him.

" 'Lo, Dick," replied the marshal, his eyes on the
two low-hung guns on Watkins's thighs. "You drinkin'?" he asked the stranger.

Watkins looked at him in surprise, and while he was
framing an entirely appropriate answer to an imperti-
nent question his new friend answered for him, and
somewhat hastily.

"Just one glass, Bob; that's all."

The marshal nodded. "Hope you like our town,
stranger," he said to the visiting puncher. "When you
do start drinkin', be shore to hang up them guns behind
th' bar." He turned slowly, his gaze resting on Egan's
face. "Hear yo're goin' up th' trail to-morrow, Dick?"

"Yeah; bright an' early."

"Wish I was once again. Well, good luck."

The two punchers watched the officer's slow progress
toward the door, and through it to the street.

"Whitest man in th' whole county, an' th' toughest,"
remarked Egan. "Used to be a trail boss, an' there
wasn't a better one. Drove for one of them big ranches
down in Texas, an' took one herd over th' Canadian
line. Then they began to drive to th' rail heads, an'
th' rail heads kept gettin' closer to th' ranch all th'
time. Bob finally quit, an' he's been up here ever since."

"Looks like he might be a good man in a tight corner," said Simpkins for the sake of saying something.

"None better; an' he don't very often pull his gun. Mostly when he starts to talk to a feller he's in arm's reach; an' that right arm of his will win first money over a mule's kick. They go down, an' they stay down long enough for him to pick off their hardware."

Watkins chuckled, fully appreciating such a character. He found himself taking a liking to the town officer, and he hoped he would see more of him; and in this he was not to be disappointed.

Two hours moved pleasantly past, and finally Watkins was forced to admit to himself that he yearned for a bed. He mentioned it to Egan, who once again had left the pool table in the hands of more capable players.

"Time I was quittin', too," said Egan, standing up. "Got to be out of my blankets at th' crack of day."

They stopped at the bar on Egan's treat, and separated outside the front door, Egan mounting his horse and riding off, Watkins loafing toward his hotel. As he reached the lighted doorway of the building the marshal stepped out of it and turned sideways to face the incomer. His low voice did not carry to the sleepy clerk inside at the desk.

"You workin' for th' BHB, stranger?" he asked, a curious expression in his eyes.

"No," answered Watkins, indignation swelling within him at this unwarranted prying into his personal affairs. Then he remembered what Egan had said about the officer, and he suspended judgment on the inquiry until later developments gave him a cue. He, too, had a good right arm. The marshal's close scrutiny seemed to give assurance that it was not prompted by idle curiosity.

"Good-night," said the officer, and faded into the darkness which fenced in the little patch of light before the open door.

Watkins looked after him for a moment and then entered the office.

"Who was that hombre that just asked me if I was workin' for th' BHB, th' feller that just came out of here?" he asked the clerk, hoping that he might pick up some useful information.

The clerk's sleepy countenance broke into a sleepy grin.

"By Gawd!" he said, chuckling. Then, remembering that he had been asked a question, answered it. "Bob Taylor, city marshal. He's a good one, an' he's square. So he asked you if you was workin' for th' BHB? Well, well, well!" He chuckled and scratched his head. "Hah! You want yore key?"

"Uh-huh," answered Watkins, studying him closely and learning nothing. "Reckon he's mebby square, but I'm bettin' he's plumb full of loco."

"Copper yore bet, Mr. Watkins; copper yore bet!"

"Um-m-m. Mebby," grunted Watkins, and walked slowly and thoughtfully toward the stairs. Reaching his room he lit the lamp and slowly began to undress; and it was well for the progress in this line that there are such things as firmly established habits for the automatic doing of involved motions, for his mind was so busy with conjectures that his fingers worked without conscious direction. He was about to blow out the lamp, but changed his mind and dropped into a chair, marshaling the conjectures into a more orderly array.

In his mind's eye he could see the various brands of the ranches around the town of Porter, and he mentally placed one in another, changing the pairs, and seeking a master brand which could contain them all. BHB; that could absorb the IP of the Peavy brothers; the HF of Henry Fowler; but it would not take in the other four marks: the JP, BB (with the first B reversed), the CD, and the FF (with the first F reversed). Evidently the old Bradley brand was not the "big brand" he was searching for. He would have to keep on traveling; but meanwhile he would spend a day or part of a day in this town, making judicious inquiries.

After a good breakfast the next morning he wandered down the street toward the saloon where he had spent the previous evening. There should be an entire shift of personnel, both behind the bar and in front of it. Any habitués found there so early in the day most likely would be bar-flies, with no moral stamina and an eager thirst. A few dollars spent for liquor might save miles of riding. It is surprising how garrulous some of this type prove to be; their tongues are hinged in the middle, and very often they give information with malicious eagerness, being unclean mentally, morally, and physically. In the final analysis gossip usually is malicious, and, to paraphrase, holds a mirror up to human nature. Petty spites, envies, unintentional slights, and scores of small things accrete into a motivating mass from which come verbal crimes, and persecutions deliberate and cruel.

Watkins, alias Simpkins, alias Nueces, entered the big room and looked carelessly about him. A young and gloomy bartender polished glassware mechanically and was the only person in the room. He placed the glass behind him on the backbar and stood ready to serve.

Watkins gagged when he thought of drinking whisky at that early hour and on top of his breakfast.

"Sack of Longhorn," he said, his eyes on the tobacco piled behind the bar, and he caught the sack as it slid toward him. Opening it, he rolled a cigarette and leaned against the counter.

"Just my luck," he growled, busy with his thoughts. The bartender glanced at him, said nothing, and picked up another glass.

"Big trail herd goin' hell-an'-gone up th' country, an' no room for another rider. Huh!"

"Hard luck," grunted the bartender, caring nothing whatever about trail herds or the happiness or welfare of the customer.

"Th' old Bradley outfit is plumb full up, too," mused the customer. "Hey! You know any other ranch hereabouts that's hirin'?"

"No."

"Seems to me that with a full trail crew missin' from th' BHB they shore oughta need riders to fill a few places. Hadn't they?"

"They've mebby got 'em," grunted the bartender casually, with that impersonal touch which is a sign of their craft. He looked at the street through the window, where a horseman had stopped and was now dismounting. "You can find out right pronto: here's th' *segundo* of th' BHB, right now."

Watkins looked around as the newcomer entered the room, and he nodded.

"Any chance of a top-hand gettin' a job ridin' for th' BHB?" he bluntly asked.

"No. We're all littered up with top-hands now," answered the *segundo,* and thenceforth ignored the inquirer.

Watkins grunted, turned, and went out. As he stepped through the door the only thing he could see for a moment was the *segundo's* horse, since it almost blocked the doorway. His gaze drifted over it, saw the brand, flashed back to the mark and rested there for an instant.

Watkins's face did not change, and he scarcely checked his slow stride, but on that instant all his troubles took on a definite form and all his puzzles seemed destined to be solved. The BHB, as a conjectural brand, was as innocent of evil as a baby; but the real mark, with its reversed first letter and its economical H, came into the court of his mind with very unclean hands. The perpendiculars of the two B's were the perpendiculars of the H. It was a monogram instead of three separate letters, and Watkins found himself again engaging in the old pastime of superim-

posing brands. Peavy's IP, Pettingill's JP, Bolton's
ᗺB, Fessenden's ⅎF, and Fowler's economical ⊢F, all
fitted neatly into the Bradley brand.

Watkins entered the marshal's office and found that
officer at ease with his feet cocked on the top of an
old battered desk. Without waiting to be invited he
dropped into a chair, placed his Stetson on the floor
beside him, stretched out his legs, and crossed his ankles.
The marshal was regarding him calmly, with a detached
curiosity, much as he might have regarded a strange
bug.

"Well," sighed the visitor, grinning amiably.

"Well," echoed the marshal.

"You asked me if I was workin' for th' BHB," said
Watkins.

The marshal said nothing at all.

"I just had a try for a job there. I braced their
segundo for it. He said they was full up. You seemed
to be curious, last night, so I figgered I'd come in an'
tell you about it."

"Thanks."

"Don't mention it."

Silence enfolded the little office, finally being broken
by the caller.

"Is their brand th' same as it was when old man
Bradley owned th' BHB?" asked Watkins curiously.

"Yes; with a few changes."

"Yes?" The caller cogitated. "With a few *changes!*"
One could see he was struggling mentally. "It's th'

same," he muttered, "with a few *changes!*" Another period of cogitation. "In other words, it's just th' same, only different. My Gawd!"

"BHB," said the officer, his keen eyes peering through mere slits. "Then, an' now; but then it was three separate letters: B H B. Now it's still BHB, but kinda run together; kinda combined."

"Which makes less strokes with a runnin' iron," said the visitor, "but don't save nothin' but a little space with a stampin' iron."

"They don't stamp," said the marshal, still watching.

"Figgered they didn't," admitted the other. "Combinin' brands is right handy."

Here was a double-barreled remark which, in some situations, would be likely to scare up anything from a jack rabbit to a mountain lion; but, barring an almost imperceptible narrowing of the slits through which the marshal's eyes were peering, it developed nothing.

"They drive heavy?" asked the visitor.

"They're a big outfit."

"Private outfit or corporation?"

"Corporation."

"Know th' members, of course?"

"No. Easterners, I hear."

"Know th' foreman?" persisted the caller.

"To speak to. Yo're damn' curious."

"Hell, I ain't begun to git curious, yet. Folks here in town think a heap of you."

"Hope so," replied the marshal.

"Bein' a city officer, you don't meddle with things outside its boundaries."

" 'Course not. Try not to meddle anywhere."

"Sheriff of this county a friend of yours?" asked the caller, his own lids dropping.

"Not special," answered the officer, and little muscles tightened around the mouth. "Just what kind of a game are you dealin'?"

"Solitaire," grunted the visitor, and uncrossed his ankles, drew up his long legs, and reached down for his hat. "Us little ranchers shore do have our own troubles," he said, getting to his feet. "When we lose ten, fifteen head, it means somethin'. I was admirin' that fancy BHB brand, an' just dropped in to tell you about it. Th' drinks are on me th' next time I see you."

"Thanks. What's *yore* brand?"

Watkins thought swiftly. "Bourbon," he answered without batting an eye.

"Ah, yes; of course. Yore favorite brand of *whisky*," said the marshal, talking aloud to himself. "I see. Th' brand I was askin' about was—ah—hump! Bourbon, huh?" He chuckled and his eyes were now fully opened, frank and calm and friendly. "You tried to get a job with any other ranch?" he asked curiously.

"Yeah; with th' IP, across th' county line; but they wasn't hirin', neither."

"My Gawd!" said the marshal softly. His expression bespoke admiration. He dropped his feet to the floor and stood up. "Any time yo're lonesome, drop in."

"Gracias. I will. Well, so-long," said Watkins, turning toward the door. He stopped abruptly, his eyes on a map tacked on the wall by the side of the door casing. "Well, well," he muttered, moving toward it. The marshal joined him, and side by side they admired the accurate work of the government.

"That would be th' trail I followed comin' over," said Watkins, his big finger swiftly indicating a line on the map.

The marshal nodded. "Reckon so: it's th' old drive trail."

"Yeah; so it is," commented Watkins. "Now, then: suppose I wanted to go home another way?" He leaned closer and peered at the fine lines. "Hah! There's th' old trail runnin' parallel with th' Rio Grande. She turns here an' runs north. An' about *there* is a ranch called th' CD—feller named Charley Dailey owns it. Suppose you wanted to drive a few head of cattle from here to Dailey's, an' to keep off th' reg'lar trail, how would you go?"

"Wouldn't want to," answered the marshal. "There ain't no water nowhere on it."

"Yeah," grunted Watkins thoughtfully. "But suppose you left it a little, an' sidled off to that spring, *there.* An' suppose there was a pond there. that never went dry?"

"I'd still take th' old trail," said the marshal, in no way indicating that he was following the visitor's line of thought.

"Yeah; I know," persisted Watkins, grinning; "but

suppose you didn't *want* to foller th' old trail? Suppose
you didn't like that there gap in them low mountains?
Let's see: you say it's a dry drive. All right: th' best
way to cover a dry drive is at night, when th' air's cool
an' th' sun ain't blazin' down. Some folks would rather
drive at night, anyhow. What I'm tryin' to get at is
just where, on this map, you would drive a herd between here an' Charley Dailey's ranch, if you didn't
use th' reg'lar trail, liked to drive at night, an' found
water where I pointed."

The marshal chuckled and drew on the knowledge
of nearly a third of a lifetime spent in that part of
the country. He had punched cattle, he had prospected,
he had cooked for range outfits; and he knew every
mile represented by the map.

"I'd go like this," he said, slowly tracing a line with
his finger, and explaining the more prominent features
of the country as he proceeded. At the conclusion of
his talk he stepped back and smiled.

"That's right interestin'," admitted Watkins, rubbing his chin thoughtfully. "Downright interestin'. I
allus like to look at new scenery, so I reckon I'll go
back that way. Much obliged, Mr. Taylor."

"That's all right. By th' way: what kind of a sheriff
is young Corson makin'?"

"Purty fair, for th' upper part of th' county," answered Watkins; "but he don't pay much attention to
th' south half."

"Like th' sheriff before him," muttered the marshal,
frowning.

"Yeah, like th' sheriff before him," repeated Watkins. "Well, glad to have met you. Thanks, an' so-long."

"So-long, Watkins; an' keep yore eyes skinned," said the officer.

The horse-like face grew hard as granite, and then a warm smile broke over it. Shaking hands, the caller slouched toward the door, stepped through it, and headed up the street toward the hotel without even a glance at the horse tied to the rail before the saloon down the street.

The marshal stopped in the doorway and looked after his departing visitor, and on his face was a grim smile; friendly, withal, but grim. He snapped his fingers, glanced at the BHB horse standing before the saloon, and chuckled. He seemed to be greatly pleased about something; as, indeed, he was. He turned, strode to his desk, and searched through a drawer. The letter was near the bottom, under an accumulation of papers. It was a casual letter from a friend who lived in Willow Springs. Scanning it rapidly, he found and read a paragraph which humorously described a puncher who worked for the JC, Sheriff Corson's ranch, a puncher who went by the name of Nueces. Tearing the letter into fine bits, he dropped them into the wastebasket, and then looked thoughtfully through the window, his eyes on the BHB horse, his mind on what he suspected about the owners of that brand.

"G—— d—— you!" he muttered in fierce satisfaction, and sought the comfort of his chair.

CHAPTER XIV

NUECES, once more to be known as Simpkins, had no further interest in the town of Bradley. He had found out what he had sought: the "big brand," the general location of the ranch, information about the lay of the country, and knowledge concerning a potential cattle trail leading across the mountains and desert from Jim Pettingill's little ranch.

To pay a visit to the BHB was not necessary, since it would tell him nothing of an essential nature that he did not already know; details at this end of the operations of the gang were not vital to him. On the other hand, if he paid the ranch a visit, there was always the chance that he would meet with some member of the crowd who had seen him in Porter, and thus provide opportunity for a suspicious mind to connect him to things which properly, in his present identity, should be of no interest to him. Also, his authority as an officer of the law had ceased when he had crossed the county line; and any steps taken against the BHB would have to be taken through the office of the local sheriff. When things were right Corson could get in touch with that official, give him the facts, and let the other officer do what he chose.

He paid his hotel bill and departed, but he did not

ride westward. There was a trail leading into the southeast, and this he chose. To follow the eastern trail as an exit from town would be to run the same kind of risk, in lesser degree, as would be suffered by a visit to the BHB itself; to follow the same trail westward toward Porter would be too risky for the same reason, and would also suggest that he was returning from a visit to the BHB range.

The southeastern road was a neutral route, and his only recourse. To strike across country would not be in keeping with the rôle he was playing: a stranger, possessing only the stranger's casual knowledge of and interest in a temporary stopping place, would keep to the trails in his riding. He kept to this one, but after about ten miles of steady traveling he came to a rocky ridge, where his tracks would not show, and he left the trail to strike west.

In due time he reached one of the landmarks marking the potential cattle trail, and thenceforth rode swiftly but alertly along this route from landmark to landmark. He estimated that it was all of fifteen miles shorter than the established route, which had been prolonged to reach the little creek farther north for the sake of water.

It was late in the afternoon when, from the top of a ridge, he saw his own range and the little adobe shack. There were no signs of life to be seen. The corral was empty, but that did not mean much to him: the horses likely would be hidden. He circled widely, and again on a smaller radius, at no time coming within the range of vision of anyone in the house. On this second circle a movement in the brush of a draw caught his attention. Two hobbled horses showed themselves and he chuckled. The enemy still held his house against him.

He was tired and very hungry. He could ride on to town or spend the night with Bolton. Either was the sensible thing to do, but he had been sensible for too long a time. He had been playing the fool and the harmless; it might be well to relax and become himself. Besides, it was his house, held against him by force of arms. For a few moments he sat watching the two animals, thinking out the best course to pursue; and suddenly he laughed aloud.

Dismounting, he hastened to the hobbled animals and, after a little effort, caught and held them one at a time. When he had finished his attentions their hobbles were untied at one end and dragged on the ground. Back in his saddle again, he headed off the horses and drove them toward the adobe. Reaching the bottom of the hill on the other side of which stood the corral, he urged them up it and, with cuts from his quirt, sent them over the crest and running down the farther slope. He himself wheeled and rode swiftly down the hillside at a tangent, and when he struck the level plain again he was following a draw which led to the rear of the shack.

Big Jake was at the stove, cooking the evening meal. Behind him on the floor, ranged along the wall, were the supplies, generous supplies. It was one thing to provide one's own food out of one's own pocket; but it was quite another when someone else paid the bill. Big Jake liked to eat, and when he had been told by one of his bosses to stock up the shack and hold it against its new owner, he gave his imagination free rein. He and Paso Tom were living on the fat of the land and did not care how long the job lasted. They were living so well, indeed, that it would be a calamity if Simpkins were to return. This was a contingency bound to come, which they had discussed off and on, and rather thoroughly. To themselves their skins were precious: they would take no chances with Simpkins, but shoot him down as quickly as they could, whether* he made a play or not. He was a dead man the moment they caught sight of him.

Paso Tom was hungry, and the smell of the cooking food wafted to him through the open door. He sat on the wash bench, his ankles crossed, at peace with the world. The early evening was as beautiful as those hours can be in a desert country. The long shadows were soft and pleasing to the eye, the erstwhile heated air had cooled, stirring eddies of it bathed him gratefully, and he was in the mood when even a man like himself could quicken with appreciation of the rare beauties of a glory of color in the western sky, a riot of breath-taking tints on the desert and hills. The distant mountain range was a magnificent mass of mauves and lavenders, with golden crests, and a creeping belt of purples along the base. A little swirl of frying ham odor played about his nostrils, and he stretched out luxuriously, such a look of peace and contentment on his face as to make him look almost idiotic. He sniffed eagerly and chuckled.

"Man! That smells good!" he called.

"Th' water bucket's empty!" replied Big Jake, stirring flour into the browning grease of the frying pan. As a maker of ham gravy he had no equal in the country roundabout, as Paso Tom could testify.

"All right," grunted Tom, lazily getting to his feet. He picked up the bucket, but his eyes and nose were busy with the frying pan. It looked and smelled so good that it almost pained him. His laziness disappeared, and he stepped briskly out of the house and headed for the big spring. This, indeed, was an ideal situation; sweet, ice-cold water, plenty of first-class food, and a good cook to work miracles with it.

He filled the bucket and was halfway back to the house when a sudden roll of flying hoofs made him turn and look over his shoulder. Down went the bucket. He faced the house long enough to shout a warning, and then ran toward the two racing animals. Big Jake could cook, but when it came to fastening hobbles he was a damned fool.

Jake popped into the doorway, hand on gun, ready for the return of Mr. Simpkins; but what he saw was his horse and Tom's running toward the little path leading to town. With the instinctive distaste of a horseman for being left on foot, he raced back to the stove, removed the frying pan, and then dashed out to assist his companion. As he passed the corral a lean, tall, horse-faced person slipped along the end wall of the house, turned the corner, and in an instant was out of sight inside the building. Once inside, he almost flinched as he became aware of the delightful odors meeting him, and his stomach clamored. One look through the window showed him Tom and Jake growing smaller on the trail, the horses barely eluding them and luring them steadily away from the ranch.

"Phew!" exclaimed Simpkins gustily, his eyes turning to the smoking ham and the still bubbling gravy near it. Death and destruction might be in the air, but he felt that he could meet them better on a full stomach. Some idea of the quality of the man might be had from the calm way in which he went about eating his supper, with two paid and hostile gunmen due to return at almost any minute. He drew up a box to the larger box which served as a table, and fell to. The ensuing interval was ecstatic, filled with harmonies of taste and smell. Steadily the ham and gravy shrunk, and he congratulated Big Jake on his prowess as a biscuit maker. Fresh, hot biscuits hidden by ham gravy, backed by first quality ham and excellent coffee, made a meal worth while. His contemplating and appraising gaze passed along the supplies on the floor: cans of peaches, apricots, cherries; jars of marmalade and jelly, bottles of ketchup, and other pleasing sights caused a faint smile to flit to his face. He slipped a hole in the belt of his trousers and lifted up the heavy belts holding his guns to ease their tension, appreciating the dislike of a horse for cinches and girths.

The last of the ham had disappeared, the last fragment of biscuit had mopped up the last trace of gravy, and, not satisfied with eating two men's supper, he looked speculatively at the canned goods. Before deciding upon a choice of dessert, he glanced once more out of the window, and made up his mind to let the dessert come later, if he was alive to eat it. Two men afoot were coming down the trail, straight for the house.

He watched the pair calmly. He was the owner of the little ranch, and he was in possession. If he should defend his tenancy he would be within his legal and moral rights. He felt no particular animosity against Tom and Jake, although he was certain that they were mixed up in the cattle-stealing operations of the county; and from what he had overheard them say, in this same shack, they would show him scant mercy if the opportunity permitted. Well, that was their affair: a matter of individual viewpoint. His affair was to defend his possession of his own ranch, if he cared to; to defend his own life, if he had to; and since he now could do nothing else he would do both to the best of his ability. First, he would warn them through their eyes and ears; and then he would, if the occasion permitted, give them a sterner hint of his intentions; and then—well, after that they would be the arbiters of their own fate.

Tom and Jake was arguing heatedly as they hastened, as well as their fatigue and shortness of breath would permit, toward their supper. It seemed that there was a decided difference of opinion concerning the proper tying of two sets of hobbles. The argument was handicapped by lack of breath, a mutual handicap; but the temper of the spirit behind their words was only improved by the physical miseries. Running in high-heeled boots was an exercise not conducive to physical well-being, and neither of the two men had done any real walking in years.

They passed the corral, still arguing; and their type, lacking ingenuity in verbal debate, falls back on personalities. Their descriptions of each other were edifying to the interested listener in the shack. Halfway between the corral and the house their wrangling ceased as if their throats had been gripped by a giant hand. There followed a moment of stupefied surprise.

Simpkins had stepped into the doorway, the height of which was not enough to let him stand erect, and this forced him to step through it and outside the building. His hands rested on his narrow hips, and he was regarding them with a cold and level gaze, so calm as to be almost impersonal. His confidence was superb: with the odds at two to one against him he held to his determination to let them make the first overt act, to let their hands move first. So he stood and looked at them, his calmness and immobility in sharp contrast with their rage and movement.

"Vamose!" he called. "I'm keepin' this 'dobe."

Their stupefied surprise came to an end, as the

sum of the whole situation came to them simultaneously. Their rage swept up the scale, and they ceased
conjecturing and went into instant action. They jumped
apart, their hands streaking downward. The distance
was perhaps twenty paces, insuring deadly accuracy.
Their guns swung up roaring, in gunman fashion, firing
as the muzzles cleared the tops of the sheaths. From
the doorway came two answering roars, and the generous smoke of black powder spurted and spread out
over the ground.

Big Jake staggered back, his gun dropping from
his hand, his elbow numbed and temporarily paralyzed
by the bullet which had scraped it. Paso Tom, struck
through the shoulder, whirled halfway around under
the heavy impact, his second and third shots going
into the air; but he was made of stern stuff. He staggered, straightened, and faced about again, his weapon
swiftly leveling. Another spurt of flame and smoke
from the doorway, and this time a little puff of dust
sprang from the left side of Paso Tom's vest, and its
owner sagged and fell, his face in the dirt.

Big Jake had recovered his gun and had crawled
behind a scraggly sagebrush near it, lying prone, the
weapon in his left hand. This hand was the less dexter-
ous of the two, and he was desperately anxious to
make his next shot count. He was raising the gun level
with his eyes, believing that Simpkins's attention was
engaged with Paso Tom and would give him the necessary split second, when a sudden burst of leaves and
twigs sifted down in front of him from the passage

of the bullet which instantly put an end to his thieving existence. He lay motionless and the dust of the sage-brush still sifted downward.

Simpkins automatically punched out the used shells and reloaded the empty chambers. Then he shoved the guns back into their holsters, frowning as he stepped forward. The fools! Why hadn't they paid attention to his warning? Why hadn't they stopped after the first exchange and put up their hands? He had given them two chances for their lives, and they had thrown them both away.

What would he do with them? If he quietly covered them up, which was something he did not care to do, their continued absence, while giving him a little more time, would in the end be explained in only one way: they had been guarding his house against him, holding his ranch against him, and therefore the questions arising from their disappearance would soon be solved by the men who had hired and directed them.

Should he catch the horses, a matter easily accomplished by a mounted man, lash the bodies across the animals' backs, and head them toward town? If he buried them he would have a little breathing spell in which to lay his plans against the reaction, a little time free from pressure, a period of calm before the storm. Should he take the peaceful interval?

What he had just done had been necessary to preserve his self-respect and to save his life. His conscience did not bother him, since it had been molded by the ethics of the frontier. He had met the threats, faced and whipped them; but to bury the bodies quietly was a secretive act which ran against the grain—an act which somehow seemed to be a sign of furtive guilt. By his standards there was a great difference here, a differentiating between the justified killer and the assassin. The man who killed his enemy in a stand-up fight, giving him the better of the breaks, did not hide bodies: he still stood up, face forward, accepting the full responsibility for his actions. He had crossed his Rubicon, cut his knot. The time for secrecy had gone. Henceforth he would have to work in his true light, if the others were keen enough to pick up and connect the threads which coupled him with the sheriff's office. This was a crucial moment, and was worth all the thought he could give to it. Here the trail divided, and he had to make his choice and abide by it.

He dropped upon the wash bench, leaned back against the wall of the adobe, rolled a cigarette, and gave himself up to cogitation. He could leave the bodies where they had fallen; he could carry them away and cover them with stones, disposing of the riding gear and the horses with but little effort; he could send them all to town. Minute followed minute as he traced out in his mind the result of each choice. None seemed to suit him. And so he sat until darkness fell, and the growing cold of the night suddenly made itself felt and sent him to his feet. He stood still for a moment, looking out into the darkness, and then, wheeling, entered the house and closed the door behind him.

CHAPTER XV

DAWN found Simpkins awake, his mind resuming the problem where it had been left the night before. He cooked and ate a substantial breakfast, cleared up after it, and went out to sit on the wash bench. Everything was as it had been left. Several cigarettes were rolled and smoked before he came to a decision, and then, having settled the questions in his mind, he arose. He had allowed them to force his hand, and now whatever course he took would be distasteful. He had chosen the open and more manly way out, even if it threatened to thwart his plans.

He obtained supplies from the house, picked up his saddle and gear, and not long thereafter he was riding toward Porter. When he had come to a suitable place he turned from the trail and, riding at a wide angle, circled until he was west of the town. Here he cached his supplies in a good place and rode on again.

He dismounted in front of the Royal Palace and entered the big barroom. Hitchins and Ike Peavy were seated at a table and watching him with a close interest that they had not displayed before. He had the feeling that they had been discussing him, and the expressions on their faces were not pleasant. He joined them, dragging up a third chair and dropping onto it.

"We'd figgered you'd gone on about yore business," said Peavy coldly, his gaze shifting. Something blazed far back in his eyes.

"Well, I was about my business," replied Simpkins, grinning. It was his nature to be able to grin and to kill at the same time. He was taut, alert and expectant. "I've now come to reckon that my business ain't no-where near this town. You damn' fools have been yel-lin' about a man that never bothered you: El Toro don't come within a day's ride of this place. That means that he stays away from here; an' that means that I've got to go where he is if I want to lay eyes on him. I'm pullin' out for San Ignacio, an' I'm pullin' out to-day."

"Great Gawd!" snorted Hitchins, his expression betraying incredulity. It seemed as if he could not believe that any human being could be so utterly foolish; and then his face gradually betrayed another thought, based on what he believed to be the truth: this puncher was lying. It would betray Hitchins's hand to put that thought into words, so he played along on the an-nounced theme.

"After all, I reckon that's th' quickest way to find him," he said, feeling foolish in keeping up such an asinine pretense; "but do you know what yo're goin' up ag'in?"

"Reckon so," answered Simpkins, stretching out his long legs. "It'll be safe enough for a while, until I make my play. I'll be a stranger, nobody'll know anythin' about me, an' I'll keep my fool mouth shut. When things break right I'll get that greaser. Th' reward still stand?"

Both men nodded, trying not to smile. Peavy was frankly incredulous and lacked the wit to hide it.

"My Gawd!" he muttered. Fools rush in where angels—aye, they did! They did, if they rushed in at all, and somehow he had the feeling that this particular fool was really going off to hunt for the bandit on the latter's own range.

Hitchins thought otherwise and was casting around in his mind for the safest way in which to have Simpkins killed. Things were so complicated, and his own game so involved and hard pressed that he did not dare to load it with any more risks. It was balanced too precariously to carry another heavy load. Since the ranchers over west had banded together and were taking turns watching the pass, it was imperative to abandon his entire system of movement and to find another quickly. There was a dangerous accumulation of cattle to be gotten rid of, and time was fast becoming as important a factor as safety. He was watching Simpkins closely, a disarming smile on his hard, gambler's face. Once get this prying fool to San Ignacio, away from Porter and its vicinity—aye, that was the thing!

"Well, Simpkins," he said, forcing a chuckle; "if you go down to that town, you'll mebby never come back ag'in. What'll you take for th' JP, cash down?"

"After what happened last night I won't sell it!" snapped Simpkins angrily.

Both men looked curious and Peavy showed apprehension.

"Last night?" he inquired, his thoughts racing.

"What happened?" asked Hitchins uncomfortably.

"What happened?" repeated Simpkins, sneering. "I had to kill a couple of range jumpers—that's what happened! Hell of a note, when a man can't ride up to his own ranch in safety! They both loosened at me, an' even after I gave 'em a chance to pull out an' save their mangy lives they kept on shootin'. I had to kill 'em. There wasn't nothin' else I could do. They're out in front of th' house, where I left 'em, for their friends to bury. That's *one* of th' reasons why I'm pullin' out of this damn' country! I ain't waitin' till some of their friends shoot me from ambush. San Ignacio may be dangerous, but it's shore a lot safer for me than this part of th' country. I'll meet anybody in a stand-up fight, but there's a lot of cover along that south trail. I'm pullin' out, that's all."

"Range jumpers!" exclaimed Peavy in a vast surprise; too vast, thought Simpkins.

"You killed two men!" said Hitchins, his eyes glittering. "Who were they?"

"Couple of saloon bums named Big Jake an' Paso Tom," answered the puncher. "Livin' in my house, with grub enough to last 'em a month! Livin' on th' JP, an' waitin' to kill me when I showed up! Ain't that a hell of a note?"

"You done just right!" snapped Hitchins, hiding the raging anger within him. Big Jake and Paso Tom,

dead! "Th' town's better off without 'em. Range jumpers, huh?" He laughed nastily. "I'd like to see somebody jump a ranch of mine!" Then he leaned forward,
his eyes fixed on those of the puncher. "Better sell it
to me, Simpkins. *I* can hold it!"

"I ain't sellin' to nobody," grunted the puncher.
"I might want to settle down some day; an' there's
right good water on th' JP."

"But it's no good to you if you go off an' leave it,"
objected the gambler, still inwardly raging over the
deaths of his two men.

"That's true, too; an', as you say, I may never come
back," muttered Simpkins. The look of perplexity
faded, and he smiled at a sudden thought. "Suppose
I lease it to you? I'll lease it for a year, but th' lease
will run on till I return. You savvy? Until I come back
ag'in. If I don't come back, th' lease renews itself year
after year. If I never come back, th' ranch is as good
as yours, unless it's been proved that I've been killed.
I'm fixin' it that way so I'll live till I get out of town,
anyhow," he coldly explained, his hard eyes on the
gambler's face. "I'm speakin' plain, like business should
be spoke. I figger my life wouldn't be worth a plugged
peso if my death would give you th' use of that ranch.
I wouldn't trust either of you out of my sight. If you
want to lease th' JP on them terms, say so an' dig up
one hundred dollars, cash."

"I wouldn't lease it, or buy it, *now,* to save yore life!"
retorted Hitchins. "I like to speak plain, too! I hope
you get yore damn' head blowed off in San Ignacio,

if you go there! I got a feelin' that you ain't got guts
enough to go there. I'll bet you that one hundred dollars that you don't go there! I'll do better than that:
I'll bet you five hundred to th' JP that you don't go
to San Ignacio! An' I'll bet a thousan' to th' JP that
if you do go there you won't leave it alive!"

"Who you got picked to do th' killin'?" calmly asked
Simpkins, watching closely.

Hitchins's hand leaped up from the table, but both
he and Peavy were looking in surprise into the muzzles
of the puncher's guns; and the bartender across the
room felt his stomach squirm: he was certain that both
weapons were aimed at him. He did not move.

"If you can't let that shoulder holster alone, I'll
take it away from you," said Simpkins. "You don't
need it, nohow. I'm pullin' out of this damn' town an'
not comin' back; but I'm not sellin', or even leasin', th'
JP to a coyote like you. I got a feelin' that you sent
them two fellers down there to hold th' ranch ag'in
me. Don't you make a move, Hitchins! Don't you try
to signal! Th' man you signal to will ride to hell
astraddle a .45. You keep yore face straight an' yore
hands quiet unless you want to ride to th' same place
in th' same saddle! If you ever heard th' Gospel, you
shore are hearin' it now."

"How did this damn' fool argument start?" demanded Peavy, surprised by the swiftness of the developments. "Can't we talk business? Can't we act
like sensible people? You got a ranch, Simpkins, that
ain't worth nothin' to you, things bein' like they are.

It's worth somethin' to me, though; its water controls th' grazin' of a right big territory, an' it's territory so far east that no greaser will try to raid it. We'll buy it or we'll lease it."

"We'll do nothin' of th' kind!" snapped Hitchins, still raging.

"All right, then: *we* won't," replied Peavy; "but *I* will, if Simpkins is willin'. I'll pay two hundred dollars for th' use of it for one year; three hundred dollars for th' third an' other years. Th' lease will run for ten. Either that or I'll buy it outright, an' pay you a cold thousan' in cash."

"I reckon I can do business with you," replied the puncher, drawing a distinction where he knew that none really existed. "She's yourn for one year for two hundred dollars. Th' lease will renew itself automatic *as long as I am away*. While I am away th' money will be deposited in th' bank to my account, an' th' bank will be empowered to make th' new leases in my name while I am away. If I die, or don't come back for three years, I'll have things fixed so that th' ranch goes back to Jim Pettingill. If that suits you, we'll go over to th' bank right now, an' send for a lawyer."

The two men arose, Simpkins keeping the room under his guns. He backed to the door, through it, and stepped quickly to one side. Peavy emerged and led the way to the bank. An hour later everything was arranged, and the lanky puncher slipped out of the rear door of the financial institution, looked carefully around, and then went to his horse, a gun glinting openly in his right hand. He was not molested, as he felt that he would not be while he remained in town. Mounting, he wheeled, crossed the dirt sidewalk, and dashed along the blind side of the Royal Palace, and soon left the town behind him. By the terms finally agreed upon in the bank he had leased the JP for one year, the lease to renew itself unless he returned within that time. If it could be proved that he died within that year, the ranch went to Pettingill subject to the one-year lease.

Behind the departing puncher, keeping at a safe and comfortable distance, and back far enough not to be seen by the man they were following, rode deputy sheriffs George Brady and Jim Huston. They were to make certain that Simpkins really entered the town of San Ignacio, for reasons known only to Hitchins, and they were to hang around the town and report on what occurred there. And miles in front of Simpkins rode a young, lithe Mexican, bearing a message from Ad Hitchins to a man the gambler never had seen. To understand this message and the reason for it, and also how it chanced that Simpkins was only the second man on that trail, it will be necessary to go back to the barroom. It is about five minutes after Peavy and Simpkins left to go to the bank. Hitchins had called for and dispatched a man to the Mexican part of the town, and very soon thereafter a slim Mexican youth entered the Royal Palace from the rear, and, walking to the proprietor's table, stopped and waited.

"Manuel, you know El Toro by sight?" abruptly asked the gambler.

"*Si, Señor.*"

"You know where to find him?"

"Een San Ingacio, *si?*"

"Mebby," grunted Hitchins shortly. "Well, any-how, if you go there, you can find a way to get word to him, can't you?"

"*Si, Señor.*"

"You've seen this Simpkins hombre that's been around town for a week or so?"

"*Si, Señor.*"

Hitchins glanced around the room, and then mo-tioned for the Mexican to bend down, closer to his lips.

"You ride like hell for San Ignacio, startin' *now*. You get word to El Toro that this hombre, Simpkins, is headin' for his town to get him. Savvy? To *get* him! To kill El Toro for th' reward. I do not appear in this a-tall. Savvy? You overheard Simpkins boastin' about it, an' that's how you know. Savvy?"

"*Si, Señor.*"

"All right, then. Get agoin'. Beat Simpkins to San Ignacio. You don't weigh very much, an' a good hoss ought to jerk you along four miles to his three. A *good* hoss. Vamose!"

"*Si, Señor.*"

Hitchins watched the youth hasten away, and then he leaned back in his chair and smiled with cruel satis-faction. He had begun to have grave doubts about this man Simpkins. They had been strengthened by very recent news from the town of Bradley. Hitchins took no chances. Now he gave his whole attention to the problem presented by Jim Pettingill, and after a few moments he nodded his head and smiled. A quit-claim deed from Pettingill would do it, and he felt that he could get one at any time.

The Mexican youth hastened into an adobe house wherein resided one Felipe, a countryman of his. They conversed for a few minutes and then Felipe, showing his beautiful white teeth in a smile of delight, patted his visitor on the shoulder.

"You stay here, Manuel," he said in Spanish. "I will take the Señor Hitchins' message to San Ignacio myself. Now that Señor Simpkins has left this town, I have no more business here. Even if he should return, no Mexican will molest him. You stay inside the house for three days, not showing yourself to anyone not of our own race. Then you can go and tell Señor Hitchins that El Toro is very grateful for the warning. El Toro is a good guesser, and he guessed who sent the word. That is fast riding, three days in which to go and come; but you are a good messenger, and you have Señor Hitchins' interests at heart. You rode six horses almost to death. You did not go along the regular trail, but chose a way which was no longer and led you past the homes of your friends; and these friends all have good horses. That is how you rode a distance in three days that would take a gringo five days to cover. It is clear to you? Then, adios."

On the second day Simpkins knew that he was being followed, and he was beginning to understand the reason for it. His pursuers had not molested him, had not even tried to close up the big gap between them and himself. At first he had been puzzled, but now he understood it. Somebody wanted to make certain that he had really left the country.

He was smiling as he entered the ford across the river, glad that the water was low enough to cross without swimming his horse, and glad that there had been no freshet to fluff up the soft, treacherous bottom. Three miles away on the other side of the stream lay his destination, the heroically evil town of San Ignacio, the turbid backwater of many vicious and ill-spent lives. Here almost anything could happen to a man, if that thing were not good. This condition of affairs, however, caused him no anxiety. Aside from his entirely sufficient ability to take care of himself in swift company, the undisputed boss of the town was a very good friend of his, so good a friend that he eagerly looked forward to meeting him again. He had a deal of respect and admiration for this particular cattle thief.

He left the ford and rode slowly up the sloping bank, on dry Mexican soil at last. From a little rise back of the river he looked northward over his own back trail and saw a thin cloud of dust barely discernible against the dark hills. The trailers were still following him. If they bothered him in San Ignacio they were due to experience a very great surprise. Turning, he loped down a gentle slope, his face toward San Ignacio; and then he pulled up sharply in surprise and dragged the rifle from its long scabbard. A dozen armed horsemen were cantering out of a draw about long rifle shot away, and while he was trying to figure out their purpose, their leader raised a hand to him.

"By Gawd!" chuckled Simpkins, greatly pleased. "El Toro, hisself! He don't overlook nothin'!"

He pushed on swiftly and soon was shaking hands with the best dressed man in the north of Mexico. The amenities over with, he found himself listening closely and in surprise to what the smiling bandit was telling him, and at the conclusion of the recital he laughed aloud.

The possibilities of the tale gripped him, and his racing mind saw the solution of a problem which had begun to bother him: the problem of his own identity and further investigations. With one motion he could sweep the board of suspicions and be in a position to start anew. He swiftly placed his hand on El Toro's arm, gripping tightly.

"No, no!" he chuckled. "Don't capture me! *Shoot* me! Shoot me, right in front of their eyes! Don't you see it, *amigo?* Shoot me down, right in front of them; and then throw a few shots in their direction, an' chase 'em back ag'in! I've still got time to get back across th' river before they show up. Wait till I leave th' ford before you shoot: I don't want to play dead under water, an' mebby drown myself."

El Toro spoke swiftly in his own tongue, and in

scarcely more than a moment there was not a Mexican in sight. The bandit himself gripped the puncher's shoulders and squeezed, a delighted grin on his swarthy face. Then he, too, disappeared.

Deputy sheriffs Brady and Huston rode up to the top of the low hill just north of the river, and drew up. Down below them they saw the man they were following. Having eased the cinches to rest his horse, he was now tightening them for the ride of the last few miles. They sat quietly, watching him. He swung into the saddle, glanced around and saw them. Placing a thumb to his nose in derision, he wheeled, entered the ford, and splashed toward the farther bank.

"Any use of us follerin' him any closer to town?" asked Huston, his eyes on the rider in the river. He was a little uneasy about visiting San Ignacio.

"Shore! Th' orders are plain. Besides, ain't we got to hang around an' see what happens to him? Come on, Jim: let's git across."

They pushed down the slope and had reached a point within two hundred paces of the stream when Simpkins left the water and turned in his saddle to wave derisively at them. As he faced around again, his arm still raised, there came a cracking volley of shots from a mass of sagebrush, and the man they were following jerked in the saddle, fell forward, caught himself, and then toppled sidewise to the ground, where he sprawled grotesquely and lay still. The sounds of the shots were still in the deputies' ears when a group of Mexican horsemen, a dozen in number, dashed up out of a deep gully and galloped toward the river. Two of them dismounted at the side of the prostrate puncher, but the others, firing rapidly at the amazed spectators on the north bank, entered the water at their best speed and splashed determinedly forward looking for two more victims.

"My Gawd!" shouted Huston, wheeling in panic. "They're after us! Come on, George!"

Brady obeyed the command so well that in ten jumps of his horse he was leading the way; and he held the lead, and for the next half score miles the two deputies rode for their lives, flat reports from the rear spurring them onward. At last their pursuers halted and turned back, but the two deputies, taking no chances with any possible fickleness of the Mexican mind, kept going, and going fast. When they again saw the town of Porter and made their report in the little back room of the Royal Palace Saloon, there would be lacking no conviction in their words or actions. Simpkins was dead, and they themselves barely had escaped a like fate.

CHAPTER XVI

EVENTS were stirring into life in and around the town of Porter. The three days, insisted upon by one Felipe, expired; and Manuel, leaving his adobe habitation after three days' voluntary imprisonment, slipped out of town just after dark on the evening of the third day, and returned riding hard and fast. He dismounted at the rear door of the Royal Palace and entered the building. Hitchins and the two Peavy brothers were talking at the big round table in the gambling room when the Mexican appeared, and the three, rising like one man, motioned the courier to enter the little private room and followed him in.

"Well?" asked Hitchins a little tensely, as he closed the door.

"Señor El Toro ees ver' grateful. He sends hees thanks an' good weeshes."

"You told him what I said, and that *I* said it?" demanded the gambler, his eyes boring into the black ones before him.

"He ees a smar-rt man, an' he guess who e-sent the message. I tol' heem thees, an' notheeng mor-re," and Manuel repeated the message almost word for word.

"Right," replied Hitchins, smiling grimly. "An' he's grateful: well, there's no harm done in gainin' th' good wishes of a man like him. Did he say anythin' else?"

Manuel's white teeth flashed in a smile, and his right hand, dropping swiftly, went through a significant series of motions. Then he shrugged his shoulders and waited.

"All right, then," grunted Hitchins, nodding. "You made right fast time, Manuel. That's a long journey."

"Seex horses," replied the courier, smiling proudly. "What you call re-lay. I have fr-riends between her-re and San Ignacio, Señor; an' they have ver' good hor-rses!"

Hitchins nodded again, a smile twitching at the corners of his mouth. He dug down into a pocket, pulled out a roll of bills, and peeled several layers from it. He could afford to be generous. Manuel accepted the offering with a flashing smile, bowed, and looked toward the closed door. Hitchins stepped forward and let the courier out of the room, and then, closing the door again, faced his two companions.

"Well, that play is over. Simpkins won't bother nobody no more," he said. "Get th' boys busy on th' JP. Throw a bank across th' crick about where we decided on. I'll take care of Pettingill when th' time comes. A little reservoir will do th' work—we don't need a big one. Get them cattle herded up, drive 'em south, roundabout, an' then hold 'em north of th' river in that little valley for their brands to heal. Th' other herd will join 'em there. We can water 'em an' rest 'em on th' JP, an' run 'em over th' desert when we're ready. There's been a lot of worry taken off me, thanks to El Toro."

The JP was pretty well off by itself, and there was

no excuse for any alien rider to visit its territory unless
he had a specific reason for it. Most of the riding was
done west of town, where the smaller ranchers and
the IP ran their cattle. Even the old, abandoned trail
up from the southeast passed some miles from Pettingill's adobe shack; and even the general round-ups,
thorough as they were, ignored the range around the
JP headquarters. A year or more might easily pass
without anyone, not a member of the gang, visiting
the place.

A day after Manuel's report to Hitchins, two dust-
covered deputies clattered into town at noon and hastened to the Royal Palace Saloon. They stopped at the
bar and sighed with deep satisfaction at the breaking
of the drought, and turned to see the gambler watching them from a little table against the side wall. They
smiled knowingly and joined him, and then looked at
each other curiously, each waiting for the other to
speak.

"Go ahead," said Brady, nodding to his brother
deputy.

"You tell it, George," said Huston, chuckling, and
he looked swiftly about the room.

"Better go inside," suggested Hitchins, glancing at
the door of the private room.

"Keno!" exclaimed Brady, leading the way.

The door having been closed behind them, both men
started to talk at the same time, but gradually Huston
subsided and let his companion relate the story. At its
conclusion Hitchins was smiling, his gently shaking

head paying homage to the forthright nature of the Mexican cattle thief.

"My Gawd!" he muttered. "That's th' way to do a piece of work! No hemmin' an' hawin' in that greaser's make-up! Th' news was hardly cold in his ears before he called th' play! Like th' strike of a rattler! I shore hope we never have to stack up ag'in that hombre!"

The two deputies burst into words again, and their employer let them talk, enjoying the vividness of the tale and their own reactions to the amazing showdown. But when they started to tell it for the third time he stopped them with a gesture.

"Well, all right, all right. You got away, safe an' sound. Now you better take th' trail to Dailey's, turnin' off th' JP a couple of miles beyond th' reg'lar JP trail. There's work to be done, an' Ike Peavy's doin' it. He can stand a little more help on th' shovel end of it. That dam's got to be packed, an' th' pond puddled so it'll hold water."

Hitchins waved them from the room, walked to the street door with them, saw them mounted and on their way, and then returned to the bar.

"I'm breakin' my rule," he said to the man behind the counter. "I'll have another drink, an' have it now. Take one with me. We're celebratin' a slick piece of work, 'though we ain't sayin' what it is. Between you an' me, however, I'll say that th' old southeast trail, up past Dailey's, is comin' back to life ag'in. We're extendin' our operations, an' extendin' 'em wide an' handsome. Drink hearty!"

The ranchmen west of Porter still maintained their vigil on the road through the pass, and maintained it well. From their station they could see both slopes, rising to the crests on each side, slopes almost free from vegetation. It is doubtful if a lone cow could have gotten through unseen, not to consider the passage of a herd of them. The outlet was blocked. This vigil, however, meant men on guard; and men on guard meant less men riding over the range. None of these small ranchers could afford to carry an outfit; indeed, it was all they could do to take care of their own personal needs. While these men were gravely congratulating themselves upon the solving of a serious problem, the problem was increasing without their knowledge, and increasing in a way that would bring despair to their hearts.

On the night following the report of Manuel, which was the night following the return of Brady and Huston, a shadowy crew of riders moved cautiously over the western range and dissolved into single units. All night long these riders drifted cattle before them, steadily southward toward the river; and the moving herd, once started, grew in size with each mile covered. This was to be a clean-up, a thorough combing of the range. After this night's work there would be but few cattle left, and utter ruination of the hopes of the small ranchers.

When dawn broke the last animal was across the river and being driven deeper into Mexico, to get beyond the low range of hills south of the stream, so that curious, searching riders north of the river would see nothing to interest them. After a rest this herd moved southeastward, parallel with the stream, and two days later it turned north, recrossed, and came to a halt in a natural basin well beyond the threat of the loco fields. Brand changing now engaged the outfit, and while the cattle were held for the new iron marks to heal, most of the crew rode off down the trail, to raid a placid and totally unsuspecting range far beyond the limits of their usual operations. Thanks to the reservoir on the JP a new territory was being opened up.

*   *   *   *   *

Far to the west of this stolen herd and the nocturnal raid; far to the west of the JP and the town of Porter, a tall, lanky puncher picked himself up from the sand of the river bank and grinned into the face of the Mexican dandy who smiled at him. The pursuit across the river had passed out of sight over the hills, although the intermittent firing was still audible. There were no hostile eyes to see this miraculous awakening of the dead.

"Reckon I came down purty hard," said the puncher, ruefully feeling himself over. "I ain't much used to fallin' off of hosses."

His companion, showing white teeth in a wide smile,

clapped the puncher on the shoulder and laughed loudly.

"I can well believe eet, *amigo*. Deed you ever fall off a hor-rse?"

The second Mexican had disappeared to go after and capture Nueces' mount, and it was not long before the three were riding toward San Ignacio, El Toro and Nueces well in front. The two men had a deal to say, notes to compare; and the bandit listened intently to his companion's plans, nodding assent from time to time and promising to give his aid. They entered the frontier hamlet, the cynosure of all eyes; and whatever doubts there might have been in regard to the status of the gringo they were dispelled by the sight of him riding side by side in friendship with El Toro. From that moment Nueces could range around the town at any hour of the day or night as safely as he could walk the streets of Willow Springs.

Night fell, and the cantina was ablaze with lights and filled with the sounds of stringed instruments, the shuffle of feet, and the low murmur of conversation in several different tongues. Mexicans, fugitive Americans, and the scum of other nationalities mingled, drank, gambled, and danced.

Off in one corner of the room sat three men, one of whom wore the air of holding court. His second in command served as a buffer between his chief and those who from time to time intruded with their questions and petitions.

The third of the little group was a gringo, a tall,

lanky, horse-faced individual who keenly watched the room and its activities. A deal of the talk in the room concerned him, for the story of his afternoon adventure had become nosed around and was arousing quiet laughter. Men smiled at him, and he was surrounded by an atmosphere of friendliness. A stranger, a gringo, and a man known to be a deputy sheriff, sitting in peace and friendship in the cantina in San Ignacio! Truly the friendship of El Toro was well worth while.

A peon approached the corner, sombrero in hand, his eyes on the face of the bandit leader.

Federico interposed himself and spoke swiftly in Spanish.

"What now, Pablo?"

"My family is sick. I need money. We starve."

"That is, indeed, like a tale I have heard before," replied Federico, but he was interrupted.

"Is this the same family that you had before?" interposed El Toro sarcastically in Spanish, his eyes challenging those of the supplicant. "Yes, you say? Hah! And the money I gave to you but two nights past for this family? Where is it?"

"It is gone, Excellency," answered the peon, his gaze on the floor.

"Of a truth! It is gone, eh? Washed down in mescal! Give him the money, Federico; but let him earn it. There is no mescal in Arroyo Verde; send him there to work with the cattle. Stay! Do not give *him* the money: send it to his house, and send him to the camp, quickly, where he will learn to control a thirst!" He looked after the departing man, who was now under orders that he did not dare to disobey.

"Children they ar-re," said El Toro, turning a smiling face to his American companion, "whose brains ar-re een their thr-roats and stom-achs! Now hees family weel get the money, and Pablo—hah! He weel get sometheeng he needs eef he does not do as he ees tol'. I have many such, and the tr-roubles of them all ar-re my tr-roubles; but they ar-re like children, and they would die for me. I am the father of a beeg family!" He laughed contentedly, glanced toward the door, and back to his companion.

"Eet ees time we hear-rd from the east; and I expect, also, some news from the south. The news from the east ees for you; the news from the south, for me."

"Well, th' sooner we hear from the east, th' better I'll like it," said the puncher, stirring restlessly. "I want to get back right soon."

"But why?" quickly asked the bandit. "You ar-re dead. Ver' dead. Reedled weeth bullets, no? Then why not e-stay dead, so you weel not be really so, and let your fr-riend El Toro put an end to thees beezeness? I can do eet like that," and the speaker snapped his fingers.

"No," emphatically replied Nueces, shaking his head. "I'll be glad of yore help in th' matter of sendin' news to Bob Corson, an' gettin' it from th' east; but I aim to tie th' knots in their tails myself. That's my job; an' I'm shore goin' to do it."

"Eef you retur-rn, they weel see you, and you weel be dead no longer, no?" replied El Toro.

"Not if I go back south of th' river, an' lay low durin' th' day," said Nueces.

"Ah, yes! Eef you do! So, eef you must, then you must. And, my fr-riend, eef I send a guide weeth you, to e-show you the way, they weel never see you teel you e-show yourself. Of that you may be asure'." El Toro chuckled and rubbed his hands.

"Good," replied Nueces, smiling. "I'll take th' guide till I turn north to cross th' river. But are you shore that you can get th' news to Corson quick enough? Things might be movin' fast."

El Toro laughed aloud, spreading his hands expressively.

"That ees a joke, Señor! Me, I have re-lays north, south, east, and west; and some een between. What you call pony expr-ess, no? Send news quickly? Hah: you would be sur-rpr-rise!" He ceased abruptly, listened closely, and then loudly clapped his hands. The cantina fell instantly silent. Hoof beats grew louder in the street and neared the door. He nodded his head quickly, smiled, and clapped his hands again, waving them grandly, and the noise returned.

A dust-covered Mexican, a slender, light-weight youth, entered the room and hastened toward the corner. He and El Toro exchanged a few sentences in Spanish and then the youth wheeled and went out again.

"There!" exclaimed the bandit, smiling with pride. "Fr-rom the south, he ees. Seventy-five miles een five hours. News quickly? Hah!" He looked intently at his American friend. "That ees a thought. When you leave her-re you take two men weeth you: one to guide, one to breeng back news, or to take eet wher-re you weesh. Ther-re ees no use for heem to come her-re fir-rst. Let heem go str-raight fr-rom ther-re."

"Damn' if you ain't got one ring-tailed system!" exclaimed Nueces admiringly. "Yo're a wonder!"

"Yes? Eeet ees my beezeness to be such. Eef I am not, then I am stood against a wall, and e-shot. One meestake ees too much."

The minutes passed with no news from the east, and Nueces again grew restless.

"I hate to sit here, doin' nothin'," he remarked. "I feel that I oughta pull my stakes an' get back where I belong."

"You ar-re like a cat weeth a fit," retorted El Toro. "You have depend on yourself so long that you do not know how to depend on others. One man cannot do eet all. Every Mexican een that par-rt of the countr-ry has hees ear-rs open, and hees eyes, as well. Notheeng ees done that somebody does not see or hear. Then I am tol' about eet. Then I tell you. When everytheeng ees right, then you reach out your hand—and tweest the tails! Two days' riding, and you ar-re ther-re."

"Wonder why we don't get some news from th' east?" muttered the puncher.

"Because ther-re ees none for us to hear. My men do not run to me and say 'Señor Heetchens took a dr-reenk,' 'Señor Peavy lit a match'; no, but w'en Señor

Heetchens e-steals a her-rd—then I know! When Señor Peavy changes a br-rand, then I am tol'. Ees eet not good?"

The daylight hours dragged more than those spent in the excitement of the cantina after its lights were lit, but Nueces managed to survive the wait; and then came the night when the wished-for news came in from the east. The courier hastened straight for the corner of the room, spoke swiftly, answered questions with military precision and snap, and departed.

El Toro leaned back in his chair and smiled expansively, little wrinkles crinkling his face. Little glints of light danced in his dark eyes, and the gleam of his teeth was like white ivory.

"Eet ees ar-rive, that news fr-rom the east," he chuckled. "Señors Heetchens and Peavy deed not light a match, or dr-reenk a dr-reenk; they e-steal many cattle. They dr-rove them south, acr-ross the river, wher-re the tr-rail weel be plain to follow."

"Then I don't need any guide," quickly remarked Nueces, a smile on his face. "That suits me better. I'd rather not take a messenger, either. I don't like to be all cluttered up with people when I'm travelin'."

"No? Well, then why take one? Ther-re ees a way. Eef you have news to e-send, and you can get near to Porter, a man weel wait ther-re for you, and he weel go wher-re you e-say. He weel wait wher-re he ees tol' to wait. That we weel feex before you leave."

"I'm leavin' at daylight," said Nueces. "Whatever

fixin' there is to be done will have to be done now, to-night."

El Toro arose, glancing toward a small booth against one side wall. A curtain hung in front of it, now drawn to one side. There was a window in the wall. Months before a stranger had stood on a barrel outside that window in a pouring rain, and learned vital information. No more news would leak through it to the ruination of El Toro's plans, for as he glanced at the booth, an armed Mexican arose from a table near the door and passed out into the night, to stand guard under the window until he should be recalled.

The bandit turned and looked at his *segundo,* who was talking with two of his countrymen.

"Federico!" he called, and raised his hand in an imperative gesture.

The *segundo* hastened to the side of his chief, dropped back one step to the rear, and followed Nueces and El Toro into the booth, drawing the curtain behind them.

Seated, El Toro motioned to his companions to do likewise, and then leaned across the table, knocking upon it with his knuckles. Answering knocks sounded on the wall, and he nodded quickly. There was no fear of eavesdroppers under the window.

"Federico," he said in a low voice, "you know the country around the town of Porter. We plan a re-lay, and a messenger to e-stay een one place onteel he ees e-sent about hees beezeness. When he ees not ther-re,

a man mus' be een hees place, day and night. We mus'
e-spik of thees theengs so ther-re weel be no mistak'.
Now let us talk them over, ver' car-reful, for mooch
depends on thees. Fir-rst, let Señor Nueces say w'at
he ees to do, for on that depends w'at we do."

Nueces began to speak, his companions listening intently, nodding their heads from time to time as the
points were made and found to be good. The conference lasted until nearly midnight, and when it broke
up a detailed course of action had been determined
upon, and everything checked. The relay would be established, and a messenger would wait day and night,
at a spot known to all the actors. If Nueces found need
to send news either to San Ignacio or to the county
seat, he had only to get to the waiting messenger and
send him off.

As the three men stood up to leave the booth, El
Toro smiled at his companions and shrugged his shoulders expressively.

"He mus' do eet by heemself," he said to Federico,
but looking at Nueces. "I tol' heem that we could do
eet ver' queeck, and ver' well; but no! *he* mus' do eet.
One man, he ees; we, we are ar-re many. But he ees
right: the sher-reef should do the sher-reef's wor-rk.
Then eet ees onderstood? Ther-re ees notheeng we
have overlook? No? Then *adios,* my *amigo;* and may
the Virgin keep you br-right een her mind. Good luck."

The brown hand rested for a moment on the shoulders of the tall puncher, and squeezed lightly; and then,
knocking again upon the outside wall, El Toro wheeled

abruptly, flung open the curtain, and bowed his American friend out into the big room, watching him stalk across the floor and disappear through the door into the night.

"He ees my fr-riend," he said in a low voice, and then, realizing that he was talking only to his *segundo*, he continued in Spanish: "He is my friend. Señor Corson is my friend. Good men, they are. We must never do anything to make them believe that we are not good friends of theirs, Federico. Never! We must never raid across their county line while they are officers of the law. For my freedom and my life I am in debt to them both." He paused a moment, picturing the night he sat in the JC ranch house under the guns of Corson and his deputy. "If they would only join with us, eh, Federico? What a tune we could play for the dancing of others! Hah!"

CHAPTER XVII

NUECES was on his way east when the sun came up, holding to a course several miles south of the river, and not worrying about water because it was always within reach. The ride was wearying, seemingly interminable; but he pushed on at a steady, moderate gait, riding well into the evening before camping. He could camp when he chose, seeing that he only had to ride north a few miles to find water; but he preferred not to reach the bank of the stream while there was light enough for some chance rider on the other side to see and recognize him: he was "dead," and wanted to remain so. He had no need for haste, for the reason that he was covering three or more miles to the herd's one, and he did not want to overtake it while it was on the move.

It was the evening of the second day when he struck the signs of the trail herd, the herd spoken of by the messenger back in San Ignacio. Now he grew more alert, and on the third day he reached the country roughly south of the JP ranch and circled farther into the south, abandoning the trail signs for half a score miles, and came to the river to water his horse after dark. That done, he struck south again and made a dry camp. On again the following dawn, he swung back

until he picked up the trail again, and followed it dog-
gedly at a slow pace mile after mile.

Eventually the signs led him to the river, but he
stopped south of the shielding hills until dark, and then
crossed the stream, watering his horse on the way, and
made another dry camp a few miles north of the river
and well to one side of the newly made trail. The tracks
were getting fresher, as they should; and on the evening of the next day he saw a thin streamer of smoke
piercing the horizon. Leaving his horse in a draw, he
went forward on foot, cautiously and deviously. Crawl-
ing up to the top of a small hill he peered over it and
saw the herd in a little grassy basin below him and
a mile away. It was of sizable proportions, had been
split into two parts, and was being worked by a full
crew of men. Two branding fires were burning between
the two parts of the herd, and the cook wagon and
camp at one side gave the operations the semblance
of legality: truly they must be well assured of their
safety to establish a camp like that.

He slipped down the hillside and worked around to
where he could get a closer view, and from this new
point of vantage he could recognize some of the outfit:
the two Peavy brothers, deputy sheriffs Brady and
Huston, half a dozen hangers-on of the Royal Palace
Saloon. The others he never had seen before. There
were too many men for this work, for a herd of this
size, based upon his judgment; but it might be that
they were pressed for time. However, pressed for
time or not, they could not hasten the healing time of

the new iron marks. While he lay watching and thinking, the work ceased and the men who were to night
herd rode off to camp, to eat their suppers and to
return.

He crept back until the top of the hill made it safe
for him to stand erect, and then returned to his horse
and rode a few miles west before heading for the river.
There was no question in his mind as to the signifi-
cance of what he had seen: the brands of the herd, perhaps half a dozen different marks, were being altered
and changed into the master brand of the Bradley
ranch. The intent and scrupulous care with which the
iron handlers worked told of old brand lines being continued, of cross lines connecting older parallels; in general, of artistic alteration. He figured the time necessary for the brands to heal, and the time needed for
the new marks to attain something of the appearance
of the old. He figured the time it would take to drive
the herd northward through a country where there was
no one to find fault or to be curious of nearly healed
sections of brands, otherwise old. It would be fruitless
to hang around this part of the county and to risk the
possibility of being seen, or trailed, before the herd
was ready to move. This was an interval he easily
could use for scouting around Porter and the JP ranch.

The next morning found him ready to leave, but he
decided to take another look at the herd and the camp;
and once more in his vantage point on the hill he saw the
herd guards changed and the cattle allowed to spread
out to graze. Now that the work was over there was

no need to close herd them. There was considerable
activity around the camp, and while he watched he saw
a round dozen men mount and ride eastward, and drop
from his sight over a little rise. This puzzled him, and
the more he thought about it, the less he understood
it. He finally decided to follow them and to try to learn
where they were going, or at least to get their drift.

In the saddle once more, he circled widely and got
around to the eastern side of the camp, where he cut
and followed the trail made by the departing dozen.
It led him straight east, and after two hours' riding
he came to what he believed was the old cattle trail,
the trail he had followed southward from Dailey's
ranch, and the one which avoided the loco fields and
paralleled the river. What could they be doing on this
road, and why were they heading directly away from
Porter? The nearest settlements in the southeast must
be all of four days' ride away. He could follow and
learn, perhaps; but he did not believe the effort and
risk were justified: the things in which he was interested
lay in the other direction. Just now, when things were
going so well for him, he did not care to follow any
established trails and take the risk of being seen. He
left the road, turned, and headed back toward Porter
and the JP ranch, riding cross country under the guidance of a plainsman's instinct.

It was noon of the next day when he espied the
adobe hut of Charles Dailey's CD ranch, and he pulled
up and dismounted, going on foot to a place which
gave him a closer view. There were no signs of life

about the house, no smoke, no horse. The door was closed and the place looked to be abandoned. There was nothing to be discovered here, and so he went back to his horse and struck off across the hills in a direct line for the JP.

He cautiously approached the hill on the north of the ranch, and soon looked down upon the little water course. The first thing he saw was a small herd of cattle being driven around and around in a muddy pond. This pond was held by a small, freshly made dam of earth. He chuckled: it had not taken them long to get to work after the news of his death. He watched the rider, and although the distance was too far for definite recognition, he believed the man to be Dailey.

Nueces now had established several points in their line of action, the line they would follow with the herd. Here was the place they would pause to rest and water the cattle after the long dry drive; from here to the Bradley ranch he had their course pretty well mapped out. But why had that dozen men ridden down that old cattle trail, heading away from their home range? If he was to catch the gang and get them all this was something he should find out. To follow them over the flat country in the southeast would be foolhardy: they could see him miles away; and, besides, it was now too late for trailing them. He could go down and force the truth out of Dailey; but what could he do with the man afterward? He could not kill him in cold blood, and he would not dare let the man loose to carry a warning. Pettingill might know something; but to find that budding gambler he would have to enter Porter and search through its saloons and risk being seen a dozen times.

Dailey continued his monotonous work, drifting the cattle around and around in the puddle, packing the bottom so solidly that it would become water-tight. He appeared to be the only man on the ranch. Since there were no cattle on the JP he must be driving some of his own; but however that was, his present occupation linked him up, in Nueces' mind, with the gang. Now he understood why the CD was not bothered by cattle thieves, and how it was that Dailey could make a living playing rancher with but a handful of cattle.

Nueces crept back, down the slope, arose, walked to his horse and mounted. It was too early to go to town, which must be reached after dark; but he would gain nothing by remaining here. He had a deal of time to kill, which was not to his liking. He wondered if Pettingill knew anything worth listening to, worth the risk of being seen. Now a gambler, and trying to earn a living at his new trade, he would not be particular with whom he associated, so long as they had money to risk. It might well be that Pettingill had overheard a great deal of piecemeal information which, being connected by a man who knew the keynotes, might throw some light on the reason for the mysterious departure of the dozen riders from the re-branding camp.

If only he could get word to Pettingill! Why, of course: there was the waiting messenger, under El Toro's instructions to do what he was told to do. Still

Pettingill would have nothing to do with that type of Mexican; and for him to be sought out by and to engage in a confidential conversation with a peon, might arouse unwholesome suspicions. That would hardly do, unless there were no better way. How to get word— ha! there was Bolton, who knew Pettingill well and who associated with him occasionally. The ranchman was trustworthy, and heart and soul in sympathy with the man he knew as Simpkins. Bolton was the man for the job.

It was past mid-afternoon when Nueces circled around the BB ranch and found nothing which disturbed him. No one was in sight, and the corral was empty. After a period of cautious spying he drew nearer to the house and stopped in a brushy draw not far from it. He had been waiting for perhaps an hour when he saw the ranchman riding toward home on a course that would bring him within four or five hundred paces of the waiting puncher. Nueces kept a keen watch over the range, but saw no other rider. When Bolton was even with the draw the puncher pushed up out of it, raising one hand in the air. It was a moment before he was seen, and then Bolton's roving glance took him in, and the ranchman involuntarily drew rein, waiting for the puncher to ride up to him. Dawning recognition was expressed on the ranchman's face by looks of disbelief and bewilderment; and reflex action sent his hand dropping to his gun.

"Don't shoot!" called Nueces. "You can't hurt a dead man!"

"Great Gawd!" muttered Bolton, his hand still on the walnut and reluctant to let go of it. "What— how—— I heard you was *dead!*"

"I am," chuckled Nueces, "to some people, which is th' way I want to stay. They'll feel better, believin' that; an' so will I. But just now, dead or alive, I'm wonderin' if you'll ride to town for me an' tell Jim Pettingill that I want to see him after dark, half a mile down th' south trail. It's right important."

"What for?" asked Bolton, who had not yet discovered the proper functioning of his reasoning faculties.

"For you, an' th' rest of th' honest ranchers down in this part of th' county," answered Nueces, his face hardening.

"Hell! I didn't mean to blurt out no question like that," replied the ranchman apologetically; "but seein' how you answered it, I'm right glad that I did. You got onto somethin', Simpkins?"

"Almost everythin'," answered the deputy. He pushed a hand down in a trouser pocket and, drawing it out, opened it for his companion's inspection. It was a six-pointed star, each point ending in a little ball; and stamped into the center of it were the words "Deputy Sheriff."

Bolton whistled under his breath, and his eyes gleamed.

"Then we been doin' Corson an injustice!" he growled. "Man, I'll take a message to Pettingill, or to th' devil hisself. What you want me to say to him?"

"Come back into that draw with me," requested Nueces, his uneasy gaze moving around the range. "I don't want to be seen, an' I want to ask you some questions."

Bolton's reply was expressed in action. He rolled his spurs along the horse's flanks and shot forward like an arrow from a bow, Nueces crowding him closely. They dipped down into the depression, and the fringe of brush closed after them. They faced each other, Bolton's countenance wan and dejected. He looked like a man who had surrendered in a hopeless fight against Fate, and cared little what the future held in store for him. The momentary interest and surprise in seeing a dead man alive had worn off.

"What's th' matter, Bolton?" asked Nueces, knowing the answer when he asked the question.

"I'm licked, Simpkins; licked, an' busted; busted in pocket an' in spirit. So are my friends. We're all cleaned out. There's hardly a head of our cattle on th' range. Lock, stock, an' barrel. While we watched th' pass, like a lot of damn' fools, they ran a raid on us a few nights ago; an' they left nothin' behind them but th' memory. We had helped 'em, too: figgered our stock would be safer on the south part of th' range, away from th' pass, an' we drove 'em there. They were right handy for th' thieves. Th' Peavy boys must 'a' lost a fortune, judgin' from the size of th' trail we follered to th' river."

"Don't reckon you an' yore friends would care to run any risks if you figgered that you could get all them cattle back ag'in, would you?" asked Nueces, smiling.

There came a gleam in the spiritless eyes, and the ranchman's jaw set, the muscles standing out in little ridges.

"What you mean?" he demanded eagerly.

Nueces nodded with satisfaction.

"You got plenty of spirit left," he said, smiling grimly. "Now you listen to me," and forthwith he told what he thought was proper for his companion to hear. It had to do with his activities since coming to Porter.

"You say that gang ain't greasers, an' that——" began Bolton as the tale was ended.

"You know, of course," interrupted Nueces, "th' men you can trust?"

"Yes; but who are behind these——"

"Let me do th' talkin', Bolton. You'll find out th' answers to all yore questions when th' time comes. Th' game that's bein' played down here is as big as any I've heard of, an' it'll be a man's job to call th' play. Th' showdown will need a big crew. When I send for Corson an' th' posse, things have got to be ready to move pronto. I want everythin' oiled an' ready to work. On th' way down to me I'll have Corson an' his crew ride past yore ranch house. Th' messenger that I'll send up for him will pass yore house, an' give you yore cue. He will say 'Es verdad, Señor?' to anyone who comes to th' door; an' he'll keep right on ridin' fast. After you get that sign, you collect yore good friends, an' hold 'em right there on yore place till Bob Corson comes along an' picks 'em up. That means that there's got to be a man in yore ranch house all th' time from now on, day *an'* night. You figger you can fix it?"

"It's all fixed right now, Simpkins! We'll all be there, loaded for bear. Even if we don't get back our cattle, we're itchin' to empty some saddles!"

"I reckon you'll get th' chance, an' th' cattle, too, mebby. If you've got it all straight I'll drift off to a different part of th' range, nearer to town. Don't forget that I plumb died down near San Ignacio: I'm dead to everybody but you an' Pettingill—*everybody!*"

"Yo're a damn' lively corpse. I'm pullin' out for town. Good luck, an' so-long!"

"Same to you," replied Nueces.

Bolton left the draw warily, scanning the range. No one was in sight, and he changed the innocent course he had set toward his ranch house and headed for town at a good speed. Nueces waited until the ranchman was out of sight and then left the draw on the farther side and kept off of rises. He rode slowly, jogging along, buried in thought.

CHAPTER XVIII

DARKNESS settled down, slowly shortening the view. A light gleamed in the town, another and another. Near-by vegetation grew indistinct and then disappeared. Nueces pushed up out of a hollow and rode at a walk toward the trail which left town on the south. He angled toward it in a direction which would bring him to it about where he expected to meet Pettingill. The night life was beginning to stir: rustles here, squeaks there. The rider stopped, dismounted, dropping the reins over the horse's head, and moved forward slowly on foot. He could see nothing at a distance of a dozen feet, but he was a plainsman and he knew the tricks. He felt the trail underfoot, and then dropped down to lie prone alongside it, his face close to the earth. His range of vision was instantly lengthened, for now he was peering along the ground with the faintly luminous sky to serve as a background. He waited patiently and silently.

Uncertain steps came along the road, their maker feeling his way. To Nueces he loomed up as a fairly silhouetted shadow against the sky. Pettingill owned no horse, and no man who did own one would walk the half mile from town when he could ride; and to this particular place at this particular time. Therefore the man on the trail must be the erstwhile owner of the JP.

"Red?" asked Nueces softly.

The walker stopped and whirled, searching about him with eyes that were useless.

"Pettingill?" persisted the voice, followed by a short series of closely connected, metallic clinks. To the man in the road they rang out like bells.

"Simpkins?" asked the walker.

"Come over here, off th' trail, Red. Anybody see you leave town?"

"Where th' hell are you?" demanded Pettingill, stumbling forward. "No; nobody saw me. I took right good care of that."

"This way. To th' left. Ah. How are you, Red?"

"Rich, an' gettin' richer. If I only had that collar button I'd be ownin' th' whole town right soon."

"You heard anythin' worth listenin' to?" asked Nueces.

"No; only snatches here an' there."

"Th' snatches only have to be joined up," reminded Nueces. "Tell me what they are."

"There's a right good lot of th' boys missin' from th' dumps in town."

"Any of 'em come back?" asked Nueces.

"Yes; a couple. They went around huntin' for some of their friends, found 'em, an' took off with 'em."

"Any idear where they went to?" asked the deputy.

"Somewhere a long way off. I heard Dirty Pete arguin' with th' bartender in Smith's, askin' for more credit in wet goods. He wanted to stock up an' take some along with him. Bartender was strong set ag'in th' idear, but at last he weakened an' gave Pete what he wanted, an' that was a-plenty."

"What was Pete's argument?" asked Nueces.

"Said there was one hell of a big game on, hundred miles or so down th' river. He said they was goin' to make some kind of a big play, clean up before anybody knowed they was there, get out quick, an' stay out."

"Hear anythin' else?" persisted the deputy.

"Yeah; somethin' you spoke to me about before; an' that's why it sticks in my mem'ry. Ike Peavy got into a game in Hitchins' private room, an' won over seven thousan' dollars. Just after that last raid, over west."

"That checks in with th' rest of it; but he really didn't win a damn' cent," chuckled Nueces grimly. "Gosh, Red, wouldn't you be surprised if we even got yore collar button back?" He laughed softly in the darkness.

Suddenly he froze, his hand swiftly reaching out and gripping his companion's arm, and squeezing like a vise. Again a twig snapped. He leaned forward, his other hand going out and reaching around Pettingill's neck, and drawing the gambler's head close to his own.

"Stay here, an' talk in a mumble. Don't shoot no matter what happens. If I call out, answer me. Keep on talkin'!"

Pettingill instantly was alone, mumbling to himself in the pitchy darkness, his hand on a gun he had been forbidden to use. There was no consolation in that injunction. Sitting up, he felt as tall and prominent as the highest building in the county; and then, rolling over, he cautiously lay down, spreading out as much as he could in an endeavor to gain thinness. During this time he kept up the mumbling and tried to imitate a second speaker. He found he could see fairly well from the prone position, good enough to spot any person who walked within a dozen feet of him.

A shadow of average height moved across his tiny horizon, and he knew that it was not Nueces. At that instant a voice rang out as Nueces challenged, and the shadow narrowed as the man turned sideways. There came a streaky burst of fire from the shadow, and another, as the intruder shot by ear; and the answer came from a point a dozen paces to the east, two shots cannily aimed by the flashes of the other's gun. The shadow sank toward the earth with a choking groan and disappeared from Pettingill's sight.

Pettingill's blood seemed to freeze at the ensuing sounds, and when they ceased he found that his face was wet with sweat. His whole body was moist, and the cool night air suddenly struck through to his skin and made him shiver and shrink.

Silence. The darkness, suffocating; cold trickles of water going down his spine. He found his nails cutting into his palms and relaxed his grip. A swift scurrying broke across the silence as a frightened lizard darted to a new cover. His straining ears told him nothing about the subjects he was interested in. The strange, terrifying gurgling breathing which had stopped so suddenly did not sound again. He wanted to call out; and then he jumped as a hand touched his shoulder.

"All right," said Nueces' low, reassuring voice in his ear. "Let's see who he was."

"Is he—is he——?" quavered Pettingill.

"Ought to be; I shot twice, once on each side of his gun flash, in case he was left-handed."

"My Gawd!" muttered Pettingill. "An' you thought of *that?*"

"Shore; why not? It's thinkin' of them kind of things that keeps a deppety sheriff alive. Come on: mebby we'll know who he was."

The gambler followed blindly, and found himself staring at the little patch of light made by his companion's match, shielded in cupped hands. He went closer and bent down.

"It's Jennings!" he whispered. "Jennings!"

"Yeah? An' who was Jennin's?"

"Worked for th' Royal Palace; but I don't know what he did. Worked nights, but I've never seen him in th' place. Come to think of it, he goes in an' kinda disappears."

"Yeah? Wonder what that means?"

"Don't know; but I've seen him come in th' place, night after night; but never saw him around. He's bad: a killer. I've allus heard he was mighty handy with a gun."

A little breeze swept through the sage, and a bending twig touched the deputy's neck. In his mind's eye he could see the sage undulating in the wind; and the undulations became those of a tapestry, gently moving. He could see the Angelus, stirred by a little draft of air from behind.

"Hah!" he exclaimed. A plan leaped to his mind, and he stood erect, swearing gently under his breath. Luck had smiled upon him, and only a fool would hesitate; a fool or a coward.

"What's th' matter?" asked Pettingill, arising in haste, his hand under his coat.

"Nothin'," answered his companion, chuckling grimly. "I got an idear, that's all."

"Why did he foller me? Why did he come out here?" asked Pettingill.

"Mebby he figgered you'd planted a cold deck an' was comin' out to dig it up," said the deputy with a laugh.

"But why did he?" persisted Pettingill.

"Reckon you know th' answer to that better'n I do."

"But I don't see how anybody could 'a' seen me leave town! I slipped along behind th' buildin's, right cautious, from buildin' to buildin', a little at a time."

"You go past th' Royal Palace?" asked Nueces with interest.

"Yes; it happened to be right in my course."

"That's th' answer," replied Nueces thoughtfully. "You was th' owner of th' JP. You was slippin' out of town in its direction. If you had walked out, openly, an' been seen, nobody might 'a' bothered about you, but when somebody saw you sneakin' along, tryin' not to be seen, they got suspicious an' follered you. Th'

JP is a right important ranch these days, an' it ain't healthy for anybody to head toward it, 'specially sly-like. An' you passed th' *back* of th' Royal Palace?" The last sentence was muttered and so low that Pettingill did not understand it.

"But I ain't got nothin' to do with th' JP any more!" persisted Pettingill. *"You* own it."

"I don't own it," replied Nueces, feeling in a pocket. "I'm givin' it back to you to-night; but nobody's to know that. Understand, nobody a-tall. You act like it is mine, an' you keep away from it like you'd keep away from a rattler. Anyhow, what do them fellers think? They think that I left it to you in case of my death. I'm shore supposed to be dead."

"What a damn' fool I am!" exclaimed Pettingill. "That's why they did it! That's why they wanted that deed! An' that's why they made me date it ahead!"

"What deed?" demanded Nueces.

"That quit-claim that I signed. They offered me five hundred dollars for it, an' it looked like easy pickin's, seein' I wasn't losin' anythin'. Right then I was havin' a run of hard luck, an' th' money came in handy. Th' ranch was a hoodoo, anyhow; an' th' next day I hit a run of good luck an' it's stuck to me ever since."

"Damn you an' yore good luck an' yore bad luck!" growled Nueces. "What was th' date on that deed?"

"Seventeenth: yesterday. Why?"

"You beg, borrow, or steal a hoss; an' you go up to th' county seat, an' you record this bill of sale," ordered Nueces. "Then, th' first chance I get I'll sell it back to you for one dollar. Let's see how good their quit-claim will be after that. Anyhow, that's somethin' for a lawyer: I may be wrong. If I am, I'll keep th' title to that ranch, an' lease it to you for ninety-nine years for that same dollar."

"I don't exactly know what yo're talkin' about," said Pettingill.

"Neither do I," said Nueces. He stared down in the darkness at the night-hidden object on the ground, and his thoughts returned to it.

"So you don't know what this feller Jennin's did, what his job was?"

"No; but mebby he worked in th' kitchen."

"Th' kitchen is closed at night. He had a better job than that, an' one that suited him, I reckon. Well, it'll mebby suit me, for to-night. Let's go to town."

They parted on the outskirts, Nueces hiding his horse, while Pettingill went on. After a short wait the deputy moved forward, taking advantage of whatever cover the buildings afforded, and working in a round-about way toward the big gambling hall and saloon. He approached the place from the rear, scouting it thoroughly, and then, opening the unfastened kitchen door, stood quietly in the semi-darkness. Between the kitchen and the gambling hall was another room through the open door of which fell light from the gambling hall. Looking around him, Nueces saw two other doors in the kitchen. They were in the side wall and as close together as they could be.

The first one he opened revealed a pantry, and he

closed the door gently. The second opened upon a narrow passage, which had a faint glow of light at the far end high up in the wall. Nueces remembered that there was a very small window in the outside wall of the building. He stepped into the passage, softly closing the door behind him, and moved forward with deliberate slowness. He came to the little window and turned a corner; and another faint patch of light lured him on. It became brighter, and distinct rays shot through the semi-darkness at a sharp downward angle.

He stopped in front of a small glassless window, in front of which hung a heavy fabric, and in this fabric were eye-holes. The conversation in the big room came to him clearly, as clearly as if he was out there in it. He stooped to peer through the holes, and the handles of one of his guns bumped against the wall. At the faint sound Ad Hitchins looked up from the big round table, his frown followed by a look of satisfaction. Jennings was on duty.

The games were not well patronized on this night, and Nueces thought he had a partial solution for it: too many of the gang were out of town. The faro dealer closed his box, took it up in his hand, and moved lazily toward the proprietor.

"Reckon it ain't worth while runnin' a game to-night," said the dealer, his statement a question.

"No, reckon not. Put it away an' amuse yoreself," answered Hitchins, his gaze going to the monte spread, where a single player wasted the dealer's time. "Jennings might as well quit, too: I want th' room to my-

self." He raised his voice and called to the monte table.
"Close that fool game an' take th' night off. An' when
you go out, close those doors, an' tell 'em, outside, to
let 'em stay closed. There ain't no gamblin' to-night.
They'll know who to let in."

Nueces thought swiftly. Hitchins wanted no ears
but those he himself chose to listen to whatever might
be in the wind. He wanted the room to himself, and
the double doors closed. The dismissal of Jennings
meant that the gunman behind the Angelus was to leave
his post. Would Hitchins take the trouble to see that
the post was vacant? He might. Nueces quietly slipped
along the passage, gained the kitchen, opened the pantry door and closed it behind him, standing close against
the wall on the hinge side. It was well that he did so.

The lagging seconds passed into minutes, and he
was about to move when he heard brisk footsteps growing plainer. They passed the pantry and went along
the secret passage; and then, returning, moved to the
outer door of the kitchen. The sound of a dropping
bar came to the listener's ears, and then the steps passed
the pantry again, grew softer in the direction of the
gambling hall, and the sound of a closing door wiped
them out.

Nueces gently opened the door of his hiding place
and as gently closed it behind him. He cautiously entered the passage, and took a full twenty seconds to
close its door behind him. He felt his way slowly, and
at last stood before the opening behind the tapestry,

being careful this time that no gun butt should rap
out a warning. His hand touched a box, which he believed had served Jennings as a seat. He was grateful
for the discovery, for now his watch would be much
more comfortable. Sitting down, he relaxed and gave
thought to the present situation, and a grin threatened his face. He had cursed the man who had intruded
upon him and Pettingill; now he was thankful for the
intrusion.

Hitchins sat idly at the table, his fingers nervously
drumming. He was restless, and kept looking at the
big double doors, and listening. Finally he picked up
a deck of cards, shuffled them, and began a game of
solitaire; but his mind was not on cards, and after a
few moments he impatiently brushed them aside. He
got up and walked around the room, pacing to and
fro; and then, stopping abruptly, thought for a moment, and strode into the little private room. When
he came out he had papers in his hand and an account
book.

The round table was not a dozen feet from the
Angelus, and the bright light above it lit it perfectly.
Hitchins resumed his seat and sorting the papers, laid
them to one side. Among them were three canceled
checks, and Nueces did not have to be blessed with
second-sight to know what they were. The other papers
looked like bills of sale; and among them was a folded,
printed form which bore all the appearances of being
a deed. Nueces knew what that was, too, and his grin
reappeared; it had not yet been recorded, and if Pet-

tingill started for the county seat the next morning all would be well.

The nature and contents of the account book were mysteries to him, but he found interest in Hitchins's absorbing scrutiny of the volume. Very likely it would contain records of cattle sales, and, if it did, would be of vast interest to Bolton and his friends. Hitchins closed the book, put it aside, and began to figure on the back of an old envelope; and so the time passed, with Nueces watching, and the gambler figuring, and listening, and looking at the closed doors, every footstep which approached them in the barroom engaging his intent interest.

Then there sounded footsteps in the outer room of a different quality from the others: short, loud, purposeful. They came rapidly nearer with intentional directness. A knock sounded on the double doors, and Hitchins's command was instantly obeyed.

"Well?" he asked, facing the newcomer. "Close th' door!"

"They've got started, all right. I'd 'a' been here sooner, only I went with 'em a ways," said the courier, who was not yet in Nueces' field of vision. He moved forward in reply to Hitchins's gesture and dropped into a chair across the table from the gambler, removing his coat. Nueces never had seen the man before, but a little flash of color in his collar button brought a smile to the deputy's homely face; unless he was greatly mistaken, Pettingill's lost luck charm was found.

"Ike slowed up an' sent a couple of men ahead, to

feel out th' way for th' boys," said the courier. "He's right cautious, Ike is."

"Yes," grunted Hitchins; "whenever his skin is anywhere near danger. That section of th' country has been peaceful so long they won't be lookin' for nothin' like that. It'll be all over before they wake up. Reckon this will be our last raid, for a while, at least. We've cleaned up around here, an' we dassn't run another raid down in th' Tres Alamos section for a long time. They'll be like hornets after this."

"How many head are we figgerin' on gettin' down there?" asked the courier. "I've heard all kind of talk, but nothin' that meant anythin'."

"If we've timed it right we get a whole trail herd," answered the gambler. "I've been kept posted right close. Th' last word that I got was that twenty-two hundred head were on th' trail; an' when they get eight days out we ambush th' crew, swing th' herd, an' drive like hell. By th' time it's missed, say in a week or ten days, they'll never find hide nor hoof of it. That trail boss won't be expected to report till he gets to a post office; an' that gives us all th' time we need."

"How's he drivin'? East?"

"Straight north. We turn th' herd west, hit th' abandoned trail with all tails up, water an' rest at th' JP, rebrand between th' JP an' th' big ranch, let th' sores heal, an' then some night we push them cattle onto th' outlyin' Bradley range an' let 'em scatter."

"What about th' herd we already got?" asked the courier.

"That throws in with th' other," answered Hitchins. "It'll change th' figgers for us in case of accidents. Instead of twenty-two hundred head there'll be nearer twenty-seven hundred."

"I reckon we can afford to let up for a while, after we tuck that bunch of cattle in its bed," said the courier. He burst into laughter and slapped his thigh. "How much money you figger we're handlin' on th' hoof?" he asked.

"They'll average twenty dollars on th' Bradley range, if my figgers are right," answered Hitchins, picking up the envelope. "Play safe, an' call it fifty thousan' dollars."

"Peavy's cattle will cut that down, though," suggested the courier, remembering that IP cattle were always included in every theft in order to divert suspicion from that ranch. "We'll have to pay him back."

Hitchins laughed contentedly.

"You didn't see no IP cattle in that bunch, did you?" he asked.

"Why, no. Come to think of it, I didn't; 'though they might 'a' been there, for all that."

"They were not there this time," said Hitchins. "Peavy's boys drifted a big bunch to th' northwest part of his range, to make th' other end of it look kinda bare." He laughed at something which came into his mind, and then mentioned it. "Peavy's big poker winnin's didn't mean a thing this time. We was just gettin' folks used to th' idea of big play. When this bunch is sold, we'll have another big game, so Ike can justify

his bank deposit. I scatter my deposits an' let 'em ride
as th' winnin's of th' house. Why, I ain't banked all
of that last raid yet: have to feed it in a little at a
time."

"Who you figger that feller Simpkins was?" asked
the courier, crossing his legs and rolling a cigarette.

"I don't know, an' I don't care, now," answered
Hitchins. "I couldn't figger him a-tall; an' when I can't
figger a man that goes 'round pokin' his nose in where
it don't belong, I get right suspicious. I stopped everythin'. Then he got killed by th' greasers, an' we started
in ag'in. Purty soon we quit, an' I figger it'll be sudden
an' permanent; an' when that time comes I don't care
who rides in a-lookin' for Simpkins an' askin' questions."

The courier now looked at the Angelus and spoke
directly to it.

"Hey, Jennings: I got that money I owe you."

"Yo're talkin' to yoreself," said Hitchins. "Jennings ain't there. If yo're lookin' for him, you'll find
him around town somewhere, playin' poker." He considered a moment, and then explained, "I didn't want
*any*body outside of us few to hear us talkin'. That's
why I didn't use th' little room: it's got a window."
He leaned forward, looking at the other's shirt collar.
"Ain't you got no sense a-tall? Put that button in yore
pocket, an' keep it there!"

"Gosh; forgot all about it," apologized the courier.
"I come near losin' it out of my pocket two, three
times, so I put it in there to save it while I was down

on th' range." He removed it and tucked it into a vest pocket. "I never owned a diamond before, but I've allus wanted to. They're right valuable, ain't they?"

"Some are; but I reckon that chip's worth about one dollar, or less. I'll give you five for it, just to get rid of th' damn' thing."

The courier's eyes became wise and crafty.

"Oh, you will, huh? If it's worth five to you, it's worth a hell of a lot more to me. I wasn't born yester- day."

"You act like you was, anyhow," retorted Hitchins. He stood up, collecting the papers and the account book. "Keep sober while yo're in town, an' don't stay here long. They'll need every man."

"I'm pullin' out at daylight," said the other, moving toward the door. "I reckon I'll set in a few hands with th' boys after I find Jennings."

"Keep sober!" warned Hitchins sternly. "Th' man that messes *this* play won't live to mess another."

"Them's my sentiments!" replied the courier, and left the room.

Hitchins waited until the door closed, and then carried the papers into the little private room, locked them in a desk drawer, and came out again. He flung open the doors into the barroom, put out the lights, and went out to lean against the bar.

Nueces waited patiently until he was convinced that Hitchins would remain in the outer room before he attempted to leave his post. He could hear the proprietor talking with the bartender, and then a sudden increase in the number of voices told him of newcomers joining the pair. A round of drinks was called for, and Nueces took this as his cue to leave.

He moved cautiously along the passage, entered the kitchen, and had his hand on the bar across its outer door when a sudden thought made him drop the timber as if it were a hot iron. That bar must be in place when the next man saw it. He tried a window, unfastened the catch, and raised the sash slowly. Looking out, he slipped through, lowered the sash gently behind him, and waited for a moment with his back to the wall, peering into the night.

The moon was rising, a thin crescent of silver. Its power of illumination was weak; but it had lightened the darkness several degrees, and objects which had been hidden only an hour before were now faintly discernible. Nueces, now wishing only to get to his horse and leave the town, worked his way along the rear wall toward the farther corner, intending to slip across the open space between the Royal Palace and the next building. As he reached the corner he stopped instantly, his hand dropping toward his belt. Two men had just left the street to cross the open space on a diagonal course which would bring them to the same corner of the building.

Nueces took a backward step, whirled, and ran at top speed along the rear wall, cursing his peculiar type of architecture: there was not another man in town as tall and thin as himself. Let them get one good look at him and he would cease to be dead, and there was no telling where their suspicions would carry them. He had his choice of the corral, the other side wall with the moonlight on it, or the kitchen. He knew there were horses in the corral, and one of the men strongly resembled, in general outline, the courier he had listened to but a short time before. If it was the courier, then the corral likely would be his objective. The far side of the building would be safe if they both rode away; but if the man with the courier should return to the street, he might choose that side.

Under the present condition of affairs Nueces could take no chances. He swiftly but noiselessly raised the kitchen window, stepped through it, got it closed just in time, and stood with his back against the wall to await developments. The voices came nearer, and Nueces peered through the window to catch sight of them. He saw them step into his range of vision and head for the corral. When halfway there they stopped.

"If I could 'a' found Jennings I'd 'a' stayed in town," said one of them. "Where th' hell he is I don't know. Well, I'll break up one damn' long ride into two parts. I'll stay on th' JP to-night with Dailey, an' have that much less to cover to-morrow."

What the other man said Nueces never knew, for approaching steps from the front of the building made him whirl like a flash and sent him across the little room like a frightened cat. He chose the pantry, closed the door behind him, and stood pressed against the wall on the hinge side of the door. The footsteps entered the kitchen. He heard them stop, heard the bar scrape, and the door open.

"Hello!" called a voice challengingly. It was Hitchins.

"Hello, Ad; this is Jim."

"Oh. What you doin'?"

"Leavin' for th' JP. Can't find Jennings, an' I might as well get a start on to-morrow's ride."

"Shore; all right. Who's that with you?" asked Hitchins.

"It's me," said a third voice.

"*Is* it?" asked the gambler sarcastically. "An' who th' hell might that be?"

"Lefty. I'll be with you in a minute." The speaker was true to his word. At the end of that interval, having said good-bye to his companion, he turned and walked toward the house, leaving the courier to go on to the corral. He entered the door, talking earnestly with Hitchins; the bar dropped into place and the two men moved across the kitchen and into the other part of the building.

Nueces sighed, slipped into the kitchen again, opened the window, and waited for the courier to get away. After what seemed to be a very long time a horseman left the corral and rode toward the street on the moon-lighted side of the Royal Palace. Nueces, sighing again, once more stepped through the open window, once more lowered it behind him, and once more moved along the rear wall. Again he swore under his breath.

An unsteady inebriate was staggering toward the corner and not more than ten feet from it, muttering to himself about getting his horse and riding to some ranch.

Nueces had more than average patience, but averages had ceased to operate at this corner of the Royal Palace. If he struck the drunken man with a gun barrel, or choked him, or shot him, there would be visible physical proof of the act; and the deputy wanted no signs of his prowling, or of any prowling at all.

The unsteady puncher turned the corner, had both feet kicked out from under him as a long arm pushed with speed and energy. He went down on his back with a suddenness and force which left him temporarily stunned. After a few moments he rolled over, jerked out his gun, and began shooting with no particular choice of direction. A window across the street said *phut!* An innocent passer-by ducked the second bullet, grabbed his hat tightly, and did the eight yards between him and shelter in two jumps; a group of card players near the open window of a building on the rear street dove from the table according to each man's instinct, and cursed unanimously at the shot that had passed between them. A roaring of hiccoughed curses came from the rear of the Royal Palace, and some foolhardy individual took it upon himself to investigate them. He reached the corner just as the outraged inebriate managed to stand erect, was taken for the assailant, and was instantly one half of a two-man fight. There was a rush toward this excitement, and a circle formed to enjoy it; but friends intervened and separated the combatants.

Explanations were jumbled and hectic, but the decision finally arrived at was that the inebriate was drunk, had tripped over his own feet, and then endangered the peace of the town. He was forthwith fined a round of drinks, and forcibly led toward the street to pay the fine.

From the deep shadow of a distant building a mounted man, sitting quietly in the saddle, watched the noisy, laughing crowd start toward the street and, chuckling softly, rode around the corner of the building and disappeared.

CHAPTER XIX

NUECES left the town behind him, a grin wreathing his face. So far everything had gone all right, and there was nothing for him to do until the time came to send for Corson and the deputies. He now had a better idea of the interval which would ensue, and an interval which would find him idle, so far as any necessity for action was concerned. This made him think of the waiting messengers, the day and night riders who awaited his orders. He struck into a lope and rode straight for that rendezvous, and long before daylight he reached it. No one was in sight, and he cast around curiously, riding a little farther on, and then drew rein abruptly as a challenge rang out.

"*Quien es?*"

"*Amigo.* Simpkins—Nueces—th' *Americano.*"

"Ah, Señor: I wait," said the voice, and a Mexican rode up out of a draw.

"There's no message yet," said Nueces. "There won't be any for three, four days. There ain't no use of you stayin' out here till then. I just rode down to tell you to take it easy in town. This is Tuesday, ain't it?"

"*Si, si, Señor.*"

"All right. You lay off till—Wednesday, Thursday; Friday, Saturday. Say Saturday—*sabado. Comprender?*"

"*Si, Señor: sabado*—Satur-rday. I onder-stand." The Mexican spread his hands helplessly. "Thees I cannot do. I hav' or-rders. I e-stay her-re. Me an' my fr-riend. Eet ees or-rders, Señor."

"Mebby so; but there ain't no sense to it," persisted Nueces. "I'm pullin' out of this part of th' country for three, four days. I won't be here to use you. You might just as well stay in town and take things easy. *Comprender?*"

"*Si, si:* I onder-rstand; but I e-stay. Day an' night ther-re weel be a man her-re, Señor."

"Judas Priest!" snorted Nueces, keeping his face straight. "Here! You was told to do what I said, wasn't you?"

"*Si, si.*"

"All right. Here's my orders," said Nueces, chuckling. "You an' yore pardner stay in town, or wherever you do stay, until Saturday when the sun goes down. *Sabe?*"

"*Si, si, Señor!*"

"Good. Then you or yore pardner come out here an' wait like you have been, till I tell you to do somethin' else. Understand? Savvy?"

"*Si, Señor; si.* Eet ees good. *Gracias, gracias.*"

Nueces raised his hand, wheeled his horse, and rode off, conscious of a kind deed done. Reaching the top of a little rise he looked back curiously, and swore as he saw the messenger sitting motionless on his horse in the moonlight, still waiting.

"Gee-wheeziz! That man El Toro shore trains 'em

right! Bet he told them fellers to wait for a message from me. He didn't tell 'em I could send 'em home, or have 'em do anythin' for their own comfort. That damn' fool or his pardner will set there till I give 'em a message, come hell or high water. Wonder what would happen to 'em if I never came back?"

Back in the little draw a sleeper stirred under the prodding toe of his alert companion, and a short conversation took place in Spanish.

"Is it time?"

The man who had just ridden in nodded.

"Yes. Day has come. Take you the watch, and use your eyes and ears. Señor Simpkins was just here. He says he will not be back for at least four days. Gringos change their minds, and our orders are plain. When I wake up I will ride in and get us more food. Four days is not long, and I would rather stay here than to lose my skin."

"With the food bring some mescal, pulque, or——"

"Shut your mouth! You wish to be shot? No liquor till this duty ends; and then we will get drunk together for a whole week. Eat, and watch!"

Nueces rode on, swinging farther to the west to go around the town at a safe distance. He had been without sleep for a long period, for him; but somehow he did not feel the need of it: that would come later in the day, after the sun had risen and beat down upon him, adding its warmth to the motion of the horse. He was bound for the county seat, to explain things before the press of action interfered with the passing of necessary knowledge. It was mid-forenoon when he found himself nodding, and with one thought for himself, and another for his horse, he sought for and found a thicket of brush, pushed into it, and not long thereafter was sound asleep, his big hat shielding his face.

*   *   *   *   *

The town grew plainer, sprawled on a hillside to the south, and the rider who had taken the trouble to circle around it, so as to ride in from an innocent direction, heaved a sigh of relief. Before he reached the outskirts lights were springing up in the windows, and he drew down to an even slower pace.

No one paid much attention to the elongated cow-puncher who jogged lazily up to the courthouse and lazily dismounted. The clerk in the sheriff's office looked up at the sound of the step on the floor.

"Sheriff Corson in?" asked the newcomer.

"He's over at th' hotel, at supper," answered the clerk shortly.

"Eatin' kinda late, ain't he?"

"Well, suppose he is?" asked the clerk acidly.

"I like to see a man take his boss's part," replied the newcomer calmly. "Suppose you rustle over there an' tell Bob that Nueces is waitin' here for him?"

The clerk got to his feet, his expression a mixture.

"Sorry. I didn't know you," he said apologetically.

"My fault," grunted Nueces, looking around the room. "Got any drinkin' water?"

"Shore! Take a seat an' I'll get you some."

"I ain't helpless. Where is it?"

"Just inside that door," answered the clerk, turning to indicate which door he meant. "Be right back," and he was gone.

Nueces had his drink, two of them; then he emerged from the little washroom, looked around, saw the door marked PRIVATE, and opened it. A big desk, several chairs, and various other articles of furniture met his inquiring gaze. He walked to the desk, opened three drawers before he found what he wanted, and then smiled pleasantly at the box of cigars. Five minutes later when Sheriff Corson entered the room he found six feet six of homely cowpuncher leaning back in the easiest chair, his legs crossed on the desk, and a first-class cigar cocked in the corner of his mouth.

" 'Lo, Nueces; how are you?"

"Fair to middlin', Bob," answered the deputy, not changing his position. "Yo're smokin' better cigars these days than you used to."

"Yes, I'm learnin' a few new tricks. Those cost me two bits apiece."

"Worth it; worth every cent of it," grunted the deputy, letting a little smoke drift down through his long nose. The Havana stung him, and he blinked pleasantly. He cleared his throat. "An' how's yore taste in likker these days?"

Corson chuckled, stepped to the door, and spoke to the clerk.

"Better go home, Tim; close th' door behind you, an' spring th' catch."

"Yes, sir; but we're waitin' for that writ," prompted the clerk.

"Office is closed; an' now that writ can wait for us. Put out th' light, pull down th' curtains, an' go on home."

The sheriff swung back into his private room, drew the shades, and threw his coat into a corner. He stepped to a closet, unlocked the door, and when he faced around again he had a promising-looking bottle and two glasses in his hands. He put the bottle into the big, outstretched hand of his companion and chuckled.

"Car Stairs," muttered Nueces. "Never clum 'em before. Good treadin', Bob?" He smelled the cork and the lines of his homely face softened, his eyes twinkling in anticipation.

"I'll let you be th' judge of that," answered Corson, holding out the glasses.

Nueces gravely filled them to the very top, took his own, held it under his long, predatory nose, and sniffed energetically.

"This here smells like drinkin' likker, an' not like gulpin' likker," he said, and let a third of the glass roll around in his mouth. The facial lines softened still more, and there was a friendly glow in the hard eyes. "Hah! We should 'a' 'lected you sheriff years ago, Bob; well, now we got a good reason to keep you here. Luck!"

"Luck!" echoed the sheriff. He put down the glass

and, reaching into the opened desk drawer, took a cigar, and then seated himself facing his cheerful deputy. "Don't you be in no hurry to talk, Nueces; you take yore own time, for we shore got plenty of that."

"I'm aimin' to, Bob. I never was much of a feller for steppin' on my own feet. After eatin' desert dust, an' fryin' during daylight, an' freezin' durin' th' nights, an' eatin' outa cans, I kinda feel lazy an' full of kindness. This here is shore a man's smoke, Bob. 'R-o-m-e-o-y J-u-l-i-e-t-a,' " he spelled, turning the cigar in his huge hand. "Fancy, ain't it? There ain't no corn shucks in that, I betcha. Have another drink!" He refilled both glasses and grinned. "My, but ain't you fixed nice! Got everythin' you need."

"I'd rather eat bacon an' beans out in th' sage," growled his boss tartly.

"Yeah," endorsed Nueces, putting down his glass with reverence. "Yeah, I betcha. Th' reason there is so much edge on this here combination is because a feller ain't used to it. Reckon it gets blunt right soon."

"I've found that out," replied the sheriff, his eyes lighting suddenly. "I've been hopin' you'd turn up right soon with a job to be done."

"Well, I've shore turned up, an' I've got th' job," drawled the deputy, his hand going out toward the bottle. "Just one more, to make her three-cornered," he apologized.

"Help yoreself," said Corson, who had no fear whatever of the effect of three small glasses of whisky on his attenuated friend. When Nueces started on the

second bottle would be time enough to became apprehensive. "You've chewed that cigar all to hell. Throw
it away an' take another."

"I like to chew some cigars, an' this here is one of
'em," chuckled the deputy. "They cost so blame' much
there ain't no sense in wastin' any part of it. An' you
notice, mebby, that I'm swallerin' the juice?"

"Man, it's shore good to see yore homely face ag'in,
an' to hear you talk!"

"Well, yo're goin' to hear quite some talk before
th' night's over. Afterward, mebby you could dig up
a little poker game that ain't too stiff for a common
cowpuncher to horn in on."

"We'll find one, old-timer; an' you'll go to it with
a bottle of that in a pocket, an' a box of them cigars
under yore arm."

"My Gawd! Won't Shorty be mad when he hears
about this! Say, how is th' little runt, anyhow?" He
did not wait for the sheriff to answer. "You know,
I been missin' him."

"Want me to send for him?"

"Yeah. I want to see him when he smells that cork."

"How long you figgerin' to stay in town?" asked
the sheriff.

"Couple days."

"He'll be here before you leave. Now then, what's
on yore mind, if anythin'?"

There was a great deal on the deputy's mind, and
it took some two hours to get it off and to discuss
it from all angles. Maps were brought out and studied,

and marked, and figured in terms of miles per hour on horseback; camp spots were located, and the slopes and hollows and general conformation of the ground at several places were gone into thoroughly. The Tres Alamos section was next tackled, and a certain drive trail studied. The rough memoranda grew, to be polished and checked and rechecked on the morrow. As Nueces had said, it was to be a big job, and it would require a large force of men. The more men they could get from the northern part of the county, the better it would please both of them. This was a detail which could not wait, for there was no telegraph leading north from the county seat, and a horseback messenger would take valuable time. They made out a list of names, and Corson wrote a letter to go with it, and then, the more pressing matters attended to, they stood up, Nueces with his eyes on the bottle.

"Help yoreself," invited Corson, as he stepped to the locker. When he turned, an unopened bottle was in his hand. Nueces was putting down an empty glass.

"What's that one for, Bob?" asked the lanky puncher, his gaze on the new bottle.

"For yore pocket," answered the sheriff, grinning. "In th' bottom drawer, on th' right-hand side," he continued, indicating the big desk, "is a full box of cigars. Stick it under yore arm."

"Shucks, no!" expostulated Nueces, grinning widely. "Put that bottle back, Bob. I'll stick a few smokes in my pocket, an' call it all square."

"Mean that?"

"Hell, yes!"

"All right; but we can drop in here after th' game. I want to get a rider started north to-night. You still figger th' boys hadn't oughta come here to meet us?"

"Shore do. That gang's got too many friends, an' some of 'em are dead shore to be located in th' county seat, right handy to th' sheriff's office."

"Reckon so. Then this letter goes as it's writ. They can make camp where we've told 'em to, an' I'll pick 'em up when th' word comes."

"There won't be time for that, Bob. You make camp with 'em, an' stay with 'em."

"All right; yo're th' boss in this game."

They walked down the street to a small house on the outskirts of the town, and the sheriff's knock was answered by a slim, red-haired deputy. He listened intently to his instructions, pocketed the envelope, and was out in his stable before his visitors had walked fifty paces. They saw him ride past on a wiry buckskin, a range-bred animal with the hardy characteristics of a goat. He swept from their sight over a short cut leading to the northern trail. Things were moving.

The following morning found the two friends in the sheriff's office again, elaborating upon the plans adopted the night before. There was no telegraph wire leading north from the county seat, although at the time one was being strung; but a wire entered the county seat from the east, from a town well across the county line, and from that town it ran south to a station newly established on a transcontinental railroad.

The railroad itself had been in use only a few years. Once in touch with the railroad station, Corson hoped to be able to get word to the sheriff of Tres Alamos County. Corson could not take his authority across the state line, and would have to wait for the more distant rustlers not only to cross the state line with the Tres Alamos herd, but would also have to wait for them to enter Cactus Springs County. They might change their minds, they might receive a warning; and to make their capture certain, he had decided to have them taken care of as soon as possible. Besides, it might be possible to stop their attack on the trail outfit, and save lives.

The sheriff and his deputy went down to the telegraph office and held a conference with the operator, who thereupon found the best way to get a connection with the county seat of Tres Alamos County; and in less than half an hour Sheriff Corson was exchanging words with Sheriff Twitchell, of Tres Alamos. The wire was kept hot, for at each end of it the respective officers were sitting with the operators and using the instruments almost as they might use a telephone.

When Corson finally left the office he had the satisfaction of knowing that his distant allies, by handling the raid in their own territory, would leave him men enough to take care of his own problems. The eight-day interval of silence on that far-off drive trail, the eight days which must elapse before the owners of the herd could expect to hear from their trail boss, was now cut in half.

The day passed in taking care of the details, and the evening in further consultation. The next morning saw a short, squat, dust-covered puncher riding into the county seat from the north. He dismounted before the courthouse, entered the sheriff's office, and bumped into his long-lost friend.

" 'Bout time you sent for me, you damn' ham-head!" was his affectionate greeting.

"Yeah? An' it shore took you long enough to get here, you runt!" retorted his bosom friend. "Say hello to Bob, change hosses, gulp some grub, an' don't waste no more time. We got a job to do!"

"Seein' you invited me to help you do it, it must be a dirty one!" retorted the squat puncher. "Well," he said, moving toward the private office room, "it'll shore be done right, *now*. 'Lo, Bob, how are you?"

"Right smart, Shorty," answered the sheriff. "If it wasn't before breakfast I'd ask you to have a drink."

"It'll mebby gimme an appertite, Bob," replied the man who had ridden all night and part of the afternoon without a bite to eat. "Where is it?"

"Oughta give you a cramp," said a voice from the outer room. "Hell, come to think about it, I could use one, too."

"Well, nobody asked you to stay out there," retorted Corson.

"Let th' ham-head stay there—man, oh, man! *That's* likker! Now I know why Nueces has been hangin' 'round this part of th' county. Fill her ag'in!"

"You don't know nothin'—an' that's a lot, for you!"

retorted the lanky puncher, coming through the door. The big hand darted out, took the bottle from the short person, and held it high in the air. "You've had enough! Get that breakfast into you, an' don't waste no more time!"

"Some day me an' you are goin' to have it out," said Shorty, wistful eyes on the bottle against the ceiling. "Bob, get a hoss rustled for me while I kill off some ham an' aigs. Be right back."

"But you've ridden all night now, Shorty," objected the sheriff; "an' I figger you was awake all day yesterday. Don't you need some sleep before you tackle another all-day ride?"

"I come from a tough fambly, Bob," replied Shorty, grinning.

"Let him sleep in th' saddle," growled Nueces. "You don't never want to pamper him, Bob."

"You go to hell," said Shorty, wheeling and striding through the doorway.

Nueces watched his friend reach the street, and then, lowering the bottle, filled a glass for himself, and smacked his lips.

"I'll put his gear on that fresh hoss while he's eatin'," he said. "Take my pick of th' hosses in th' stable? Good! Good! I'll pick him out a hoss that'll shore keep him awake!"

Fifteen minutes later Shorty returned, egg drying in the corners of his mouth, to see his grinning friend seated on a good horse, and holding the reins of another.

"Wait a minute, Nueces. I want to say hello an' good-bye to Bob. Where is he?" asked the newcomer, his memory keenly preserving the flavor of that whisky.

"He's locked it up," said Nueces. "You climb up here if yo're goin' with me!"

"Yeah?" asked Shorty in a rising voice.

"Yeah!" snapped Nueces, his voice falling.

"Who said so?" demanded Shorty, cocking his sombrero over one eye.

"*I* did!"

"For two bits you could go by yoreself!" rejoined Shorty, and without another word he climbed into the saddle. Striking into a distance-eating lope, the two friends left the town behind them.

CHAPTER XX

NUECES and Shorty, crossing the Rio Grande, turned east, following the course which Nueces had followed on his ride from San Ignacio. They had passed around Porter, well to the west of it and its outlying ranges, and to the best of their belief no one had seen them. On the way, Nueces had told his companion just what the situation was, and how he hoped to shape it and the destinies of the men involved. With something of interest to occupy their minds, the miles and the hours had passed quickly. Now they camped where Nueces had camped, and pushed on again shortly after daylight, recrossing the river where he had recrossed it, and following his former course northward toward the position of the stolen herd.

From the top of the same little hill they looked down upon the peaceful herd grazing in the small valley. At that distance they could not see the brands with any clearness; but from the interval which had elapsed since their alteration they knew that the marks had not yet healed. Six men were in sight, idling in their saddles as they rode on the outskirts of the scattered cattle.

"You pore damn' fool," said Shorty, taking in the scene with one comprehensive glance.

"Much obliged," said Nueces without turning his head. He showed a little interest, however. "What's itchin' you now?"

"Sendin' up for a posse to *take* that handful of rats! Hell, with Bludsoe an' Burns we could slip down there after dark an' get th' whole bunch. Six bums, an' *you* want a posse!"

"What about th' dozen down in Tres Alamos on that raid, you runt?" asked Nueces. "I told you about 'em! I didn't know that Bob would telegraph that sheriff, did I? When they got back there'd be three times as many as there are here now. Besides that, there's more hangin' around Porter an' th' IP that'll likely show themselves when things break. An' suppose that Tres Alamos posse fails to connect up with that bunch? Huh? Suppose *that!* Our posse won't be none too big."

"It'll be as big as yore head, an' that's too much!" retorted the squat puncher. He looked suspiciously at his friend. "What *you* figgerin' on doin' when th' showdown comes?"

"I got to do a job up in Porter, an' it's a good job!" retorted Nueces.

"Yeah, I betcha! All hand-picked an' special. A right good one-man play, which means there oughta be at least two to do it. I know yore hoggin' disposition!"

"Hell you do!" snapped the lanky puncher.

"Yes, I do! You got somethin' picked out for yoreself that's got more excitement in it than in all of th' rest put together!" accused Shorty.

"Well, what of it?" demanded his bosom friend with heat. "What of it?" he repeated challengingly.

"What of it?" snorted Shorty sarcastically. *"I'll tell you what of it! This* is what of it: Beginnin' right now yore private job ain't private no longer: it's a two-man job, an' *I'm* th' other man. You get my drift?"

"Yo're th' other *what? Man?* Old woman, you mean!"

"Then that makes us a pair!" retorted Shorty earnestly, "but I'm th' other one, whatever it is."

"Well, I'll make it a two-man job, rather than argue with a sorehead like you. Yo're allus wantin' to horn in."

"I ain't *wantin'* to horn in, a-tall; I've already done it. Now, you tell me all about that Porter job, hamhead."

"Didn't I tell you all about it, on th' way down here?"

"You told me about everythin' but that; an' you know it."

Nueces grudgingly complied with his friend's thirst for knowledge, but as he proceeded the grudging faded; he had known all along that Shorty would be in on that play; but to let Shorty know it before he had to was another thing.

"And you said it was a one-hand job?" asked Shorty in vast disbelief when the tale was concluded. "You figgerin' you could split yoreself in half, an' be in two places at once?" He chuckled grimly. "If you don't have somebody coverin' yore play, they'll be diggin' an extra long grave th' next mornin'! What about th' barroom, you damn fool?"

"Bludsoe an' Burns!" muttered Nueces. "We can use 'em both, Shorty! There's one thing that's been botherin' me, an' it wasn't th' barroom, neither; an' it wasn't my play in town. It was that somebody might get away in th' fight with th' posse an' carry th' news to Hitchins—an' *he's* th' boy *I* want to get! With Bludsoe an' Burns we can stop that. They're in it, too, Shorty."

"Put 'em to watchin' th' trail?"

"Yes; to stop anybody from ridin' along it toward town on *that* day, or night."

"They'll do it, an' do it right," said Shorty. "Now you gimme th' layout of that town an' that saloon."

Nueces complied, going into minute details and even making drawings in the dirt. When he had finished Shorty had a comprehensive knowledge of the situation in Porter, but——

"Huh!" he snorted. "Lot I know about it from yore tellin' of it. I oughta go up there myself, after dark, an' look around. Th' picture of a man an' a woman, standin' in a field, with their heads bent down. I want to see that picture for myself; an' I want to look over that saloon."

"You'll see it when th' time comes, an' not before," replied Nueces flatly.

"You've knowed me for years, an' you don't know me yet!" jeered his companion. "I'm goin' up to Porter right pronto, an' yo're stayin' here; but why th' hell yo're hangin' 'round here is more than I can figger. You kinda admirin' them bums down there? Huh! What good does it do to stay here, anyhow? Tell me that."

"You'ain't got th' brains of a horned toad, you damn' fool!" retorted Nueces politely.

"Then that makes me smarter than you!" came the quick rejoinder.

"Ain't I been tellin' you that there's a dozen hombres figgerin' to rustle a whole trail herd an' bring it up here?" demanded Nueces. "Ain't I, huh?"

"Keep a blattin'; keep a blattin'," replied Shorty. "What about the Tres Alamos posse?"

"That posse may miss fire. Th' gang figgers on mixin' up th' two herds an' goin' on from here in one body," explained Nueces patiently, as if he were talking to a child. "Twenty-seven hundred head, with eighteen men drivin' it, an' all ready for trouble. Does that sound like somethin' worth lookin' for?"

"Mebby it does, ham-head," retorted Shorty; "but it don't tell me why we can't take one day an' go to Porter, instead of hangin' around here wastin' our time."

"You'll get all th' whisky you can hold *after* this trouble is over," countered Nueces. "Until then you don't get a drop. That take out th' itch about goin' to Porter?"

"Can't a feller ride to town once in a while, an' mebby have a little excitement?" asked Shorty defensively.

"Any gun-play at this stage of th' game might spoil th' whole thing," replied Nueces. "Them fellers have got brains!"

"They ain't got many if they let you out-guess 'em! But that don't tell me why we're stayin' *here.*"

Nueces sighed resignedly and looked at his companion with great pity.

"We're hangin' out here, Shorty," he said with painstaking slowness, "to see th' two gangs meet an' mix; to see how many got away from that Tres Alamos sheriff. When we find that out we're sendin' off a messenger to Bob's camp, tellin' him what's what. He picks up Bolton on his way, an' Bolton's friends, an' tells Bolton our message. Bolton knows th' country, an' he'll guide th' posse; an' he'll guide 'em to a little place I got in my mind."

"It shore must be a little place if you've got it in yore mind!" jeered Shorty cheerfully.

"It's that JP ranch I've been tellin' you about," continued Nueces without even hesitating for Shorty's interruption. "That's where they'll hold th' herd over if they get th' chance. It's at th' end of one long dry drive, an' at th' beginnin' of another. They got to make th' second dry drive in one jump, an' they got to time it so they'll be passin' around Bradley in th' night. Th' cattle will have to be rested, grazed, an' watered; an' there'll be time for that because that Tres Alamos sheriff can't cross th' state line after 'em."

"Yeah," said Shorty. "An' when they get to th' JP, after th' way they mebby have been travelin', they'll be all tired out: hosses, cattle, an' men."

"Shore," endorsed Nueces. "It'll be as easy as *that*," he said, snapping his fingers. "It will be if they don't get suspicious an' send to Bradley for more men, an' to Porter, too. They can double their force if they have to: an' *then* how much too big will our posse be?"

"Yo're figgerin' right good, for you," said Shorty. "Damn' if you ain't got a long head on them shoulders. Well, all right; you stay here an' watch 'em," he continued, starting to slide backward down the slope of the hill. "I'll rustle up to Porter an' take a look at that picture hangin' on th' wall. I want to know somethin' about th' lay of th' land before I start whoopin' my war cry."

"All you got to do is to wait and go there with me," said Nueces. "I'll take you to th' buildin', an' all you got to do is to go 'round to th' front door while I head for th' kitchen. When you see me step into sight in th' gamblin' room, you come in through yore own door. That's all you got to know."

"Yeah!" snorted Shorty, pausing in the slide. "An' how about th' street behind me, with me in th' light of th' door, an' darkness outside?"

"I figger you'll know how to take care of that when th' time comes. My Gawd, what do you want? A regiment?"

"No, I don't want no regiment!" retorted Shorty, preparing to slide again. "I want to look around in that town; that's all."

"Shorty," said his companion with great earnestness, all banter gone out of his voice. "Shorty, up in our part of th' county we're a kinda joke———"

"Who says so?" demanded Shorty truculently, and checking his progress. "Who says so?"

"You know what I mean," explained Nueces. "We're th' long an' th' short, an' folks grin when they see us together. We're kinda famous, that way; right well knowed. Everybody knows us, *or has heard about us.* It ain't been very long since I left Porter; th' tall, lanky, horse-faced Simpkins. I got killed. Yo're my pardner. What will a pardner likely do when he hears that his friend has been shot? Then you breeze in: short, chunky, squat, fat-faced. Somebody that is suspicious couples us up. Suspicious minds jump right quick, an' sometimes they jump right. Here's another thing: if they couple us, they'll know in a flash that my name wasn't Simpkins. Nueces an' Shorty! Bob Corson's friends! Bob Corson, th' sheriff; an' Nueces an' Shorty, his deppeties! An' a big cattle steal on! Have you just *got* to go to Porter?"

Shorty turned and continued to slide. He looked back, and the grin on his chubby face was a beautiful sight to his worrying companion.

"Hell, no," said the slider. "But let's get back to camp an' eat; I'm hungry."

"All right, runt," chuckled the horse-faced puncher, starting a slide of his own.

"Don't you call me that no more, ham-head!" warned the other, the grin growing.

CHAPTER XXI

THE sheriff of Tres Alamos County had acted instantly when the telegraphic communication had ceased. Fore-warned of the raid, and knowing the number of the raiders, he was able to make his plans without guess-ing. By elimination, and from what Corson had said about the eight-day interval of silence from the trail boss, he was able to determine which herd was threat-ened; and, as it happened, there was only one herd in that part of the country where such a raid was prac-ticable.

His first duty was to protect lives and property by peaceful means if possible. If he could get a strong force of men to reinforce the trail outfit before the attack, and by sheer strength of number to discourage such an attack, that would be far better than to force a fight, risk lives, and perhaps lose part of the herd as well. In less than an hour after he had received the word he was on the trail at the head of a score of heavily armed deputies. The herd was several days ahead of him, measured in herd miles; but herd miles were less than horse miles; and he believed that he could catch up with the trail outfit in two days or less, throw his men around the cattle, and be ready to face the raiders when they arrived. He knew that he had no time to waste and that his margin was very close.

In the latter he was correct, for the sound of gun-fire struck his ears before he could see the herd. He had ridden hard, and the horses of his little contingent were well spent; but he forced them into their best pace and raced to the scene of the fight.

The herd was running and scattering to the four winds. Two riderless horses were passed, and the searching eyes of the posse failed to discover their riders; but that was something which would have to come later. The gunfire was very near now. It came from the other side of a small rise. Knowing the condition of his horses, the sheriff knew that he could not hope to make a showing in a running fight. He stopped the posse, divided it, and sent one half of it along the bottom of the rise to circle around and attack from the other direction. While he waited with his own contingent girths were looked to, arms examined, and impatience held down by sheer will.

A sudden increase in the firing told him that his friends were charging and, shouting an order, he led his men over the rise and down the other side.

Before him in the little depression between the two rises was the chuck wagon, surrounded by a small circle of dead horses, a bulwark of flesh to somewhat shield the desperate defenders. Powder smoke hung like a cloud over the little fort, through which came the pale flashes of spitting guns. On a wider circle, fair rifle range away, isolated figures fired and crawled, centering on the wagon.

Instantly this outer circle broke, the attackers leap

ing to their feet and running for their lives to their distant horses. One of them dropped, and another, and a third. Another, failing to catch his frightened horse, made a gesture of rage, faced about and hugged the earth, to sell his life as dearly as he could. The posse broke into smaller groups, charging the rustlers nearest to them. Two saddles were emptied before the spent horses were reined in and the hopeless pursuit abandoned. Four fleeing riders shrunk in size in the west, and, finally topping a rise, were seen no more.

The posse collected about the wagon, shaking hands with the defenders. Two men lay quietly behind the fleshy barricade, and all the others were wounded more or less. Somewhere out on the plain two of their number lay dead, shot down in the first rush, killed before they had known they were in danger. An hour later the herd was held where it had been checked, and scattered cattle were being rounded up and added to it. The contents of the wagon were piled on the ground, covered with the tarpaulin; while the wagon itself creaked along the back trail with its grisly load, flanked by wounded riders, who in turn were flanked by deputies. The fight was over and the herd was safe, but four of the trail crew and eight of the raiders had gone over the Great Divide.

*　　　*　　　*　　　*　　　*

Shorty squirmed restlessly and swore under his breath. His companion lay quiet, calm, stoical. The sun blazed down upon them and their thirst grew steadily. Below them the scene had not changed: the grazing cattle, the lazy riders, the faint smoke from the cook's fire at the distant chuck wagon. Noon came and passed; and some of the riders, taking advantage of an opportunity to eat a midday meal, rode in to the camp. They ate and then relieved their friends.

"My Gawd!" growled Shorty. "Couple more days of this an' I'll go loco! Wouldn't you reckon they'd scout around a little, instead of lettin' us hang around up here?"

"Why?" asked Nueces tonelessly.

"Why?" echoed Shorty in surprise. "To find out if anybody was spyin' on 'em. That's why!"

"There's nobody around to spy on 'em," replied Nueces, sighing. "They run th' county, an' they are let alone; besides, they're down here where nobody would ever look for 'em. Simpkins is dead."

Shorty snorted in disgust and squirmed anew, cursing the sun. Time stood still. . . .

"But they oughta have a man out scoutin'," he growled a quarter of an hour later, indicating that the trend of his thought had not changed.

"Yeah; but they ain't," grunted Nueces. "What's th' matter with you? Got th' itch?"

"Oh, go to hell!"

Another quarter of an hour went by.

"My Gawd, but it's hot!"

"Glad you told me," grunted Nueces, shifting a little to find a better position.

"Th' damn' fools! They deserve what they're goin'

to get! Six bums, without brains enough to have a man ridin' 'round loose, keepin' watch."

"But there ain't nobody to bother 'em inside of near fifty miles," replied Nueces patiently.

"*We*'re here, ain't we?" demanded Shorty.

"This place is away from everythin'. If they had a man out, they'd have him on th' trail, over east."

"*We*'re here, ain't we?" persisted Shorty, his words clipped short.

"They ain't got no reason to reckon so. Will you shut yore whinin' face! I've got troubles enough without listenin' to you bleatin'."

"Go to hell!" snapped Shorty, and then his interest shifted to a little stone under his hip. He rolled over, flinching as the scorching earth stung him, dug the offending stone from under him, and hurled it down the slope. He muttered savagely and then let himself drift into silence. He squirmed again, shifted his arms, and relaxed. Lying prone on his stomach, with his arms crossed out in front of him, he raised his head, smoothed out a wrinkled sleeve with two impatient sweeps of his cheek, let his head fall again, and in a few moments was dozing lightly.

Nueces maintained his vigil without interest, a detached, mechanical vigil. His eyelids dropped and then went up again from an increasingly difficult act of will. The six riders, endlessly riding; the placid cattle, endlessly grazing. Another day of this would tax all his will power. He yawned and again his heavy lids drooped. It was almost torture to keep them open;

and then they flew up and the man became galvanized with interest. Four men popped into sight over the hill east of the camp. Their nearly exhausted horses stumbled and dragged down the gentle hill, and the six riders in the basin snapped into life. The racing half dozen met the four newcomers and crowded about them in a bustle of excitement. After a few minutes of milling the ten men rode on toward camp.

Nueces strained his eyes, holding his breath in an effort to increase the power of his vision.

"*Now* what you think, Shorty?" he asked in a whisper, not realizing that whispering was unnecessary. He received no answer and, turning his head, glanced at his silent companion. His long arm moved and a huge hand grasped Shorty's ear, and twisted.

"What th' hell?" muttered the sleeper, his eyes popping open.

"Look yonder," said Nueces, obeying his own injunction.

"Four more, Nueces! Wounded, too, if them bandages mean anythin'! Who are they? Where'd they come from?"

"Looks like th' two Peavy brothers, that pair nearest th' wagon; can't place th' other two. They've been in a fight, an' eight men are missin'. That Tres Alamos sheriff didn't waste no time; nor lead, neither, looks like. Our wait is over! Slide down, runt."

"Thank Gawd!" muttered Shorty, promptly obeying. He was the first to reach the horses and the first in the saddle, but he fell back to his companion's side and they pounded ahead, stirrup to stirrup, eating up the miles. Their quarry was ready to move, and with haste, if they guessed right; it was now their own duty and privilege to set the trap.

Night fell, and still they pounded on through the dim light of countless thousands of stars. Their total of miles had grown to dignified proportions, but still they swept on. At last Nueces reached out and rested a hand on his companion's shoulder.

"Pull up, Shorty; we're there, or thereabouts." He raised his voice and called. There was no answer. "Keep on, at a walk," he said. Five minutes passed, and then they drew rein spasmodically.

"*Quien es?*" demanded a voice almost under their feet. There was a ring to the challenge which suggested that a prompt answer would be wise.

"Simpkins; Nueces!" answered the tall rider. "Are you ready to ride?"

"*Si, Señor.* I go now."

Nueces spoke slowly, making certain that his message was thoroughly understood. It was a short message and not complicated with a lot of detailed directions. The Mexican repeated it, word for word.

"All right," said Nueces, nodding in satisfaction. "Get goin', pronto."

The Mexican disappeared, and it was several minutes before they heard the sounds of his moving horse.

"Stalked us, on foot, till he was purty shore who we was," said Nueces, chuckling. "An' yet there are a lot of damn' fools that copper Mexicans."

"Where we goin'?" asked his companion. "To town?" his voice rose hopefully.

"You gimme a pain!" sharply retorted Nueces. "You'll get to town when I take you there, an' not before. Right now we're headin' for Bolton's, an' takin' it easy. These hosses are tired."

It was nearly midnight when they rode up to Bolton's ranch house, but they had no more than passed the corral when a challenging voice told them to stop and to raise their hands. They obeyed instantly, Nueces calling out and revealing his identity; but the man in the house was taking no chances. A light suddenly gleamed around the edges of a curtain in the kitchen, and then the curtain shot up and let the rays stream through and outside. A moment passed.

"Come ahead slowly," said the suspicious person from the dark main room.

Nueces led the way toward the lighted window, pausing when the rays fell upon his face.

The lamp went out and the door opened, and Bolton bade them enter. They stripped off the riding gear and turned their horses loose to graze, knowing that one of the rancher's animals was in the corral and could be used to wrangle their own in the morning.

Bolton closed the door behind them, pulled down the curtain again, and relighted the lamp. He nodded to Nueces and then looked curiously at his companion.

"Shorty," explained Nueces, waving his hand. "Brother deppety an' Corson's friend. That Mexican get here all right?"

"Yes, an' went right on ag'in," answered the ranchman. "You fellers hungry?"

"Yeah; an' damn' thirsty!" blurted Shorty, a smile breaking across his face.

"You can hand him th' grub," said Nueces; "but I'll pour out his likker."

Shorty nodded, but said nothing.

Bolton busied himself in the kitchen, Shorty lounging to the door and watching every move. The beans were cold, but he liked cold beans; the biscuits were cold, and that was all right, too; but cold coffee did not appeal to him.

"Hadn't I better start a little fire under that coffee pot?" he asked.

"Why, yes; if you want to," answered Bolton.

"Did you get word to yore friends?" asked Nueces, stopping against the door frame in Shorty's place.

"Hen Fowler was here with me, an' he lit out right pronto after th' messenger left. Gosh! I could eat somethin', myself. What you say we heat up th' beans, fry some bacon, an' eat like white men oughta?" He scratched his head thoughtfully. "Be just as well to have a fire goin' in case some of th' boys git here ahead of time." He lifted the coffee pot, appraising its weight, and nodded.

"They oughta get here quite some time ahead of th' posse," said Nueces. "Our boys will feed before they break camp, an' be ready to go right along. You'll have plenty of time to waste with us."

"Is Corson holin' up very far off?" asked the ranch-man.

"Dutchman's Springs."

"You know this part of th' country better'n I reck-oned, for bein' here such a short time," commented Bolton.

"Dutchman's Springs was picked out for me by th' best damn' cattle thief that ever sat a saddle," replied Nueces.

About to place the frying pan on the stove, Bolton held it suspended while he looked at the lanky deputy.

"That so?" he asked curiously, very curiously. "Well, we got some right good ones around here, but I wouldn't go to compliment none of 'em that much."

"El Toro picked out that spring for me," chuckled Nueces; "pervided that messenger, an' offered to clean up this mess by hisself if I reckoned th' job was too big for me an' th' rest of th' boys."

The frying pan struck the stove with a ringing clatter and the ranchman's jaw tightened ominously.

"El Toro?" he demanded. "What do you mean?"

Nueces slouched into the room and dropped onto a chair, and, crossing his ankles, told the ranchman a sketchy account of recent events not covered by his previous recital in the brush-filled draw some days before.

"By th' Lord Harry!" exclaimed Bolton as the tale was finished. "Then *that's* why you wasn't killed, down there near San Ignacio!"

"Every bullet missed me," chuckled the horse-faced deputy. "You can thank a Mexican cattle thief for what's goin' to happen around here in th' next couple of days. We figger there's five hundred head in this last stolen herd, an' I'm figgerin' that you boys can pick out a lot of yore cattle on that ranch over near Bradley. That is if they ain't all been sent up th' trail."

"They wouldn't keep re-branded animals on their range if they had a chance to trail 'em off som'ers," growled Bolton pessimistically.

"That idear struck me just after I spoke," said Nueces, recrossing his ankles. "But, Bolton, th' Peavy brothers have got lots of cattle, ain't they?"

"Yes, damn 'em!"

"An' you boys know about how many you lost?"

"Yes!"

"An' th' Peavy boys might be persuaded to sell you fellers some of their best criters at, say, well—a cent a head."

"A cent a head!" growled the ranchman. "Like hell!"

"A hot iron is right persuadin'," interrupted Shorty, grinning.

"Shut up!" ordered his bosom friend, and turned again to face the ranchman. "A man thinks a lot of his neck, Bolton. If he understood that th' guards might get careless, an' that a fast hoss was picketed right handy for him; or if he was persuaded that things wouldn't go too hard on him in court—well, I'd say that a cent a head was too much." He laughed gently. "Besides, there's an account book in Hitchins' little private room that may tell some tales about cattle."

Bolton gravely arose, stepped to a box fastened to the wall, opened the leather-hinged cover, and picked out a bottle. He walked to the table, slid three glasses into a row, and poured slowly and deliberately, Shorty's eyes watching every falling drop.

"*G-o-l-d-e-n W-e-d-d-i-n-g,*" spelled Shorty, squinting at the label. "Damn' if I can't hear th' music an' smell the flowers!"

Bolton handed each of his guests a glass, and held up his own.

"Here's to th' mem'ry of Simpkins!" he said.

CHAPTER XXII

THE following day passed slowly to the three men in the ranch house, but when night fell their interest quickened, for with the coming of night came Bolton's ranchmen friends. To have gathered earlier would have been to run the risk of being seen by some possible spy from the camp of the enemy. The situation was well talked over, and certain phases of the affair discussed; phases which were not to come before the official attention of the sheriff. In this case punishment was not enough; threatening poverty demanded restitution, and if their plans went through restitution would be made. Each of the ranchmen knew approximately the number of animals he had lost; but it remained for the lanky puncher to mention the factor of natural increase, and to revise the figures upward.

At last there came through the night the sounds of many hoofs, and a shadowy mass of horsemen loomed up before the little house, their low voices sounding reassuringly in the darkness. Someone among them made a witty remark, and a ripple of restrained laughter gave him answer. Saddles creaked, following the example of the leader's, and the men were now afoot; all but one man. His work well done, he wheeled and disappeared into the night, choosing a direction which would lead him to San Ignacio and to his master.

Introductions were hurriedly made in the crowded ranch house, and then came the order to mount and to ride. Rations of food, prepared against this contingency, were distributed; and the ranch house became empty almost in a wink. Again saddles creaked, and the sounds of moving horses told of an expedition under way.

In the van rode Sheriff Corson and his chief deputy, with Bolton between them. Plans were discussed, questions asked and answered, assignments made and possible contingencies provided against. Mile followed mile, and then four men left the force and pushed on at a more rapid pace, leaving the main body under the able guidance of Bolton and his friends. Four men, riding hard: Nueces, Shorty, Burns and Bludsoe.

The main body pounded on at a steady pace, miles and hours having been figured and set one against the other. It still lacked an hour of dawn when the force, dismounting, left their horses in the charge of one man, and moved on foot up the northern slope of a little hill.

In the hollow between this hill and the one to the south lay the small adobe ranch house of the JP and the newly made reservoir. Sheriff Corson, his men at his back, looked down upon it, studying it in the moonlight. He turned and gave some orders, and the force behind him shifted, some of the men going one way; some, other ways. He faced about again and spoke to the man at his side.

"Time to get him, Bolton. I won't be long."

"You goin' alone?" asked the ranchman, a little surprised.

"You reckon I need any help in a case like this?"

"Mebby not; but I'd better go with you." The ranchman hesitated. "I'm a little restless," he explained.

Corson laughed and rested a hand momentarily on the broad shoulder.

"You know th' plans, Bolton. I won't be long."

The ranchman watched him move down the hillside and across the bottom of the little basin, step by step, until the moon-made shadows of the house blotted him out in the space of a breath.

The sheriff placed a hand gently against the ranch-house door and pushed slowly. The door moved, hesitated, yielded to a greater pressure, and swung open. Corson, gun in hand, waited while one might count ten and stepped inside. The rays of the moon shone through a window, making a bright patch of light upon the dirt floor. Deep, peaceful breathing sounded from the end wall, and the sheriff's eyes, now accustomed to the dim light, made out a bunk built against the wall.

He slipped forward and stopped at the bunk, looking down upon the sleeper. In his left hand he held a gun; in his right, steel handcuffs. Chuckling deep down in his throat, he moved swiftly; and the sharp click of steel snapped in the silence. His right hand, moving swiftly from the cuffs, swept up and jerked a gun from a holster hanging on a nail at the head of the bunk.

"What th' hell's this?" roared an angry voice as

the bed clothes heaved. A man, half clothed, stood upright against the bunk, straining at the short bit of chain between his wrists.

"Easy!" warned an ominous voice from the middle of the room. "Yo're under arrest, Dailey!"

"Arrest? Arrest?" cried the prisoner, his voice pitching high. "What you mean? G—— —— you, what you mean? Who are you?"

"Mean what I said. Yo're under arrest. Don't make me shoot you."

"What you mean? Who are you? What th' hell you reckon yo're doin'?"

"I'm that no-account sheriff from th' county seat. Corson's my name. Yo're under arrest for stealin' cattle. Pull on yore pants an' boots, an' come along with me."

"Go with you!" shouted Dailey, followed by a burst of profanity. "I'll see you in hell first!" The speaker swung swiftly around, his chained hands streaking to the pendant holster, and then he cursed anew.

"Time's short, Dailey!" came the snapped reply. "You'll come with me, an' come quick, or I'll knock you out an' drag you! Take yore choice, an' take it quick!"

Dailey hesitated. He was handcuffed, and the other had a gun. Sighing and still muddled, he obeyed orders, intending to mark time until he had the right of it, and in a moment he was outside the house. He opened his eyes wide in surprise. A group of men, heavily armed, approached the house. Exchanging a few words with the sheriff, they filed in through the open door, which slammed shut on the heels of the last to enter.

"By G—d, we'll find out about this!" growled the prisoner.

"Close yore mouth! Anythin' you say will be used ag'in you. You better save yore breath, an' do yore talkin' in court. You'll need it all."

"Great G—d!" muttered Dailey. "An' th' boys are drivin' up here to-day!"

The sun pushed up over the horizon, stabbing the fleeing night with level lances of light. With it came a gentle wind, to stir the sage and to set it whispering. Cattle moved around the reservoir, placidly grazing. Time dragged. Higher rose the sun, banishing the cool of the night. On the eastern horizon there appeared a transparent film of dust, red from the sun behind it. The film soared higher, spreading sideways. Black dots bobbed in it, appearing and disappearing. On it came at a good pace, and the dots became the bobbing heads of cattle. Beside them, somewhat out of the pall of dust, were horsemen, urging the herd to its best speed, the punishing top speed of thirsty cattle on a long, dry drive. The wind, growing stronger with each passing minute, now shifted suddenly and came from the west; and with it went the scent of water to nostrils eagerly testing it. The heads bobbed more swiftly and the pace increased. No need, now, to urge the cattle forward. Their thirst, engendered by a merciless dry drive, and only partly assuaged by the meager water

supply at Dailey's ranch, drove them resistlessly against
that scent, half crazed to trace it down.

Running is not a natural gait with cattle, but the
leading ranks broke into a lumbering gallop, and the
horsemen let them go. In a flash the whole herd was
running madly and opening a gap between it and the
following riders, a gap which the horsemen did not try
to close. The hoofed avalanche poured over the slight
rim of the basin and into the shallow pond; and almost
instantly became a quiet herd, knee deep in the caress-
ing water, nosing it and lowing with contentment.

The riders bunched and came on without a change
of pace. Trail wise, they had seen that their small
horse herd had reached Dailey's water first and drunk
their fill. Horse flesh is the foundation on which all
trail-herd efforts are erected, and the needs of the riding stock are paramount, are above all else. These
horses were not thirsty and needed no restraint. The
bunched riders moved on steadily, at a sober pace.
Out of the ten, four wore bandages.

They reached the rim of the basin and paused to
look at the cattle. The low adobe house lay ahead of
them, a little to their left. Its blank rear wall was blank
no longer, although at that distance that fact was not
apparent. The two small loopholes which had been
cut through the clay wall were not prominent enough to
attract the attention of an unsuspicious man. Later,
when the sun rose higher and blocked in the holes with
shadows, they would be plain, indeed.

Ike Peavy said something to the man at his side, and

gestured widely with an arm; and the group, nodding, pushed on and headed for the ranch house. Around them were clumps of sage, and behind some of these were riflemen, crouched or lying prone. One of these riflemen, tense and nervous, moved too soon, anticipating the signal. He leaped to his feet, his rifle going to his shoulder. At the shot a horse dropped from under one of the leaders, and Ike Peavy found himself afoot. The group whirled, drawing weapons, and two shots rang out. The rifleman staggered and sank down behind his cover.

Other figures now leaped into sight, to the right, to the left, and running men closed the gap at the rear. Nearly a score of armed men on foot closed three sides of the plain. The rustlers, firing from prancing horses, split up into two parts. The first, under Frank Peavy, with his brother up behind him, raced for the ranch house to get inside it and make a stand behind its thick walls. On they rode, almost unopposed from the front, urged forward by screaming lead from behind.

The other section, racing toward one point in the wall of deputies, found their targets dropping out of sight; and found that men lying prone, with elbows solidly resting on the earth, can shoot with telling aim. One by one the horses or the riders dropped; one by one the little, desperate group grew less. Two of them still rode on, and when the horse of one dropped from under him his companion took him up behind and kept on going. And then, around the end of the northern hill, came four deputies riding hard. The two cattle thieves, threatened from that direction, swerved and swung to the east. They had no chance and they knew it; and suddenly they leaped to the ground behind a patch of sage and let the horse go on. Their little sage bush became the focal point of a circle of fire.

The other group, riding desperately, got to within nearly a hundred paces of the rear wall of the house, when two bursts of smoke puffed from the rough loopholes. Frank Peavy's horse went down, throwing its double burden heavily. The other three men, seeing that they were squarely in a deadly trap and that their position was hopeless, threw up their hands and waited sullenly.

Sheriff Corson stood up in plain sight and stepped from behind his bushy cover; and here and there over the plain deputy after deputy arose and moved quickly forward, rifles at the ready. The encircling line closed in under the ample protection of the rifles in the loopholes and of those in their own hands.

The little group of prisoners, dismounting, gave up their arms and submitted to the handcuffs, while Ike Peavy stirred and rolled partly over. His brother Frank sat up and looked around, dazed and without understanding.

Corson stepped quickly forward, a deputy by his side. Frank Peavy, weaving unsteadily, seemed to have an inkling of the situation and reached for his holster. It was empty, the gun having been lost in his fall. He groped around on the sand for it, searching blindly, and then struggled vainly in the arms that gripped him. In a moment, hands locked behind his back, he was helped to his feet, cursing in a low, monotonous streak.

Ike rolled back again and opened his eyes, and like a flash he drew his gun, as if by instinct alone. There came the vicious crack of a rifle, and the weapon leaped from his uncertain grip. In another moment he was cuffed, and helped to his feet and then joined the line-up which slowly moved toward the house.

Ike Peavy, sitting with his brother on the bunk, sneered and spoke.

"Turned ag'in yore pardners, huh?" he demanded, staring with unwinking hostility at the seated sheriff. "Well, we got that which will end yore job an' jail you with us. How come you forgot them checks?"

"Th' county attorney hopes you'll produce 'em in court," replied the sheriff, smiling. "Simpkins says they're safe in th' Royal Palace. If you don't produce 'em, *I* will."

"Shut up, Ike!" growled his brother. "Keep yore trap shut tight!"

Three men rode up to the door and dismounted. They were Bolton, Fowler, and Fessenden, ready to bargain. As they entered the room Corson and his brother deputies arose and faced the door.

"Th' changes in th' brands still readable?" asked the sheriff.

"Shore! Plain as can be!' boomed Bolton, a smile on his face. "Every last one of 'em came from our ranges. That new iron work is right prominent. They'll

get twenty years each for this, if they don't earn th'
mercy of th' court!"

"Good," said the sheriff, motioning for his deputies
to go ahead of him. "I'm leavin' these fellers with you
boys," he said, smiling. "See that they don't get away."

Bolton's eyes hardened as he scowled at the handcuffed brothers.

"They won't," he grunted. "I reckon we'll be right
easy with 'em, if they'll listen to reason."

The sheriff closed the door behind him and joined
his brother officers, winked at them, and rode off. He
had not appeared to see the piece of paper, covered
with figures, which Bolton had pulled from a pocket;
and had he noticed it, how was he expected to know
that it contained the list of stolen cattle, and a little
more, and that a sort of trading was even then going
on inside the house? How was he to know that the big
herds of the prosperous IP ranch were soon to shrink,
and that those of lesser brands were about to grow
unbelievably? How was he to know that the mercy of
the court would be asked, and given?

CHAPTER XXIII

POUNDING through the night after leaving the posse, four horsemen rode toward Porter and the trail leading out of it on the south. Nueces told the story, from the beginning to what he hoped would be the end, and outlined the strategy of this night's ride and what would follow after sunrise. On Burns and Bludsoe the success of the whole affair might possibly hinge; not only the success of the action in town, but also that out on the open range where Corson and the posse would play their parts. No messengers must come into town or leave it; the drive-trail crew must be cut off from any word from Hitchins; and Hitchins, from it.

It was late when the town came into sight, so late that only a few lights burned. Bludsoe and Burns were cannily placed at a point where the trail dipped down into a draw and turned around a thrusting point of chaparral. They moved apart, but a dozen feet separating them, a dozen feet and the trail itself.

"Don't let a man get through," said Nueces, casting one final look around.

"Don't worry; they won't," said Burns grimly.

"No chance a-tall," grunted Bludsoe, and then the two trail guards were alone, listening to the diminishing sound of galloping hoofs in the direction of town.

Nueces and his companion whirled on, neared the

outskirts of the town, and slowed. At last they left their horses and went ahead on foot. Houses and stores were dark. The first saloon they passed was closing for the night, and a glance down a side street showed the leader that even the saloon where he had won the JP ranch from Pettingill was closed. But there was light in the darkness: the windows of the Royal Palace gave notice that it was open for business, a business which at this hour was fairly brisk for a short time, and then swiftly dropped to nothing. Turned out of other places, the die-hards of the bars were wont to drop in here for a final glass and, perhaps, a final game.

Two awkwardly walking punchers slipped around the edge of the lot and made their way to the corral in the rear, where three horses were penned. They opened the gate, drove the animals forth, and started them on their way; and when certain that the animals could not be found again before morning they approached the main building and moved silently along its one blank wall.

Half a dozen horses stood at the tie-rail, picked out by the light which streamed out of the open door. Nueces worked toward the entrance, his back against the wall. Cautiously peering around the door casing, he saw that the outer room was vacant except for a sleepy bartender, who was getting ready to close for the night. In the gambling room a group of men sat around the big round table playing poker. The game was growing listless, and the signs told that it would soon break up. Nueces slipped back again and nodded to his companion. One by one the horses were untied and led out of the patch of light, and when all had been collected went down the street under Shorty's guidance, and were turned loose and started out of town.

The two friends met again at the corner of the building, whispered for a moment, and separated, Shorty to slip along toward the open street door; Nueces moving swiftly toward the kitchen.

The latter tried the rear door, found it unlocked, entered silently and closed it gently behind him. He dropped the bar and then, feeling along the wall, he found and locked the passageway door, and put the key in his pocket. Drawing both guns, he tiptoed through the door leading into the next room, where light from the gambling hall lay upon the floor.

Shorty, counting silently, reached two hundred and then walked carelessly into the saloon and up to the bar. As Nueces had said, this room was occupied only by the bar man. He placed both hands on the counter and nodded toward a bottle on the backbar.

"Whisky," he said casually. "This town shore goes to bed early."

"My Gawd, man," replied the bartender. "It's after two o'clock! I'm just gettin' ready to close," he said, scowling frankly at the card players in the next room. He mumbled something about wishing that the business was all over with so that Hitchins would go to bed at an earlier hour, and slid a glass after the bottle.

Shorty, enlightened by Nueces' explanations, understood by that mumbled remark that Hitchins was

waiting for possible news from the trail. Shorty smiled:
things had not gone right for Mr. Hitchins down in
Tres Alamos, and the man was nervous and apprehensive. Well, he had a right to feel uneasy, as he soon
would find out. And then the signal came in a roar of
sound, and Shorty's swiftly moving right hand swung
up and over and down, and the descent of the heavy
gun took the bartender with it, and he dropped behind
his counter, to have no further interest in current events
for half an hour or more.

Shorty continued the movement without a break,
leaped backward through the door to the street, whirled
with his back against the wall, and held two ready
guns against the possible arrival of the curious and
the belligerent.

Nueces, having moved swiftly across the intervening
room, stepped suddenly into the inside door, and the
roll of his left-hand gun was like the roll of thunder.
The Angelus leaped and writhed, ripped from its tacks
through its dry-rotted upper edge, and fell in a limp
mass upon the floor; behind it sounded the crash of
a falling body, and an arm flopped through the little
window and hung inertly.

The card players made convulsive movements and
froze in grotesque postures. Hands went up slowly or
swiftly, according to the natures of the individuals;
but Hitchins thought more quickly than his companions,
and he made a sudden dive sidewise from his chair,
turning in the air like a cat, both hands streaking under
his coat. Nueces fired again, and the gambler, twisted

halfway around under the impact of the heavy slug, let his hands drop to his sides and leaned weakly against the table. His right arm was useless, and he knew that it meant death to move again.

Nueces slowly lowered the empty gun and dropped it into its holster. Moving forward, the badge on his vest glittering in the lights of the room, he relieved the gambler of the pair of shoulder guns and slipped them into a coat pocket. Stepping back he jabbed his right-hand gun at the most abject of the players.

"Line 'em up ag'in th' wall, face to it," he ordered harshly. "You fellers are all under arrest, an' th' first smart Aleck that makes a quick move will get a free ride to hell. Hitchins, I'm itchin' to kill you if you give me another excuse."

Hitchins's reply was a stream of curses, interspersed with whys and wherefores: and the answer told him all that he wished to know.

The squad was against the wall, their faces pressing against it.

"Now go through 'em an' take every weapon they got," ordered Nueces of his abject assistant. "You'll get a bullet for every weapon you overlook! Pronto!"

The work was swiftly done and six men sat on the floor, their backs against the wall, Hitchins on the near end of the line. Nueces whistled, and was answered by a flurry of movement from the street.

Shorty popped into the barroom, slammed shut the door, and locked it. He leaped to the windows, one after the other, and drew the shades. Then he hastened to the bar and went behind it, and he emerged dragging the still unconscious bartender. Hauling this unfortunate person into the gambling room, he added him to the line-up, took a gun from under the white jacket, and went back to put out the lights in the big outer room.

"Watch this bunch, Shorty," said his bosom friend. "I want to look around an' get some rope."

Shorty seated himself in a chair by the big round table, a Colt resting on a knee.

"Go ahead, Nueces; an' take all th' time you want," he said cheerfully. "If you hear a shot, don't bother to pay no attention to it: it won't be *me* that'll be needin' any help," and he smiled pleasantly at the line-up.

Nueces stepped into the connecting room and passed through it into the kitchen. Unlocking one of the twin doors in its side wall. he entered a narrow passageway and went along it.

Out in the gambling room Shorty suddenly cocked his ears and listened with great intentness. He did not like the sounds he heard coming from behind a wall, and he arose, partly turned, and for an instant his eyes rested on the little window and the arm hanging through it. The creaking and steps persisted, and he drew back the hammer of the gun.

"Nueces!" he snapped loudly, as the muzzle of the weapon swung up.

"All right, Shorty: I should 'a' told you where I was goin'," said a muffled voice from behind the wall. "I plumb forgot."

Shorty gave his whole attention to the line-up, but one could easily see that he was indignant.

"You'd 'a' remembered quick enough if I'd 'a' let this hammer fall!" he retorted. "Damn' ham-head!"

The progress of the hidden man continued. There was indistinct movement behind the little window, and the inert arm disappeared, a match scratched and flared; and after a moment a horse-like face was thrust into the opening for a brief glance around the gambling room. It disappeared, and a few moments later showed up in the connecting door of the intervening room. Nueces ducked through the door with two lariats dangling from his big hands.

Dawn and the rising sun. The town came to life, and smoke twisted up from numerous chimneys and told of breakfasts being prepared. The sun climbed higher, and store doors were opened and flung back. Men moved about the streets, going about their business, and no one of them seemed to think it strange that the Royal Palace was not yet open; but it was early for that place of business; and, besides, smoke climbed up from its chimney in a long, peaceful ribbon and died of attenuation in the upper air.

Two hard-faced punchers rode into town from the south, looking about them as if they were searching for something. One of them, revealing glittering gold teeth in a sudden smile, raised an arm and pointed.

"Royal Palace," he announced, and suddenly became alert and ominous.

His companion's grin was almost cataclysmic, threatening the safety of his prominent ears. He did not seem to share in his companion's doubt, and refused to become either alert or ominous. He knew the quality of those two hombres.

"Closed tighter'n hell," he grunted.

They stopped before the door, dismounted, and knocked. A shutter-backed peekhole played with its own shadows and revealed an eye in the exact center. A lock clicked, the door opened a grudged one third, let in the two strangers, and closed again.

Down the street the keeper of the general store stopped his sweeping and held the broom in mid-stroke over the board sidewalk.

"That's pe-culiar," he muttered. "There's strange doin's goin' on in this town, an' have been, for months." He glared accusingly at the Royal Palace. "Oh, well: every man to his own business," and the broom descended.

Little Tom, the first-shift bartender, hastened toward his place of employment, chiding himself upon being late again; not that it mattered greatly, but it had happened too often recently. He turned the corner, saw two curious townsmen watching the Royal Palace, nodded to them, and stopped before the door. It was closed and locked. He chuckled: the clean-up man was keeping even worse hours than himself. His key wouldn't go in the lock—naturally, since there was one in it already. He knocked loudly, and in sudden irritation, and glanced across the street at the two curious onlookers who, satisfied by the arrival of the bar-keeper, were moving on again. When he turned back toward the door it was opening slowly, and he pushed with sudden energy and stepped across the sill. The door swung shut behind him, and he found his recent breakfast threatened by the painful pressure of a gun muzzle.

"What—what——" he began, his gulps interfering with his speech.

The gold-toothed smile of the other man was not reassuring, and the swiftly moving hand plucked a short-barreled .45 from the hand-tooled holster.

"Nothin'," said Bludsoe, one thumb jerking toward the gambling room. "Nothin' a-tall. Just go in there with yore friends an' keep yore trap shut. Step along, Mister!"

Little Tom moved forward, doubting his eyes, and silently joined the line-up, too dazed to speak. As he settled down on the floor, his back to the wall, he caught sight of another man seated in a chair against the opposite wall. This man held a gun loosely, and tried to frown. The Angelus lay on a heap on the floor, the hidden window now gaping blackly. Little Tom blinked, and at last found his tongue.

"Somethin's happened," he muttered wisely, and instantly held his peace.

"Keep yore trap shut!" growled the guard, and then he raised his voice. "Hey, Bludsoe! What th' hell's th' matter in th' kitchen? I'm near starved!"

Time passed, and a crowd collected before the Royal Palace. It had no particular purpose in forming, but its units had nothing else to do and, being extremely gregarious, and owning to a love for gossip, they just drifted up and stopped.

Their discussion covered a range of possibilities without getting anywhere, and none of them was crazy enough to hit upon the solution. Then one of the more important citizens announced that he was going to find out what had happened. He had taken three steps when a sudden movement down the street made him pause. One earnest look, and he changed his mind, rejoining the safety of numbers with great alacrity.

A cavalcade rode in from the south, and at its head was a figure vaguely known.

"It's th' sheriff!" shouted some more discerning being. "Who's that with him? Ain't that Ike Peavy? An', lookit! There's Frank! What you reckon's happened?" pened?"

"An' Bolton, an' Fessenden, an' that Fowler feller!"

Talk was fast and furious and the crowd surged forward to surround the stopping horsemen, but did not press too close; naked six-shooters and stern, unfriendly faces gave a cue not to be mistaken.

Corson swung down and knocked on the closed door. Its peekhole fluttered; and then the big door swung open, wide open, crashing back against the wall. Nueces stood on the threshold, and the crowd gasped: the dead had returned to life, and to Porter!

"Everythin' all right?" asked the sheriff.

"Shore, Bob. You ran yore play accordin' to plan?"

"Yeah. Got 'em all; some of 'em alive," answered

the sheriff. "I smell bacon: you ready to feed th' boys?"

"Hell no!" snapped the horse-faced deputy. "We got just enough for ourselves an' th' line-up. Tell 'em to go feed at th' hotel."

Corson turned, stepped aside, and waved his hand.

"Bring 'em in here, Bolton," he ordered. "Detail a couple of th' boys to guard 'em, an' tell th' rest to go get their breakfasts."

Jim Pettingill stepped from the crowd and was about to pass through the door when the sheriff saw him. Corson's arm streaked out, grabbed the intruder by the collar, and yanked. A quick protest sounded from within.

"He's all right, Bob!" yelled Nueces. "He's my pard-ner, th' owner of th' JP! Aw hell; you done tore *that* shirt collar, too!"

Corson loosened his grip, nodded an apology, and watched his lanky deputy duck down to pass through the doorway.

"Hard luck, Jim," said Nueces, holding out his hand, in which something glittered in the sun. "Just got yore collar button back from behind a wall, an' now you ain't got no place to wear it."

"Gimme that button!" shouted Pettingill, grabbing it. "If I ain't got no place to wear it, I'll make one, by G—d. My luck's come back ag'in!"

"Grub pile!" came a shout from the kitchen, ring-ing hollowly in the big building. "Grub pile; come an' get it or I'll throw it aw-a-y!"

THE END